KEEPING UP APPEARANCES

Rose Macaulay (1881–1958) was one of the most popular satirical novelists of her day. Born in Rugby and educated at Oxford, she was created Dame Commander of the British Empire in 1958. Author of some thirty-nine books, she is perhaps best remembered for the novels *The Towers of Trebizond* and *They Were Defeated*.

'Daisy Simpson, the snobbish little journalist from East Sheen, alias Daphne Simpson, the brilliant social success, alias Marjorie Wynne, the popular author of *Youth at the Prow* is one of the best characters Miss Macaulay has created.'

Sunday Times

'In *Keeping Up Appearances* Miss Rose Macaulay joyously renews her attack on the follies of her day. Her dexterity is unfailing, her derision is contagious, and her impatience with fads, cranks, and poses as brilliant as it is salutary.'   *The Spectator*

Other Rose Macaulay novels available
from Carroll & Graf Publishers

CREWE TRAIN
DANGEROUS AGES

KEEPING UP APPEARANCES

ROSE MACAULAY

Carroll & Graf Publishers, inc.
New York

First published in Great Britain in 1928 by William Collins Sons & Co., Ltd.

First Carroll & Graf edition 1986

Carroll & Graf Publishers, Inc.
260 Fifth Avenue
New York, NY 10001

ISBN: 0-88184-290-7

Manufactured in the United States of America

Three Johns.
1. The real John; known only to his Maker.
2. John's ideal John; never the real one, and often very unlike him.
3. Thomas's ideal John; never the real John, nor John's John, but often very unlike either.

Only one of the three Johns is taxed; only one can be weighed on a platform-balance; but the other two are just as important.

OLIVER WENDELL HOLMES
The Autocrat of the Breakfast Table

'Oh, I don't think that's her character,' said Miss Cotton.

'Neither do I. She has no fixed character. No girl has. *Nobody* has. We all have twenty different characters — more characters than gowns — and put them on or take them off just as often.'

W. D. HOWELLS

CHAPTER I

Daisy's Night

Daisy Simpson, having retired to bed at one o'clock in febrile and semi-intoxicated gaiety, woke in the dark yet glimmering grey of some later hour, and lay listening to the conversations that occurred in the streets of that town throughout the night and day; for Daisy was abroad, among those whom her mother in East Sheen called 'the foreigners,' and the foreigners, as is well known, rest not day nor night from speech. The throats of the foreigners are constructed on different principles from English throats, which tire and become sore, constricted and weak, as they mumble their foggy, recessive speech, owing, no doubt, to the abominable climate in which the English have elected to live. The throats of the foreigners do not tire; from them their voices ring out like resonant bells, vibrant and strong and noble, not slurred and muffled and flat, like *le murmure anglais*. It is no wonder that the foreigners like to produce this splendid sound all night, as well as all day.

Miss Simpson, lying in the dark and glimmering morning, felt like the small, cold wind that stirs mournfully about at dawn; her soul, all her life, dying away in eoan misery and amaze. Where was she, what, and why? What was the world, scurrying so strangely, so awfully, among the dreadful vastity of the stars, and what was she upon it, crawling between earth and heaven; nay, rather between earth and hell? Whom the gods would destroy they first make mad. The gods would destroy her utterly.

The gay, the agreeable evening, enacted itself in new and sinister colours against the chill curtain of the dawn. Daphne's voice rang in Daisy's ears, foolish, flat, without meaning or grace, chirping like a cicada, uttering epigrams that were not (were they?) at all amusing. Was Daphne as attractive as Daisy, her close, her bosom friend, in her more confiding moments supposed? Was she actually esteemed by others, or was she seen through and despised, as Daisy herself was surely despised? Daisy's own object in social intercourse was to take over, to escape, if she could, observation altogether, to shelter behind Daphne. But what if Daisy and Daphne were really classed together by the discerning, and dismissed as of no importance? What if they were perceived to be precisely that which they indeed were?

Born of one father, but of two quite different mothers, Daphne and Daisy looked alike, though Daphne was the better looking, the more elegant, and five years the younger. But in disposition, outlook, manners, and ways of thought, they were very different, Daphne being the better equipped for facing the world, Daisy for reflecting on it, though even this she did not do well.

At last night's party (given by some English in one of the hotels) Daphne had not been present all the time; she had slipped away too often, and, in Daphne's absence, Daisy felt cowering and uncovered, like a Purdah lady who has by accident stepped into the street. Mislaying Daphne, she mislaid her defences against a contemptuous universe.

Oh God, one should not go to parties, Daisy sighed, sinking in wan defeat in the melancholy dawn. One should not mingle with others; one should keep oneself to oneself, and thereby keep high one's vanity and pride, which now, like mournful peacocks, drooped plucked tails and weary heads.

It now seemed definitely established that the evening had been a failure.

As if this were not enough, stealthy foot falls crept outside the bedroom door; the handle appeared to turn. Someone was seeking entrance, seeking access to Daisy's room and Daisy's goods. Daisy lay more still than sleep, while waves of heat and waves of cold surged over her prickling skin. Would the frail lock hold, as through other nights it had held against similar assaults? If it should not hold, then the quiet steps would prowl into the room, stealthy fingers would grope about for what they might thieve, keeping always between Daisy and the door, so that she could not leap from the room. More still than sleep she would lie; so much more still than sleep that a face would surely bend above the bed and peer into hers to discover if she feigned, to choke the cry that might be springing from her throat. . . .

So Daisy lay, cold and hot, precarious yet without hope, blown about by the black winds from Dis, and as it were ground to morsels and poured out like water, or like that powdered soap which the foreigners have arranged to be emitted from grinding machines in the toilettes of their trains, lest soap in the piece should prove too much for the cupidity of *MM. les voyageurs*. Daisy thought of East Sheen, and cried in her soul, 'Oh, mother, mother, help!'

The light grew; the stealthy, intimate noises of thieves were lost in the honest uproar of the morning. Cocks crew, carts creaked, men shouted, women called, children yelled, mules brayed, fishermen hauling in nets execrated, dogs barked, hens laid, church bells rang; in short, day had arrived. Lulled by this friendly daybreak clamour, and closing her eyes against the day behind, the day ahead, and the peculiar terrors of the night, Daisy sought from all these the refuge of sleep, as one creeps into a warm hut that one finds on a barren and incomprehensible mountain, and drifted presently into light and broken dreams.

2

From these she awoke at the happier hour of complete coffee. The night's defeat was forgotten, reversed, as usual, by the gay, the conquering morning, by coffee and by rolls. This young woman's ecstasy in the morning hour, when the sun flooded her crumpled bed, and, through the open shutter swinging brokenly on its hinges, the smell and sound of the sea came, the strident voices came, the clanging church bells came, the shriek of wheels on paved streets came, together with that exquisite sound, the shrill blowing of the elfin horns of foreign trams – Daisy's exultation in this happy hour shivered through her trivial body and trivial soul until both felt buoyant with ichor, and winged into bliss like birds. She sang to herself between bites and sups, enjoying the felicity of the thick white bowl of foaming coffee and milk, the crusty roll, the little tender croissant. Coffee; white bread; milk; three of the poisons which doctors most condemn. They would prefer that one should breakfast, if breakfast one must, on mineral water, brown wholemeal bread, marmite, Ry-Vita biscuits, and an apple, or even a lemon. An incomparably nasty opening to the day. None of the shouting foreigners ever touched any of these medicinal viands, yet they had (obviously) preserved their health. One need not seek to live more salubriously than they.

In the large gilt-framed mirror opposite the bed, Daisy saw herself munching roll and drinking coffee, propped commodiously among pillows; a small round face, pale but for freckles and tan, little grey-green eyes set far back under light brows, straight, short, ruffled hair. An inconsiderable face; it looked trivial and insipid and English among the vivid bronze or ivory skins, black or dark brown hair, straight features, and lustrous dark eyes of the foreigners. If you admire the human face at all (which it is not necessary to do, and indeed most of nature's works present a much better appearance, but humanity has had to make the best of such endowments as it has, and has always put up a brave pretence that human beauty exists) – if you admire the human physiognomy at all, then you must admire that of the inhabitants of the neighbourhood in which Daisy Simpson was just now staying. Beauty, after all, is relative, and these people were beautiful if compared with the British, the northern and central French, the Germans, the Dutch, the Scandinavians, the Slavs, the Ethiopians, the Japanese, the Esquimaux, and the Hottentots. Daisy was British, and the British are not admired outside their own islands. For that matter, Daisy was not particularly admired even within them. But she passed, when properly dressed. As to Daphne, she was well enough in looks and more or less amusing in speech and ways. Daphne was twenty-five. Daisy, on the other hand, had inadvertently just strayed to that boundary which is commonly supposed to divide youth from middle age; that is to say, she was thirty (but well preserved). Daisy often wondered what she was doing with her life, and why; Daphne professed gay indifference on this point, maintaining that to enjoy life was all that one was called upon to do with it. 'Young people are so selfish nowadays,' said Mrs. Folyot, the young women's employer, who was not selfish at all. What she held should be done with life was to help revolutions. If you had asked her, revolutions against what, she would have replied, revolutions against anything, but particularly against governments. When in England, she and Mr. Folyot (a very gentle, nice man) applauded industrial strikes, and offered hospitality to such foreigners as sought asylum in that country from the mutual persecutions of their home governments and themselves, though she strongly deplored their occasional tendency to say it with bombs. But the British Isles (at least, since the emancipation of Ireland) were rather tame islands, in spite of periodic strikes, so that Mrs. Folyot paid frequent visits to islands and continents abroad, where there was more of what she enjoyed going on. Particularly she found agreeable the island on which she was now staying, for to it fled discontented, persecuted, and persecuting rebels from all lands, so that one could enjoy the society of anti-Fascist Italians, anti-Bolshevik Russians, Catalan separatists, French loyalists, anti-French Corsicans, German imperialists, German Alsatians, Trentino Austrians, Jugo-Slavs from Fiume, Poles from Poland, such Portuguese as desired a change in their government of the moment, such Armenians as did not care about Turks, such Dodecanese as were homesick for Turkish rule, and enough other of the world's malcontents as to form a very agreeable, if somewhat fluctuating and transitory, cosmopolitan society.

Daisy and Daphne also enjoyed this society, and the sensation of being at the heart, so to speak, of a score of revolutionary movements, even though most of the movements were at the moment mainly of the nature of rapid strategic retreats.

Well, here was arrived another day, and Daisy arose from

bed. Another happy foreign day, with the sun, the sea, the
hills, the little town, the agreeable meals, the foreigners, the
English, Mr. and Mrs. Folyot, Raymond Folyot, and Mr.
Struther. A day in which one did not (one hoped) work. To
work was nauseating; Daisy would have liked to be as
Erinna, who had left a considerable reputation as a poet, but
only a few lines of poetry, or Eriphanis, who has left one
line, only that is not a very good one. Achievement without
labour; that was the ideal. Whereas the common lot of life
was labour without achievement. Not but that Daisy, when
in the mood to do so, could pour forth verse with the joy
and élan of a young bird chirping, scribbling in pencil on
scraps of paper and old envelopes, so that the results, what
with her spidery and niggling handwriting, and what with
the faults of crasis, elision, metaphesis, and syncope into
which her pencil slipped when writing, were scarcely to be
deciphered even by her own eager eyes. What matter? To
Daisy, who had always felt that she could probably do
something very well indeed, it had not so far been revealed
what this would be. At thirty she was still able to hope that
time would show; time, that great, if not always agreeable,
exhibitor, has sometimes shown undreamt of powers to
persons of forty, fifty, sixty, even seventy. Meanwhile,
Daisy wrote verse for pastime, and lived by serving the
Folyot family, by writing novels to which she gave such
names as 'Youth at the Prow by Marjorie Wynne'; and by a
connection between Marjorie Wynne and a Sunday
newspaper, which required from her periodic articles on
one or another of those absorbing problems that beset
editorial minds concerning the female sex and young persons, as, should women simultaneously rear young and
work for their living, should they play games, can they see
jokes, have they minds or souls? Daisy despised such theses,
but, since the newspaper world required of her no others,
she had perforce to write on them, and assist in keeping that
curious ball rolling. Even here, from this distant island, she
was supposed to be sending chatty social pars suitable to her
sex about the English visitors to the island.

CHAPTER 2

Daphne's Morning

Daphne strolled downstairs, in a neat white frock, and with the deportment of debonair insouciance that distinguished her even so soon after the hour of complete coffee. In the lounge were Mrs. Folyot, kind and energetic, and a clergyman called Mr. Struther, who helped her with revolutions. They were both in their fifties, and both wrote leaflets, as was suitable to their years, for people are even as trees, and it is in the autumn of their lives that leaflets shower from them, as from trees in October gales, more leaflets and yet more, until at last in the winter they stand bare and bereft. But it would not for long years be winter with Mrs. Folyot and Mr. Struther. Besides the leaflet habit, they shared also the platform habit; they would go round Europe, and even other continents, talking and talking, denouncing, inciting to Revolution in the name of Christ, Liberty, and International Labour. Though slightly grizzled, they belonged to the League of Youth, and other eager fraternities. Mr. Folyot was as generous and noble, but quieter, and something in the British Museum.

Mrs. Folyot, who was stoutish, dark, and agreeable-looking, and had her hands full of papers, said, 'Good morning, Daphne. I wish you'd take the children to the Moleta beach this morning. They can bathe from the rocks. I have my Catalan lesson at ten, and then I must walk over to Jaccio to meet the one o'clock boat. Morelli says it will be full of anti-Fascist printers. . . . It's going to be hot.'

'Thank God,' said Daphne, who thought the hotter the better, and was at home beneath Southern suns. But Daisy did not care for great heat; it made her languid and plain, wilting her even as cold did. Daisy was no good with weather; it made her head ache. She had not Daphne's poise. Daphne was opening a cable addressed to Daisy. It

read, tersely, 'Mail 500 words to-day dead typist mystery.'
For a dead British typist had been discovered in a clump of
firs on a mountain crag of this island, and it had become
quite a question how she had come to be dead. The editor
of the paper for which Daisy wrote was not among those
who believe that when a woman is dead she's dead, and
there's an end of it; he held that death (and more particularly
a female death) is, if well handled, but a beginning. Daphne
was the only person on the island who was aware of the
furtive journalistic activities of Daisy; she put the cable
in her pocket, against the time that Daisy should appear.
What appeared at the moment, however, was Raymond
Folyot, a dark-browed young zoologist, in whose presence
Daisy very seldom, and never voluntarily, appeared, for
she felt that he regarded people like her as among the less
noticeable forms of creature life. Daphne, on the other
hand, displayed a sufficiently intelligent interest in such
things as interested him, and he found her an agreeable
companion.

'I hope no bad news,' said Mr. Struther, having seen the
cable, and connecting cables with catastrophes.

'No thanks,' said Daphne, rather languidly.

'Raymond, darling,' said Mrs. Folyot, 'I wish you'd
come over to Jaccio with us and meet the one o'clock boat.
A lot of anti-Fascist printers are on it. Fleeing, you know.'

Raymond said that he would prefer to seek for small
marine creatures on the beach. Printers were to him less
anti-Fascist or Fascist than beings who frequently failed to
spell correctly the generic names of their less conspicuous
brethren, such as the Pectunculus Inaequalis. Well might
they flee.

'You're terribly selfish, dear,' his mother said. 'No public
spirit whatever. These poor men – they've had to come
away in a hurry, leaving their wives behind.'

'Well,' said Raymond reasonably, 'I shouldn't be any use
to them. You'd better take Daphne.'

'Don't be silly, dear,' Mrs. Folyot was sorting and
gathering up important papers. She had always important
papers, like the villains and heroes of fiction, or like Rus-

sians, or the British Foreign Office, the only persons except
Mrs. Folyot to whom papers seem important.

The children, Cary and Charles, came in from the piazza.
Cary was twelve, a thin little wisp with straight, light hair,
and a plain elfish face and eyes clear and green, like sea-
water. Charles was ten, sturdy and fair, with a forehead and
chin that stuck out. They were bare-legged and already
sandy and rumpled ere the day had well begun. They
gyrated rapidly about the lounge, emitting the protracted
cry peculiar to their species, which was, approximately,
'What are we doing this morning, mummy? Where are we
going? Can we bathe from now till twelve, and go fishing
after *déjeuner*? Can we go out in the boat with Gianni in the
evening and see the net let down? Can we take our lunch out
now and not come in till supper?'

No one took any notice of these sounds, but Mrs. Folyot,
having gathered her papers, said, 'Well, I must be off,' and
went out to learn Catalan. Mr. Struther, who also had
papers, settled down to them in a large chair, sniffing the
crisp air and saying, 'Really, a morning like this is like wine.
Exactly like wine.' Upon which Cary, a clear-headed child,
began to point out to him the ways in which the morning
did, in point of fact, differ from wine; how, for example, it
could not be poured out and drunk; how its colour was less
pronounced and it lacked alcohol; and how, in brief, he had
been more accurate had he said not 'Exactly,' but 'Rather.'
Again these child-sounds passed unheeded, like the bleating of the flock of black goats in the road outside the
hotel.

'We are going to the Moleta beach this morning,' said
Daphne to the children.

'I am going there, too,' said Raymond, who visited
different beaches on different days, seeking and finding
little creatures and bringing them back in bottles.

In that case, thought Daphne, Daisy could not come.
Had Daisy come, she would have sat on the beach and
written an article on Dead Typist Mystery Developments,
and notes on the English visitors to the island. But Daphne
would join Raymond in his animal researches, and bathe,

and behave with a mixture of intelligence, camaraderie, and aesthetic sense.

2

They strolled out into the little town, which smelt of coffee, of fish, of sanitation (or of its lack), and of sea, and which sang with the loud noises the foreigners make in their towns, and with the light breaking of the ocean. Through a deep arch with tiny dark shops inset they passed on to the shore road, and the golden morning flowed about them, and it was, indeed, as Mr. Struther had said, like wine, though, of course, as Cary had pointed out, not exactly. On the shore's long, pale curve the light sea tripped, humming like honey-questing bees in clover fields, lilting up and dying down, with a gentle droning song. Nets were being hauled in, agitated here and there by a small fish. Several little bianchetti and a sardine or two had been so unfortunate as to be thus captured, but not more than enough to make one good plateful. There was a *coq de mer*, but under their eyes he flew up out of the net at the sea's edge; a leap, a flash of blue and green, and he was away.

'Sharp little sportsman,' said Raymond. 'The others can't manage that.'

The children frisked along in the tumbling white edge, ankle deep, knee deep, or on shining sands. Daphne and Raymond, bare-legged, too, but in sand shoes, walked over blue sea-holly and yellow sea-poppies and purple sea-heath. They gathered red coral, and pearl shells, and fairies' slippers, and little sponges, and seaweed balls, all the delightful litter to be found on beaches after storms.

In half an hour they were arrived at the Moleta beach, a very white cove, where the Moleta river ran into the sea, making a tiny clear lagoon, set about with tamarisks, and on its grassy banks grew golden trees, and in the blue water stood golden brown reeds. Back from the beach stretched grassy slopes, purple and pink with romulea and silene and sea-green with rosemary, and above the grassy slopes the heath, which smelt, as Mr. Struther might have put it,

exactly like Paradise; so aromatic, so keen, so sharply
diverse and so sweetly mingled were its fragrances of pink
heath, white heath, sarsaparilla, myrtle, lavender, juniper,
strawberry, cistus, honeysuckle, and no doubt a great many
more plants. Inhaling these fragrances, so exquisitely mingled with that of the ocean, Miss Simpson was giddy with
pleasure, and Cary paused in her careering to sniff. Male
creatures being less excited by scents, Raymond was
already wading in rock pools with his net, and Charles
already removing what he wore of clothes. In about a
minute the two children, a small fraction of their persons
clad in skin-tight scarlet suits, were splashing through the
river's mouth to the sea. Daphne, who had thought it only
right to find a tamarisk tree behind which to undress,
followed them in a few minutes, in her spare sea-suit and
tanned skin. Raymond waded among rock pools with net,
glasses, and jar, his flannel trousers rolled above his knees.
The shore and pools this calm morning after storm were a
rich treasury of charming aquatic life. As Daphne passed
him he held up his jar.

'Clavellina,' he said.

'Oh, let me look.' Daphne peered into the jar, and saw
sitting there quietly a charming little being, sedentary,
translucent, and two inches high.

'What a darling. Looks quite happy, doesn't he – or is it
she, Raymond?'

'Difficult to say.' Raymond carefully placed the jar on a
flat rock, and bent hovering over his shining, shadowy,
green pool.

The children, swung in the eddy where the gentle thrust
of the stream met the gentle break of the sea, shouted and
splashed, leaping and diving like bonettas at play. Daphne,
too, slipped into the sea.

Raymond stooped peering over the pool. Green weed
swayed; through the green weed and the green water tiny
scarlet crabs scurried; on the rocks bloomed big dahlia
anemones, opening and closing, opening and closing, in
deep shadow, in shafts of beamy light. A cuttle fish waved
its limbs about like a tumbler; a rotifer turned somersaults

among the sedentary limpets, among the little sea-horses swaying like birds in the branches of the dendroid weeds. What life, static and dynamic, goes on in pools of the ocean.

3

Charles, swimming, went under, caught by something, entangled, helpless, choking, beating the sea with his hands. Cary, nearer shore, shrieked, 'Raymond! Raymond! Quick!' Looking up from green shadows, turning his gaze seaward, Raymond saw Cary screaming and waving her arms, saw Daphne swimming swiftly to where Charles had been, plunging under, coming up in a moment alone, shaking the sea from her eyes.

'He's caught in something,' she cried, and sounded frightened. 'I can't. . . .'

'Raymond, Raymond!' sobbed Cary, 'Charles is sunk! Come quick!' She was swimming like a dog, scrabbling the water with her hands.

'All right,' Daphne called, 'I'll get him; I'll bring him up,' and down she dived again, as Raymond plunged into the sea. She was a minute gone this time; when she came up she was dragging Charles by the hair.

'He's drowned,' Cary whimpered, for Charles's eyes were shut and his mouth hung open. Daphne was spluttering and gasping. Raymond reached them and took Charles's weight from her; between them they towed him to shore, Cary crying behind them. They laid him on the sand and adopted the usual resuscitative measures, pumping, pummelling, running the water out of his mouth, and in ten minutes Charles breathed again and was sick.

So no harm had been done, and in future they would all be more careful. Cary, a nervous child, capable of hysteria, had lain quite still on the shore while Charles was being revived, as still and green, almost, as Charles himself. But when Charles once more breathed, she began to shiver and whimper and cough up sea water.

'It's all right, Cary; Charles is all right now.'

'He was drowned,' Cary whispered. 'He was drowned.

She didn't get him up till he was drowned.'

They rubbed Charles dry and put on his clothes, and left him resting in the sun.

'Come along, Cary,' said Daphne, pulling up the cold and shaking child. 'We must get dressed. Charles will be all right now, you know.'

Cary let herself be led away to the rock where she had left her garments.

Raymond, now that he had leisure from resuscitating Charles, thought, Daphne has intelligence and nerve. She did that well. Diving under and pulling him up and getting him to shore – all very neat. Some girls lose their heads. Daphne is plucky and cool.

He went back to the pool and fetched his jar with the clavellina in it.

4

Daphne took the children back to the hotel. Charles hung on to her arm, walking heavily, drunk with sea water. Poor little boy, dear little boy, he must lie down and rest in the afternoon. Daphne and Daisy both loved Charles. But as to Cary, Daisy, at least, was doubtful. Cary was sometimes disconcerting. Now, however, she ran about, picked up shells and sea-horses, gathered sea-holly and thyme. She was happy again now that Charles was no longer drowned.

In the hotel garden Mr. Folyot sat and read. He was gentle and kind and clever, and was writing a book about sculpture. He looked up over his glasses at Daphne and his children coming in from their walk. Cary cried to him how Charles had been caught in sea-weed and drowned.

'Daphne pulled me up,' said Charles. 'She dived under and pulled me up. I was drowned for a long time on the beach.'

'He lay drowned for hours,' said Cary. 'And they jerked his arms and hit him, and at last he woke up and was sick.'

'Poor Charles,' said Daphne. 'He did have rather a dose of salt water. He got caught in weeds and held, and it was rather a job getting him up.'

'Daphne couldn't do it at first,' said Cary. 'She came up without him, but then Raymond began to come, and she dived down again and got him.'

'Dear me.' Mr. Folyot gathered that there had been a bathing contretemps, of the kind that will occur when people go bathing. His mind was on his book, which was a German book about sculpture.

'Dear me,' he said. 'Very fortunate.' For here they all were, so the contretemps must have turned out well. Naturally, with an intelligent girl like Daphne in charge. That reminded him that he wanted Daphne to take down some notes for him. He caused her to sit down beside him, handed her a pencil and notebook, and sent the children indoors to get ready for lunch. Daphne lit a cigarette and waited, for Mr. Folyot was often slower than he believed in starting. Daphne was interested in his forthcoming treatise, which he was wont to emit in such fragmentary jottings as these; she knew a little about sculpture herself, and could have learnt more had she more time and inclination for study in her idle, gay days. She was really so clever a girl that she could have been proficient in anything to which she had given her mind. As it was, if she did not know a great deal about any one subject, she took an intelligent interest in many. When Mr. Folyot, having assembled the thoughts suggested to him by the German's wrong-headedness, began to utter them, she took them down with intelligent terseness. For her background was sound; she knew what he was talking about. She was young, and her mind worked clearly and gripped hard. Mr. Folyot did not, perhaps, fully realise how well Daphne's mind worked, how clear and apprehensive it was (probably only Daisy realised that), but he thought her a bright, intelligent girl, with enough education to take down his notes. So he emitted sculptural thoughts, dictated references, unloaded his mind of epigrams, arguments, and demolitions of the German, until his wife and Mr. Struther appeared, warm and perspiring, having returned from meeting the boatful of printers.

'They only just,' said Mrs. Folyot, panting in the trivial

shade of a eucalyptus tree, 'escaped being sent as confinati to the Tremiti. Another week and it would have been too late. Some of them *were* sent. . . . They say the dysentery on Lampedusa is appalling.' She dropped her voice, because she and Mr. Struther were involved in hatching a desperate secret enterprise concerning the confinati on the Tremiti islands. They sat daily and discussed it with Italian refugees. Mr. Folyot only doubtfully approved, because it was plotting against the law of another country, and it is by no means certain that one should do this.

CHAPTER 3

Daisy's Afternoon

Daisy, lingering in the hall after they came out from lunch, glanced at the visitors' book. Several people had arrived at this hotel by the midday boat. Mrs. Folyot had not observed them; she had taken interest only in printers and other refugees, who had not come to stay in the hotel. Daphne had asked her at lunch, seeing a party come into the dining-room, who they were, but she had not known. Vaguely and kindly she had dismissed them, as of no importance, as ostensibly not being rebels or refugees.

'But they might,' Daphne had said, 'all the same be amusing,' and then she, too, had dismissed them, forgetting about them. But Daisy, whose job it was to know and to write home about it, lingered by the visitors' book and read the new names – Mr. Gerard Ashley, Lady Anne Ashley, and Miss Mona Ashley. Having collected this information, Daisy picked up the local journal and retired with it behind a palm tree to read the list of yesterday's arrivals on the island. Quite a number of people who mattered were now assembled on the island. Most of them had been at the party last night at the Maris Hotel. Daisy, besides her story about the dead typist, meant to send a paragraph about that party by to-day's post. She went up to her room, sat down at her typewriter, and began to type.

'There was a quite amusing little party last night at the Maris Hotel, given by Mrs. Wentworth-Carr. Everyone on the island who counts seemed to be there. I saw clever Mr. Peter Jameson in the neatest of white ties; unlike many of our younger literary set, he was immaculately turned out, perhaps to compete with his smart wife, who was wearing a silver tunic over slashed beige satin and looked the very latest thing from Paris. Like all top-notchers, Mr. Jameson is most awfully easy to talk to . . .'

and so on. Daisy did not know how much her paper would print of this, but they must have it to select from, as limelight was now playing on this island owing to that little matter of the dead British typist, to which, having finished the quite amusing little party at the Maris, she now turned her attention.

'The mystery surrounding the shingled girl-typist, Vera Wilson, who was found dead in a wood here five days ago, is still unsolved, though the police are said to be at work on clues in their possession. "I cannot think," said her sister, who has come over here, "why Vera should have met with this untimely end, as she was a very bright, popular girl, of a sunny disposition, with no worries and no intimate men friends. It is, naturally, a terrible grief to my poor mother, who had not at all expected any such thing when Vera left England a month ago with a Lunn Party for a holiday." The dead girl's sister, Mrs. Albert Hammond of Walsall, is a handsome, well-dressed, shingled woman, who is naturally in a state of considerable distress. Sensational developments as to the mystery are expected shortly. The islanders are much excited about it, as murders are as unusual here as they are common in Great Britain.'

Here Daisy paused to count the words she had typed and made them one hundred and sixty-eight. She thought two hundred would look better, so added:

'The belief is general that the girl's murderer was of British nationality, though she does not appear to have been particularly friendly with any male fellow-member of her party.'

Daisy, like other journalists, believed, no doubt justly, that the murders of ladies are usually perpetrated by their gentlemen friends, and adopted the motto, '*cherchez l'homme.*' These poor dead girls, always of such sunny natures, with no cares at all, not one, and no men friends, and yet not all their sunniness and their friendlessness had availed to save them from perishing miserably.

The May afternoon, sweet like honey, sharp like the sea, washed in through open green shutters. The town cried, the Mediterranean rustled, the church bells clanged the hour. Daisy enclosed her typed pages in a long envelope, addressed them, and wandered to the window, her heart lifting with the light lifting of the sea. Mother's clever girl, earning her living by writing for the London papers, writing such bright, clever pieces, that people always liked to read. One of those vulgar little journalists who write popular feminine chit-chat in that kind of paper that caters for mob taste. Oh, what matter? She was either, according to her environment. Go to East Sheen, be Mother's clever girl, petted and admired; go to the newspaper office, be one of the smart young women journalists, writing good live articles; move along Folyots and highbrows, and be as one not realised by nice highbrows, and only recognised by less nice highbrows as a target for unkindly jests. Yet it was the highbrows that one chose: this environment that annihilated, that relegated one's activities and one's true self to the slums where common people move. This one chose, because one admired and loved. And, after all, there was Daphne, who would speak for Daisy, who would stand as a shield for her, diverting the notice of the Folyots and the Folyots' friends; Daphne, whom the Folyots accepted and liked, and who, though not herself liking Daisy, yet would always shield her.

Daisy wiped off the cold cream which she had placed on her face and neck after lunch in order to mitigate the effects of the sea. How plain she looked, all yellow and freckled from sea and sun. Some vanishing cream, a lot of powder, a little rouge; that was better. Mrs. Folyot would think she looked made-up if she met her before time had a little abated it. Mrs. Folyot never made up at all. And Daphne only used a little powder sometimes, for her skin was naturally good, and she was only twenty-five.

2

Daisy went downstairs and slipped out with her envelope to
the post. The darling town received her into its long
afternoon sunlight, its steep shadows, its rich fragrances.
She bought nespoli and cherries from the radiant pile at the
corner. Lovely children surrounded and pursued her with
the wide, scornful stare and derisive cries bestowed by
children on the female members of strange races. The faces
of the English they derided because they were not the right
colour or shape: their clothes, because they wore hats, short
skirts, and the wrong shoes; their figures, because these
were straight and scanty instead of full. Daphne and the
Folyots cared nothing, but Daisy grew cross and hot when
thus pilloried. She had that complex which is called inferi-
ority, and knew herself to look, on this island, less than the
islanders. A beautiful but unmannered people, primitively
callous as to the sufferings they inflicted, primitively scornful and derisive of any divergence from type. The English
proletariat, so uncouth, so plain, so vulgar, so lacking in
grace and charm, yet display better and kindlier manners
towards the foreigners in their midst. A kindly people!
Their very vulgarity, that vulgarity to which Daisy, with
her long buff envelope, was subscribing, was, however
fatuous and half-witted, not unkind.

Climbing one of the steep streets that led out of the town
and became a hill-path, Daisy outdistanced the mocking
herd, and forgot her English queerness, and was glad again,
amid the hot sleepy fragrances of heath and honey and
thyme, myrtle, juniper, arbutus, roses, and the sea. She lay
in the blue shadow of a clump of pines and ate nespoli and
cherries, and her heart was shaken by loveliness, and by
Raymond Folyot, whom, a distant, white, lounging figure
below on the beach, she perceived. He was joined by his
mother; she took his arm; they walked and talked. Of what
did they talk? Of sea creatures, radolarians, polyzoans,
rotifers, and clavellina? Of refugees, revolutionaries,
Fascismo, Catalans, nationalist plots? Of Daphne? Of
Daisy? Or merely of the sea, the sky, the weather, and the

island day? God grant it might not be of Daisy; God grant they might not have found Daisy out in her ignominies, her thousand shames, and were not even now saying, we cannot retain her, we must send her away, for she is not our sort, not good for the children; she is, in fact, nothing at all, and her mother in East Sheen is impossible.

To see two others whom she knew talking intimately together filled Daisy always with uneasy alarm, so ardently did she feel that she feared to be their subject, or else so envious was she of that happy stream that flowed on without her, uniting the talkers in mutual ease and love.

To numb that envy and that alarm she thrust into her mouth sweet cherries and juicy nespoli, munching them greedily, like a bear in an orchard. With fruit in the mouth, sweet smells in the air, and the hot sun on foreign hills and sea, all must be well, even though the heart shakes and the soul melts away in fear.

'O honey-sweet the wind of life against the gates of fear
    Drifts, drifts, and breaks, yet breaks not through, and eddies
        backward sighing,
O honey-sweet, and bitter-sweet, like bells upon the air,
    The morning sings against the night, the living to the dying . . .'

But Daisy knew that, instead of poetry, she ought to be writing her weekly articles on Women. Dreamily she mused on it, while the bees hummed round her in the thyme. Should Clever Women Marry Stupid Men? Should Clever Men Marry Stupid Women? Should Women and Men Marry at All? What is the Religion of Women? The Post-War Girl: is she selfish, rude, clever, stupid, drunk, thin, tall, dark, fair? Is one Post-War Girl different in any respect from another? No, that wouldn't do; the press knew she wasn't; it would regard even the question as heresy. You might admire or blame the Post-War Girl but you must not deny her existence as a separate entity. That was left to the Folyots and other highbrows, who had never heard of her owing to not reading the Human Press. To them she was as Mrs. Harris. Neither had Daphne heard of her. But Daisy wrote and read of her daily, and by now knew her simple characteristics by heart, even as she knew those of the girl of an earlier generation, who took no exercise, who fainted or, alternatively, did embroidery, all day, and always obeyed her elders. The Folyots had not heard of her either; to Daisy the world seemed largely made up of persons, things, and ideas of which the Folyots had not heard. She sometimes thought that the Folyots must be, though so clever at some things, a little dense, to see and hear so little of what is so loudly and so continuously written, often in such large and black type. It seemed to Daisy that you couldn't miss it – like the way which one is told by kind strangers in the street. Yet the Folyots would say, blankly, sincerely, and without interest: 'What's that? I never heard of that,' and Daphne would agree that *she* had never heard of it either, or only just, only by the merest chance. And all the time Daisy knew those two dreadful girls, past and present, like sisters, even as she knew the Modern Business Woman, The Mother and her Baby, the Husband, and the Smart Woman choosing her disgusting beige, silver, and jade-green frocks. A grotesque, fantastic gallery, like those waxen figures which stand in the windows of Selfridge's in boudoir caps, in immaculate evening dress, in bathing suits, their scarlet painted fingers lightly holding the handles of small bags, their faces as the faces of simpering corpses. Daisy sometimes wondered which of the figures of which she wrote she most detested. She desired very greatly to tell them exactly what she thought of them all, but this would not be accepted or paid for, and she had to go on babbling of them in half-witted phrases, explaining the modern figures with flattering blame or smarmy praise, referring to the pre-War models with pitying contempt. . . . Damn the lot of them, the silly mannequins, with their cocktails and cigarettes used as panaches, displayed as symptoms, instead of, like the drink and cigarettes of real persons, taken as refreshment; with their self-conscious independence and provocative glances at deans and elderly persons who would, they hoped, preach or write about them; with their very hair and clothes, though worn in the prevalent fashion like everyone else's, made a target for comment, somehow a symbol of some horrid thing called emancipation; with their disgusting babies or careers, their loathsome upstanding courage, and 'boyish figures,' or, alternatively, their horrible embroidery and faked fainting-fits (the connection between embroidery and fainting was clear to the press, though less clear to Daisy, who knew all about fainting but nothing about embroidery). Why was she thus doomed, she impatiently sighed, merely through an accident of sex, to write of these grotesque waxworks, of which intelligent persons had never heard? Why would they not let her write about inhuman things, about books, about religions, about places, about the world at large, about things of which intelligent persons *had* heard? 'A subject for you, Miss Simpson: Can Women have Genius? You might make something good of that, I think. The true genius of women is personal, concerned with people, not ideas – all that, you know. Make it human.' This madhouse built by journalists – had journalists built it first, and so got it into the minds of the more inane of their readers, or had they taken it over from these minds? Daisy believed that journalists had built it, out of their own fevered imaginings, and were busy trying to get it across to the public. But they miscalculated; the public, though dull, has not quite such a skull. . . . It was surely not only the Folyots and their kind who were immune from these seeds of folly; beyond the Folyots stretched the great mass of ordinary impregnable people, who took the world as they found it, and paid no attention to what 'the papers' said. Daisy's mother at East Sheen, for instance, knew that she had not fainted in her youth so often as Daisy fainted now; that she had not obeyed her parents, or led a sheltered life (far from it); that her daughters, and the daughters of her friends, were all different from one another and much what girls had always been; that women were quite ordinary people, going about their business in an ordinary human way, and again all different from one another; that fashions in hair-dressing and clothes had nothing to do with character; that cocktails were just a kind of drink, some tasty, some less tasty, symbolising nothing, and quite as likely to have been drunk fifty years ago, had they happened to have been in fashion; and that it is no more 'fast' or depraved to drink before a meal than during or after it. Daisy's mother read what Daisy wrote in the papers, and thought it fine, but all the finer in that it had no real relation to real people or real life. 'Fancy thinking of all that, you clever girlie!'

Oh, yes, ordinary people, bless them, went about their business, cynical, indifferent, and patiently sceptical, and not even the journalists and novelists (for many novelists also subscribed to this fantasy) themselves believed in their own marionettes. It was all like a foolish clattering stream, running frothily beside the real stream of life. As to that real stream, into its dark and bright shallows and depths, its slimy horrors, its dancing waves, its slow, stagnant pools, its deafening cascades, its lilies, its weeds, and its mud – oh, into the real stream one scarcely could look for dizziness. . . . In the real stream there was no coarse simplicity of types, anyhow not among human creatures, for where spirit begins types end, and each human creature is a thousand worlds, strung loosely together by some strange, frail bond.

Daisy turned her eyes from those worlds, that dizzy stream. She sat up, got out her pen and notebook, and wrote, irritably but firmly, 'The Best Age for a Woman.' For the number of years attained by female creatures on this planet was one of the subjects counted important by her employers, as, doubtless, it was. Through the sweet, hot afternoon, Daisy's pen drowsily and contemptuously inscribed comments on age: how at twenty the female does not know her good fortune; how at thirty she begins to realise youth, just as youth begins to slip by; how at forty she need not be sad, in these days when life holds so much for women besides looking well, and when, moreover, a woman can look well at any age, but should use a little more powder; how at fifty one's grandchildren are (possibly) placed in one's arms, and one must take a back place; how at sixty, one should go, perhaps, into longer dresses; and at seventy use more powder still, but never, even at eighty, let the figure go. As to the face: if the life has been sweet and the thoughts noble and kind, the face will have taken care of itself.

So Daisy wrote her human stuff, hearkening dreamily to the humming of the bees in the myrtle and the chirping of the cicadas in the grass, and the turning and singing of the island world. All was music, all was magic, all was poetry, and within the charmed circle she wrote of human ages for the British Sunday press.

CHAPTER 4

Raymond's Afternoon

On the seashore, among the boats and drying nets and sea-holly, Mrs. Folyot and her son Raymond strolled. To protect her neck from the long slant of the five o'clock sunshine, Mrs. Folyot had hung a handkerchief from her straw hat, and she was talking about the *confinati politici* on the Tremiti Islands, trying to interest Raymond in them.

'Morelli thinks it can be done. It's a big risk, of course . . . but, after all, one can't simply stand aside. The conditions there are *unspeakable*. No water, no proper beds, no anything. All flung together miscellaneously like cattle into a shed, and some of them sentenced for years, probably indefinitely, till Mussolini thinks it safe to let them back. It's all very well, Raymond, but one can't just stand aside and do nothing.'

'Well, but one has to, with other countries' affairs. If you begin interfering, look at South American prisons, or at China, or at almost anywhere. There'd be no end to it.'

'There *should* be no end to it, until governments are forcibly civilised.'

'Governments will never be civilised, forcibly or otherwise. That's to say, never what the more civilised of their people think is civilised, because decent opinion is always ahead of governments and always has been. Anyhow, I don't see that you can go rescuing the prisoners of other countries all over the place.'

'Well, what's the League of Nations for, I ask you?'

Raymond said that he was not quite sure.

'Well, I am. It's to interfere with scandalous ill-treatment and injustice all over the world, whenever it hears of them. Look at the Traffic in Women and Children Report.'

Raymond gently groaned.

'That's all very well, Raymond, and anyone can groan;

it's merely selfish. One's *got* to care and be interested. Fishes aren't everything. You think that because they have no troubles, no one else's matter.'

'Oh, mother, you're wrong about fishes. They have a hell of a time. They are frightfully cruel to each other, like all the animals. Conditions are unspeakable. But still, we shouldn't interfere. . . . Human beings, you know, are, on the whole, among the less atrociously cruel of the creatures. All but the crudest barbarians have that kind of softness that keeps them from the worst atrocities. The other animals haven't; they're damned heartless, and no one's pain but their own matters twopence to them. If you want to write to the League of Nations, write about the way the spex lays its eggs on the paralysed cricket, or the way the fox drives the badger and the rabbit from their houses and steals them for himself, or the shrike's methods at meal times, or the shrieks of the fly in the hands of the spider, or – '

'My dear boy, I'm sure it's a hell of a world. But fortunately we didn't make it, and needn't hold ourselves responsible. Now for our behaviour to one another we *are* responsible; we have to keep one another, so far as we can, in order, and protect the under-dog. You'd interfere to save children, wouldn't you?'

'Possibly, in some circumstances. All depends. So long as no one called them *the* children. I do hate the definite article when applied to generic groups. If the organisers of charitable funds realised the effect their language has on our minds they'd cut it out. The 'Save the Children Fund,' now – if it was called, say, 'Destitute Children's Fund' or something business-like of that kind, it would have got three times as much money always. I've even seen 'Save the Kiddies' sometimes. Well, it simply can't be done. One couldn't bear to help to perpetuate the kiddies in any way. Whereas to 'A Fund for Children Seriously in Need of Assistance' one might send something.'

'Don't be petty, Raymond. What's language, when it's a question of saving lives?'

But Raymond had never been a particularly ardent saver of life. When he was six and had been taken to *Peter Pan*, he had turned down his thumbs at Tinker Bell, since he did not believe in fairies and strongly disliked this one. Shortly after the apparently otherwise unanimous verdict on Tinker Bell, he had been sick and had been taken out. Either it was the raspberry frappe and the mixed fruit sundae he had had for lunch, or it was Peter and Wendy, about whom he felt much as he felt in these later days about the dancers in the Russian Ballet. Raymond was, as a matter of fact, no patron of the drama; it seemed to him nearly always sentimental, silly, and vulgar.

'Well,' he said practically, 'how are you going to set about this rescue party? What's Morelli's scheme?'

'I mustn't tell you that. We're not telling a soul. But we think it's practicable.'

'Practicable! You'll all find yourselves in jug before you've done, mother. Then father will have to pull strings to get you out. He won't enjoy that.'

'Nonsense, dear. There's no question of jug. It's all beautifully organised. Stephen will tell you that.'

Raymond looked bored. With none of Mr. Struther's views as to the universe was he in agreement, and he felt this clergyman to be too much in evidence.

'Where's Daphne this afternoon?' He preferred Daphne to Struther.

'I don't know. She went off alone somewhere. . . . What's this about Charles? Was he really long under?'

'Long enough. It took a few minutes getting him round. He quite passed out for a bit.'

'It's not safe, really, their bathing like that, with you catching crabs on shore and Daphne swimming about practising strokes. Children have to be watched.'

'Oh, it's safe enough. Nothing's safe. Daphne got him up all right, and I should have been there in time if she hadn't. Daphne's got lots of sense.'

'Oh, Daphne's a capable girl. Still, she must watch them. . . . Daphne's quite keen about this scheme of Morelli's by the way; much keener than you are.'

'Is she? I don't think so. I don't think Daphne's keen about things like that. Not really. She didn't want to damp you, that was all.'

Daphne, he thought, was keen about aquatic creatures, clavellina, rotifers, sea-horses, and rare shells. These were what Daphne was keen on, these and bathing, and walking, and exploring, and enjoying herself about the place; Daphne didn't give a damn for *confinati politici* on the Tremiti Islands or for fleeing refugees either. Still, she was a kind of secretary to his mother. His father thought she was keen on Greek sculpture. Struther thought she was a good deal interested in religion.

'I suppose she has an interested kind of mind,' Raymond admitted.

'Doesn't *know* anything,' said Mrs. Folyot. 'Not to speak of. But likes to hear. She's very sympathetic, Daphne is. Enters into things. Now I must go in. I've two anti-Soviet refugees coming for a chat. We're trying to help them get their wives and children from Moscow.'

'Well,' said Raymond. 'I shall go to a café and get a drink, and then bathe. You make me thirsty.'

'Go and drink, then. It's all these crabs and shells and things you grub about for make you thirsty, not me. Another thing, they're making you slouch terribly. You should have a turn at looking for birds, or stars, or aeroplanes. I can't think why all you young people slouch: *we* don't.'

Stout but upright, she hurried up the beach to the hotel.

From the hillside above, Daisy saw Mrs. Folyot go, saw Raymond turn up towards the town, slouching his hands in his pockets, his soft hat over his eyes. She was filled with desires to save him from drowning, to hold palm leaves over his head to protect him from the sun, to run before him collecting from the sands all the shells in the world to stuff into his pockets, to dive deep into the ocean and come up laden with rare protozoa, with clavellina, with sun-fish, that he might, having confined them in bottles, take his pleasure therefrom.

3

Daphne, strolling along the shadowed streets of the town, saw Raymond sitting outside a café, drinking beer, and stopped beside him.

'Hullo, I'm thirsty too. I'd like a lemon ice.'

'Right. Take a seat. I could do with one myself. I've had too much beer. It's good here, that's a fact. That's why I drink it, not because I'm thirsty. Have some, I advise you. It's good.'

'I know it's good. Yes. I'll have a Pilsener. *And* the lemon ice. I'm hot. I'm sweating.'

'You look it. What've you been doing?'

'Just scrambling about. I shall bathe now.'

'So shall I. I like to bathe on several beers and an ice.'

'Do you think I ought to go in first and look for the kids?'

'No. They'd want to bathe too.'

'Well, Charles can't again to-day. So I'd better leave them alone. . . . This tastes good all right. I wanted this.'

'I always want Pilsener when I'm warm. More than Lager I want it. Don't you?'

'All depends . . . I'd rather have a gin-and-ginger if I could, every time. That's one of the few mistakes foreigners make, not having gin-and-ginger. They're right about tea; it's a fool's drink really. Thank God I'm not a tea-soaker.' (Daisy, however, was precisely this.)

'You're ice-sodden, though. Hurry up with it. No, rot, you don't need another. Come on.'

'I've got to go and fetch my bathing-suit.'

'Well, don't let anyone keep you. Mother's doing rescue work; she's got Russians there – or she had; probably by now it's Catalans or anti-Fascists or discontented Portuguese. She says you're interested in that Italian prisoners' scheme. I said you weren't.'

'Of course I am. I think it's very amusing. I love Mrs. Folyot's schemes; they're so racy and distinguished.'

'I damp them. I don't want her jugged. She was always being jugged when I was small. I forget why. She rather likes it, but it makes trouble, and would hamper Cary and

Charles at school. Parents have got to think of that. One never minds disgrace again, but at school one does. I remember I did. Did you?'

'Awfully. I do still.'

'Oh, well, there doesn't seem to be such a thing when one's grown up. I can't think of anything. I mean, even if one wrote a novel, or a play, or one's memoirs, well, people are doing it all the time, and one would feel hardened. And one stops feeling in the least responsible for one's relations.'

'Absolutely.' Daphne went into the hotel for her bathing-suit. In her bedroom she met Daisy putting away the manuscripts she had brought down from the hillside.

'His relations,' said Daisy, who had heard Raymond's remark, 'are all right. They couldn't disgrace anyone. If he saw some of mine!'

She looked into the glass and powdered her face and wished she looked cooler; but it was Daphne who went out to bathe with Raymond.

CHAPTER 5

Daisy and the Boar

One afternoon soon after this, Daisy and the two children took a country walk. It was a very hot afternoon, even at five o'clock. They went up a hill path, which began by being paved and climbing in shallow steps between pink and white farm-houses, olive groves, orange and lemon gardens, fig trees, vines, and cultivated land, but after the village of Canio it became a rough track and led through open heath country and dense thickets of oak, pine, ilex, and cork. The air here was of a marvellous sweetness owing to the many aromatic shrubs that grew together, as has been before mentioned – pink heath, white heath, sarsaparilla, myrtle, lavender, juniper, strawberry, cistus, honeysuckle, and no doubt a great many more plants, all mingling as fragrantly as possible with the sharper tang of the ocean, that drifted even so high as this.

The children played in the heath, which grew to a great height, and climbed the trees in the woods, and Daisy, forgetting them, drifted lazily about the maquis, half-inebriated with the hot sweetness and the strangeness of the golden evening.

'Oh honey-sweet and bitter-sweet, like bells upon the air . . .
Oh honey-sweet and bitter-sweet, against the gates of fear. . . .'

If Raymond were up here too, all would be rapture, all would be peace. One could see a long island lying, a deeper blue against the pale-blue sea, far to the south. Almost one could see the mainland, so clear the evening was. To the north climbed the mountains, their heads in snow, their feet lapped in blue and golden meadows.

'What are you?' called Cary to Charles. 'I'm Eagle Nose, the Sioux chief . . . All about us, in the dense forest, can be heard the rustling and grunting of my hidden followers, relentlessly pursuing their victims. . . . Look out for yourself, Paleface, if I should give them the word to attack.'

The maquis was full of stirrings, hoppings, twitterings, and cries. All the birds in the world must be in it – thrushes, blackbirds, wrens, tits, finches, wagtails, robins, nightingales, and little owls. You would think all the birds on the island had been shot and eaten in pâtés, but still the maquis was always full of birds.

The woods, too, were full of stirrings, rootings, and scufflings – forest beasts, or the tribe of Eagle Nose relentlessly pursuing their victims. Bandits, wolves, and boars, or merely rabbits, badgers, and hares. Forests are never, for a moment, quite quiet; not in the hot drowsy hour of noon, nor yet in the deepest dark of night; always in forests something stirs, rustles, and roots, feet patter, bodies leap, quick eyes glance . . .

2

The gruntings and scufflings became a rending crash as the boar leapt out of the woods. For a moment he stood, heavy head raised, tusks gleaming, staring with small red eyes at the intruders on his heath. Charles was nearest to him; Cary was ten yards away from Charles, and Daisy twenty yards from Cary. Such a boar he seemed as was sent by an offended goddess to devastate Calydon, or such a boar as Heracles pursued up Erymanthus, so fierce that he would require a hundred huntsmen to despatch him, with infinite sacrifice of life, or else Heracles with his noose.

'Run, children, run,' Daisy cried to them, superfluously, for already they ran, and she too, towards the old stone wall that shambled along the edge of the maquis. They weren't safe, these wild boars; they might be harmless, but they might pursue and gore. They all ran. When Daisy reached the wall she turned and saw the children behind her, Cary ahead, Charles behind, and the boar rootling about at the edge of the heath, swinging his great head and staring at Charles. Suddenly he grunted and moved forward, lum-

bering through the heath with a crashing, tearing noise. He
was after Charles.

'Run, Charles, run,' Daisy called from the wall. There
was no danger, she thought; Charles would reach the wall
long before the boar reached him. But misfortune overtook
Charles; he stumbled over a branch and fell, and as he
scrambled up he wrenched his ankle, and now could only
hobble along, while the boar gained on him each second.
Cary had nearly reached the wall when it happened; she
screamed to Daisy: 'He can't run, it will catch him!' then
'Come and keep it off! It will catch him!'

Daisy stood irresolute; the boar was still a few lengths
behind Charles. Cary, calling out no more, caught up the
branch of a tree that lay near and ran back to Charles. She
pulled him along by the arm, waving the branch with her
other hand; then Charles fell again, and the boar pounded
up close to them, and Cary faced him with her branch,
screaming: 'Get back, get back! Help!'

Daisy had no stick with her; she stood by the wall unable
to move. Daphne would have dashed to the children's side
and defended them with her own body; Daisy had not this
courage nor the training which teaches that on no account
must we leave children in the lurch, so she hesitated by the
wall, looking this way and that for a weapon or for help,
and the boar rushed at Cary and knocked her off her legs
even as Raymond vaulted over the wall and ran towards
them.

Daisy hid her eyes with her hands; when she looked again
Raymond was coming towards her, carrying Cary, with
Charles hobbling at his side. The boar stood behind,
uneasy, sullen, beaten off by Raymond's heavy stick,
doubtful whether and how to charge again. They reached
the wall, and Raymond laid Cary on the grass on its farther
side. Cary was promptly sick. She had fallen on her head;
her nerves, strung unbearably taut, now collapsed, and she
fell to whimpering. Charles nursed his ankle, and
whimpered a little too.

'How did you get here?' Daisy asked.

'I was up on the hill above, with my mother. We saw the

whole thing. I couldn't get down before.' He answered her brusquely, without looking at her, bending over Cary. Daisy's heart turned chilly within her. We saw the whole thing: what, then, had he thought of her?

'Lucky you came,' she said. 'Though, of course, I didn't suppose there was any danger. If I'd thought there was, I'd have gone back to them myself, of course.'

Raymond ignored that.

'Well, you might see to Charles's ankle now,' he said.

How he disliked and despised her. This was the end, then. Cowardice did not do. Anything else might pass, but not that, not leaving children in the lurch.

With cold, shaking hands she removed the shoe and stocking of Charles, disclosing an ankle swollen and hot. As she did so, Mrs. Folyot arrived, fat and scant of breath, having run down the hill after Raymond. She all but pushed Daisy aside, and took possession of the situation, of Charles's ankle and Cary's collapse. Of Daisy she took no notice; for once she was that most terrifying of God's creatures, an angry mother whose young have been injured. Deftly she bound Charles's ankle with a handkerchief, then took the shivering Cary into her lap and held her in a comforting clasp.

'Still dizzy, darling? There, there, it's all over now, and mother's got you safe; just forget all about it, my lamb.' She was afraid for Cary, a nightmare-ridden child, who would for ever be haunted by a boar with savage red eyes, rushing at her. She rocked her to and fro, crooning: 'All over now, my lamb; quite safe now.'

'I'll carry Charles,' said Raymond. 'Cary'll be able to walk down all right, won't you, old lady? Still groggy? Hang on to mother's arm, then.'

'And mine,' said Daisy.

At that Mrs. Folyot flashed round at her. 'No need for yours,' and, panting, helped Cary to her legs.

So the little party trailed slowly down the hill-path; Raymond first, with Charles on his back, Mrs. Folyot behind him, with Cary, white and shaken, clinging heavily to her arm; Daisy alone in the rear.

3

This was the end. Anything else might pass. But not cowardice; not leaving children in the lurch. They hated her, they despised her, as she hated and despised herself. Daisy had a passionate admiration for courage. But in practice she was like the people in the newspapers, who stand by and watch children drown, for fear of being drowned themselves. She lacked the elementary courage which is a matter of course with people like the Folyots and their friends. They had not Daisy's admiration for it; they merely took it for granted in one another and in her. Only Cary had known, had always seen into Daisy's soul, behind her defences, and had known. Cary had not for a moment expected Daisy to go to Charles's help; Cary had known that she would not. But Mrs. Folyot and Raymond had been shocked and disgusted; they had not known.

So this was the end. They despised her, and she must leave them; she could not stay, despised. She had been unmasked as not their sort, as a lower, meaner, commoner sort than theirs, and she must go.

They were unfair. What did they know of the sick tumult of nerves that shook her when danger threatened, dizzying her brain and paralysing her will? To them decency was so easy; to her so hard. They didn't understand. . . . It hadn't been deliberate; she hadn't meant to save herself and leave Charles to the boar; she hadn't known what she was doing, blind and sick with fear. Couldn't they make allowances? Oh, yes, they would make allowances, they were generous and would be kind again, but they wouldn't trust her, they would always know her now for what she was, for Daisy, a girl who lost her head in danger, and left children in the lurch. That was how they would always think of her now, even though they would be kind again. So this was truly the end.

The island and the shimmering sea swam in tears before Daisy's hot eyes. If only Daphne and not she had been on the maquis that afternoon, how differently would the adventure have turned out! Daphne would have defended the children from the boar with all the agility and courage of the heroines of moving pictures. Daisy saw her, chivvying the creature back with her stick, keeping between it and the children till they were safely over the wall, then leaping over it herself, just in time.

But Daphne had been off duty this afternoon, for Daisy had not known that Raymond and his mother were to be on the hills. Well, it was a pity, it was all a sad pity, and life was really at an end. As to Cary, the malicious child, she would probably have an illness, just out of spite – hysteria, or meningitis, or concussion. She would be delirious, and lie raving about boars, and Charles, and Daisy not coming to save him. Mrs. Folyot, a generous woman, but a mother, would not forgive if Cary should lie ill. Mr. Folyot, only a father and a man, would forgive more easily; in fact, he would not be greatly impressed by the tale of what he had not seen; also, as middle-aged men do, he would judge Daisy as a girl, and not as he would judge a man. Women and young men know better than this; young men because they understand their contemporaries, women because they understand their sex. Neither offer young women the indulgence of kindly contempt.

'It's scandalous,' Mrs. Folyot was saying, 'the way they leave these wild boars loose about the place. I shall certainly speak to the Mayor about it. *And* write to the papers. They ought all to be exterminated immediately.'

'Oh, they're mostly pretty safe, probably,' said Raymond, who was zoolotrous, and did not care that even boars should be exterminated. 'Unless they're annoyed.'

Mrs. Folyot sniffed. 'Boars are always annoyed, I should think. At least they look it. Those horrible little eyes, and their mouths and noses and tusks. Most ill-tempered creatures.' She had forgotten Cary, whose hand tightened on her arm, and she added quickly, 'But still, I expect they look worse than they are. I don't believe they really hurt people. Only bowl them over in play, eh, old lady?'

'There's an owl,' said Charles, who, though in some pain, retained his placid interest in the world, 'on that tree.'

How calm boy children were, his mother reflected, while

girls were so often all nerves. It was a lovable quality, this
unconscious placidity of the male. It was part of the reason
why men went so far; they remained whole, did not go to
pieces as women did, under the assaults of fate. They were
less passible, less brittle, more courageous. They could
even go into battle and come out sane.

The party trailed down the hill and into the hotel.

4

At dinner they were not unkind to Daisy; they spoke to her
almost as usual. The episode was over, and the Folyots were
too generous and too sensible to bear a grudge against a girl
for losing her nerve in danger. Mrs. Folyot had, to be sure,
decided that she was not a fit person to send out with
children, but that was no reason for nagging her. As to
Daphne, she was wilted and confused by Daisy's disgrace,
and hardly knew how to take it or how deport herself,
whether to make much of it or little, whether to shield
Daisy with gay composure or to blame and accuse her. For
once, Daphne was at a loss. The young women went to bed
early, and Daisy had an abominable night. Mrs. Folyot sat
with Cary, who had a temperature and nightmares.

Next morning Daisy accosted Mr. Struther in the
lounge, reading the day before yesterday's *Times*. She could
not ask the Folyots what they felt about her staying on, but
Mr. Struther, an impartial third party, to whom Mrs.
Folyot had doubtless spoken her mind, could be consulted.
It was not an easy conversation, for both were embarrassed;
Daisy at what she had to ask; the clergyman, a kindly man,
at what he had to reply. But he replied truthfully. Yes, Mrs.
Folyot *had* doubted whether Daisy was the best person to be
with children. Yes, he was afraid he must own that Mrs.
Folyot was disappointed, and a little vexed. Mothers, of
course . . . and she had had a bad night with Cary. From
this Daisy gathered that Mrs. Folyot's expressions of
doubt, disappointment, and vexation had not been confined to last night.

'Perhaps you might open the subject with her,' he suggested. 'Explain a little how it was.'

'But there's nothing to explain. Besides, explanations never turn out well. No one believes them. I *was* frightened, and I *did* run away and leave the children, and they saw me. I'd better go back to England, I think. . . .' Her voice quavered, and she turned away to hide her rising tears, for tears came easily to her when she was tired and had not slept.

Mr. Struther protested at that. 'My dear child, no. What an idea. You mustn't make a mountain out of a molehill like that. I shall blame myself very much.'

But Daisy, really crying now, had gone. She ran up to her room and locked the door, ashamed of her tears. To cry was a disgrace; Daphne never cried.

Well, it all came to this, then. The Folyots would never think the same of her again, and she would go. The Folyots' household was no place for such as her. She would return to her cheap journalism and her cheap London rooms.

She deputed Daphne to tell Raymond that afternoon that they were going (for if Daisy went Daphne must go, too). If Raymond should ask them to stay, as if he meant it, not as if he were being polite or kind, they would stay. That should be the test.

Raymond was preoccupied with a lizard when Daphne told him, and hardly asked them to stay at all, only saying, 'That's too bad. Must you really go?' and that settled it. Daisy's heart (for she was listening) turned to lead in her, and Daphne said, indifferently lighting a cigarette, that they really must, there was so much to do at home. Daphne wasn't going to refer, even remotely, to Daisy's conduct in the matter of that damned boar. Raymond's regret was abstracted; it seemed to Daisy that he didn't care twopence; he had been Daphne's friend, he had talked to her about all manner of things, and shown her all kinds of creatures he had found, but now he was wrapped up in a lizard and didn't care twopence.

So in the evening, at dinner, Daphne told Mr. and Mrs. Folyot that they must go next week. Mrs. Folyot said that she was terribly sorry, but, of course, if it must be.

'We shall all miss you,' she said to Daphne.

'I certainly shall,' said Mr. Folyot. 'Who's to help me with my notes?'

Mrs. Folyot looked kindly at Daphne, remembering what a nice woman her aunt, who had died last year, had been. Unmarried, highly educated, an artist, and interested in all kinds of good causes, such as anti-vivisection, welfare work, and hand-weaving; Mrs. Folyot had liked Daphne's and Daisy's aunt very much. She was remorseful now about yesterday, fearing, after what Mr. Struther had told her, that she had been sharp about the boar. But she had a capable young niece who would be delighted to come out while they stayed abroad and help with everything, and perhaps this would be best. So, 'But of course if you must,' she said.

CHAPTER 6

The Boat Train

It was on the train from Paris to Calais that England began. Till then it had been abroad, Daisy felt, but the boat train was England, tourist England, returning from a Cook's tour. The second-class carriages were full of the English upper-middle and lower-middle classes. The Cook's tourists were for the most part of the class called lower-middle. Daisy was struck, not for the first time, by how ethical in speech were the English, and specially the lower-middle classes and the poor. They must be ethical, for they kept saying the word 'right.' Foreigners do not say 'right' much. The conversation of the French is not punctuated with the word *juste,* that of Italians with *ragione,* that of Spaniards with *razon*, nor that of Germans with *recht*. But the English say right, right, right, like crickets chirping, or like a drill sergeant gone wrong.

'That's right,' they were saying, and, 'It didn't seem right, did it, over-charging us like that?' And, 'It's only right, isn't it?' And again, 'That's right.'

Daisy thought, we are an unattractive people, self-conscious and prim. To be fearless, careless, and free – this is the manner to have. Daphne had it; most foreigners had it; some of the English upper class had it, and some of the poor. The middle classes were timid, careful, proper, and constrained. A crowd of them together, like this, was like a coffle of slaves; they would have the slave virtues and vices. Daisy disliked them with the intensity of one sick for abroad. They were emblems to her of that England to which she was in bitterness returning.

'But I said to them, it's only right to have the windows down a little in this heat. The convenience of all in the compartment should be consulted, I said. It's only right isn't it?'

'That's right.'

Daphne contemptuously read a French novel.

A ticket collector came round. The Cook's tourists spoke to him in halting, impossible French. He angrily shrugged, as the French do when people speak their language badly, and banged the door.

Daisy, too, despised the English for not knowing French. But, all the same, she wondered why it was considered by her, by the French, and by many English, more contemptible and laughable of English persons to speak French badly than of French persons to speak English badly. If a French woman struggled haltingly with English, English ticket collectors would help her out, all kindness and courtesy. But when English persons struggled with French, French ticket collectors were angry and contemptuous and pretended not to understand a word. *Was* it more ignoble not to know French than not to know English? Daisy felt sure that somehow it was, but did not know why. It is, of course, always stupid not to be able to talk the language of the country one is in.

Daphne's French was accomplished; she kept on reading her French novel; she preferred novels to be in French. Sometimes she half smiled, tickled by a stroke of Gallic wit.

The tourist next to her was reading an English novel in Tauchnitz. Most of the tourists were not reading at all, but talking together about their experiences, which had been, to use their own expression, most enjoyable.

It was now definitely established that Daisy disliked these people, since they were other, quite other, than the Folyots, and since they reminded her of the more repulsive elements of English life, those elements for which newspapers catered when they made her write such articles as she wrote. These were the people who were meant by editors to read her articles and find them enjoyable; these were her public. All the same, Daisy believed them to be misjudged in this matter. Unattractive they might be, but they had plenty of sound sense. Daisy did not think that they wasted their time reading articles on the habits of women; they had too much else to do. Not even these were so foolish as the newspapers thought.

'It's quite feasible,' someone was saying, 'that Harold and Lillee may meet us at Dover. Mother didn't say for certain, but it's quite feasible they may.'

Daisy, not only a xenomaniac, but a wholehearted snob, passionately over-esteeming those advantages (such as education, elegance, and correct English) which money can buy, despised these bleating uneducated voices and their catachrestic speech. She wondered if these people came, possibly, from Tooting, that so notorious suburb, of which one had heard such derogatory opinions, which had been so loudly and so often condemned by those who, presumably, knew what they were talking about. One day Daisy meant to go to Tooting and find out whether those who condemned it were right, and if it was really worse than other places.

But Daphne, well sustaining her attitude of amused indifference, read her novel. The tiresomeness of people never bothered Daphne, who was tranquil.

A group of young women of another kind of upbringing were talking in the corridor, in their deeper, crisper tones, and terser, less genteel phraseology. Daisy wondered why having more money and staying longer at school should make female voices deeper and male voices less deep. She thought of Mrs. Folyot's voice, a busy, intelligent contralto, and of Raymond's soft, light tones, but at the thought of the voice of Raymond her soul swooned away in desolation, for it seemed to sound in her ears now, above the train's clatter and the rambling bleat of the voices of those with less money who had stayed less long at school. 'Many plants can move about quite freely,' he was saying, as he had said one evening on the beach last week, and Daphne had laughed.

Between Daisy and the prim French fields a brown shore shimmered, with a purple evening sea slurring softly at its weedy edge, and Raymond, bare-armed, bare-legged, bare-headed, prodding a heap of sea-weed.

Daisy dragged her thoughts away. She thought again of class and national differences, and reflected how members of the English upper classes quite often resembled, in

appearance, fishes. They were, too, the stiffest people on
the earth's face, and did not speak unless they had been
introduced. They were not cheerful and cordial to
strangers; they were afraid of them, and caused them, in
their turn, to be afraid. No people in this world made one so
shy, or were so shy themselves. Still, they were not without
charm.

'Well, fancy, if that isn't the Channel,' said someone.
'Good old England at last. I shan't mind a nice cup of tea and
a bun again, shall you, after all those cafés and *gâteaux*?
Well, I never did, Ethel, if you haven't been sitting right on
top of the bag with the *gâteaux* I bought for Charlee. You
are a one.'

How kind, to have thought of Charlee and bought him
gâteaux. And how kind, how more than kind, to hold one
another's heads upon the Channel, which to-day was
uneasy. Daisy, too, was overcome, and if anything could
have made her plight worse it would have been to have her
head held; but still, how kind!

Dover, porters more tranquil than the porters of Calais,
and grey rain. It had been a mistake to cross the troubled
dividing seas for this, leaving abroad behind.

Daisy thought that when she should be old, if she should
have any money at all, she would be one of those spinster
ladies who reside in hotels abroad, roaming from hotel to
hotel, with their little spirit lamps, their tea-infusing
spoons, and their chatty friendships with one another and
with the chaplain. The state of these gentle nomads is very
gracious; if they become bored they have but to fold their
tents like the Arabs and silently steal away, transferring
themselves, their spirit lamps, infusing spoons, hot bottles,
and chat to a new place, where also they shall find sunshine,
a chaplain, new lady friends, and the enchanting music of
foreign tongues. Single, as the world counts singleness,
they have taken abroad for their husband; homeless, they
are freed from household cares: rootless, they flourish in
any soil; depatriate, they have for country the world. And
never have they need to cross those narrow but unpleasant
dividing seas, for they are already where they would be.

The placards of three different evening papers announced in brief to the returned English the day's occurrences. One said:

WEST-END FLAT MYSTERY SURPRISE
DARK GIRL SENSATION
AMAZING REVELATIONS

Another:

WELL-KNOWN CLUBMAN IN DOCK
MYSTERY WOMAN IN COURT
AMAZING SCENES

And the third, more briefly:

CAPTAIN COE'S FINALS
FLAPPER'S FATAL LEAP

Some of the English had been away from these cryptic sentences so long that they had forgotten how to parse them, and whether surprise was a noun, an adjective, or a verb, and whether a clubman was a man who wielded a club, like a gunman, or a man who spent a great deal of time at his club (how much time each week qualified you as a clubman was known only to news editors). In fact, the British had become unused to British journalism. But they would soon pick it up again.

Daisy, on reading the placard about the dark surprise sensation mystery flat girl, commented briefly, 'That's Ed. He's on that flat crime story.'

CHAPTER 7

Daisy in East Sheen

Mrs. Lily Arthur, of 'Thekla,' Park Street, East Sheen, W.14, hummed 'Barcelona' as she let herself into her house. She was a tall, plump, fair woman of forty-nine, and looked happy, even when she had not just been, as now, to the pictures. She had a kind of gallant and cheerful idleness, which sent her out on pleasure bound, whatever duties there might be that she ought rather to have fulfilled. Too neat in her personal habits to be a slattern, too capable to be an incompetent housewife, she only sailed, owing to her zest for life, just this side of both. Her husband and her three children who lived at home all went up daily to London to pursue their several avocations; her husband William was head of a builder's and decorator's firm in Baker Street; her son Edward was a newspaper reporter; her daugher Ada an assistant in Keith's Cheap Books Store; and Amy, the youngest, a telephone operator. All earned their bread, or some of it; only Mrs. Arthur was a contented drone.

They were all home when she came in, and had begun supper – ham, salad, buttered egg, ginger pudding and treacle, all kinds of delicious viands. Mrs. Arthur advanced on them like a sail spread to the winds, removed her hat, patted her large shingled head, which was dyed bright gold, and sat down with a sigh.

'You old gadabout,' her husband William said, with affection. 'Been to those pictures again, I suppose.'

'You've got it, Dad. It was Harold Lloyd, so I just had to be there. But if I'd of known you were all going to get home so prompt, I'd have gone after supper instead. Then we could all have gone together. You're all home early, aren't you?' Mrs. Arthur usually believed her family to be home early. 'Well, what's the news from London? Don't all speak at once. You look tired, girlie,' she added to her youngest.

Amy said, in the clear trilling notes of the telephone operator, 'You can believe I *am* tired, Ma. Nothing but trouble from morning till night. And the language! There was one subscriber said such things, when I reported it to Mr. Clark, he said he'd a good mind to cut her right off and go straight round and see her and tell her why. If it was his own daughter, he said he'd say to her, who she'd spoke to like that, he'd have her in the courts for it, he said, and he wasn't going to have us girls spoke to like that, he said. I mean, you can't speak back at them, that's what it is, so it's downright mean, really it is. One of the girls had her ear drum nearly broke to-day, a subscriber put the receiver and transmitter close together so as to make a howl. That's the meanest thing they can do to us, and they know it, too, the beasts. And us girls can't do anything back, that's where it is.'

'You can chalk up in their bills all the wrong numbers you've given 'em,' her brother suggested, but Amy returned, tranquilly contemptuous, 'Oh, we do that in any case. We're supposed to. Telephones wouldn't pay the Postmaster if we didn't do that. That's why their calls always come to twice as many as they expect, the silly cheeses. Serve them right. All that chatter about nothing. Silly, I call it.'

'Well,' her mother cheerfully observed, '*you* needn't talk about that, my girl. No one can get in edgeways when you get going. Ada, have you brought me back a nice book for the week-end?'

Mrs. Arthur, instead of belonging to a circulating library, preferred to buy her reading-matter cheap from Keith's, so that she could, if she liked it very much, retain it, or if was so minded, sell it again.

'Yes, mother. This week's Edgar Wallace. A review copy, half a crown. It's fine. Truer to life than his last week's, they say. More *likely*.'

'Oh, likely . . .' Mrs. Arthur looked doubtful. 'Not one of those realistic, everyday books, is it? I don't care about those. I mean, I like something out of the way, to surprise me.'

'Oh, it'll surprise you all right. He always does that, Wallace does. I read the first chapter . . .'

'Don't tell me, girl, that's a selfish trick, I've often told you, telling books aloud. I want to be surprised, so does Dad.'

'Oh, me. I never look at your nonsense, I've too much else to do.'

Mrs. Arthur suddenly jumped.

'Why, if I've not forgotten, Daisy's coming to-night. There was a telegram. She got into London this afternoon, and she says: "Coming to-night."'

Daisy was Mrs. Arthur's eldest daughter, by an earlier and less regular union; Daisy's father had not been Mr. Arthur, but a young literary man, who had fallen in with her mother at a farm where he was spending the summer. Mrs. Arthur was extremely proud of Daisy, who took after her father, and had been well educated, having lived during her school terms, between the ages of eleven and eighteen, with her father's unmarried sister in London and gone to St. Paul's School. Daisy now wrote for the papers, and had recently been abroad, with a Mr. and Mrs. Folyot. Ada and Amy did not think so highly of Daisy as their mother did; after all, she was thirty and not yet married, and her looks weren't much either (Ada and Amy were of that large majority who believe in human looks). Also she was stuck up, and neither had she been born in wedlock. Still, they got on with her pretty well, and so did Edward. William was kind to her, but faintly shy; he could not help regarding her as a lapse on his wife's part, and her paternal relatives were of the class whose houses he decorated, but with whom he did not hold much other intercourse. Still, William said: 'Well, that's good,' liking Lily to be pleased.

'Plenty of room for us all,' he added, with some pride, for he had prospered, and had a nice good-sized house. His step-daughter Daisy did not spend a great deal of her time in it; she had mainly lived in London, first with her aunt, who had recently died, then in a flat in Great Russell Street.

2

The door-bell rang, and they all went to let Daisy in. Mrs.
Arthur engulfed her in a deep embrace. Suit-cases filled the
little hall. Among them stood Daisy, travel-stained yet
neat, a wisp of a young woman, all over freckles and tan
from suns abroad, assured, friendly, yet faintly forlorn.
Perhaps she missed Daphne.

'You've not had supper, girl? We're just at it now. Emily,
set a place for Miss Daisy.'

No, Daisy had not had supper. Emily set a place for her,
among the lavish foods, and they all went on eating.

'You're as thin as a sparrow,' Mrs. Arthur told her
daughter, 'after all those foreign hotels. You must eat up
and get plump. . . . So you got tired of being abroad, did
you? Well, I don't blame you. A change is a change, but you
don't want to *live* abroad. How did you leave your friends?'

'They were all right,' Daisy said, and, as she said it, was
overwhelmed, borne down by her consciousness of how
right, how unassailably, impassibly all right, the Folyots
had been left, how impregnably unaffected by any comings
and goings of hers, on their happy island beneath the ardent
sun. A circle of tranquil brightness seemed to girdle them
about, enclosing them in a passionless paradise like the
saints – Mr. Folyot, writing about sculpture in his long
chair, placidly amused; Mrs. Folyot, bustling about with
Mr. Struther, surrounded by refugees, deep in helpful
schemes; Cary and Charles gambolling in the sea's bright
edge; Raymond with his net, peering darkly into pools.
Oh, yes, she had left the Folyots all right.

The supper-table, plump with English food, shone
sleekly in its glossy tablecloth beneath the chandelier.

'Coming again for ham, Ada?' said Mr. Arthur.

'No, thanks, Dad, I've done very well.'

The old familiar phrases. Daisy remembered hearing
them as a schoolgirl, to and fro between her mother's house
and her aunt's, observing the different speech that obtained
in each. Have some more, come again; had enough, done
very well; napkins, serviettes; woman, lady; man, gentle-

man, or fellow; jam, preserve; cos*tume*, *cost*ume; of'n, often; and so on and so on. It was like knowing intimately two languages. The people in the train had talked the East Sheen language. But the people in the train had been not only common; they had been dismally unattractive, genteel, and prim. The Arthurs were common, but they weren't prim, they were attractive. Daisy saw them as attractive, munching round the table, chattering, bickering, chaffing – William, grey-headed, solid, moustached, beaming across at his wife; Ada, pretty, pale, dark, rather charming, and brimful of the knowledge of all British fiction; Amy the fair, baby-faced little creature of just twenty, with her sleek cropped head, one of the kind little girls who talk to us so sweetly from Exchange, trying to get them for us, sorry there's no reply, sorry we have been troubled; Ed, the alert young reporter, neat and twenty-five, his hair slicked back, his merry eyes prepared for a joke, his brain stored with the worst newspaper tags always ready to spring forth on to paper when he went questing after a story; and, at the table's foot, Lily Arthur, merry and big; and at the gay, absurd, irresponsible grace of her darling, common, facetious mother, Daisy's heart seemed to dissolve away in love. Lapped about in comfort, she felt, befriended, petted, fed, mother's clever girlie. . . .

'That was a nice piece you had in the paper last week, Daisy, about all the different ages,' Ada was saying. 'I liked that piece. Ed did, too. Didn't you, Ed?'

Ed nodded, his mouth full of cake.

'It was the stuff all right. Ages are the stuff. Women's ages, that is.'

'If you ask *me*,' said Mrs. Arthur, 'the less said about ages the better, women's *and* men's. Depressing, I call them. We've all got to *be* ages, but why talk about them I'd like to know. The stuff you write, Daisy!'

'It's not my fault, mother; they make me. I shouldn't get paid if I didn't write what they said.'

'Oh, well, that's the thing that matters, isn't it, after all? But, Ed now – he does nice pieces about accidents and flat dramas and sensations. He had a corpse last week, didn't

you, boy? That's what *I* call the stuff, not your flapdoodle
about how short skirts ought to be, and do girls drink too
many cocktails, and can women see jokes, and the rest of it.
Your editor, Daisy, has got women on his poor brain. He
must be one of those sex maniacs, that's what I think. If a
woman went on that way about men you'd call her man-
mad. If he'd let women alone for a change, they'd like his
paper a lot better. As if we couldn't settle the length of our
clothes and our hair and what we drink without *his* help! Lot
o' nonsense. Still, if he likes to pay people for writing what
no one wants, that's his look-out.'

'Well, he does. What's more, Ed has to do it too. He
mayn't describe a street accident without saying women
were in it, and if they weren't he has to say they looked on.
Haven't you, Ed?'

'That's right. That's the stuff to give 'em. See my story in
to-night's?'

'I saw the west-end flat crime mystery dark girl surprise
well-known clubman involved. Anything else?'

Edward produced an evening paper from his pocket,
swallowed the last of his supper, and read aloud, with pride:

'ATTEMPTED SUICIDE
BOBBED-HAIR GIRL IN DOCK

That she had no friends and no one to love but her cat
was the pathetic statement of the bobbed-haired
London girl, May Wilkins, who appeared at Bow
Street this afternoon to answer the charge of attempted
suicide, smartly dressed in a beige suit ['Bet you don't
know what beige is,' Amy interpolated] and small
black hat. Following a dose of laudanum, she had
thrown herself into the Thames off Battersea Bridge,
but was rescued by a waterman, due to her cries of
fear.'

'She was probably potty,' Ada suggested, with contempt. 'Must have been, to go about bobbed in these days.
Everyone's shingled now, unless they're cropped. What's
more, I don't believe Ed knows the difference. Anyway,
why mention the way she wore her hair, you poor mutt?

Who cares?'

'Oh, we always do. The news editor's nuts on styles in hairdressing; we think he began as a barber. He always throws in a bob or shingle if we leave it out. But I think that reads all right, what? I mean it opens well – "That she had no friends and no one to love her but her cat." That's a peppy line to start with.'

'Lovely, Ed. Don't you notice what the girls say. You read us your other piece, the one about the flat crime.'

Edward read it.

'What's a clubman, Ed?' Mr. Arthur wanted to know.

'A man who puts in a lot of time at his club, I suppose, Dad.'

'Well, what's a *well-known* clubman? Who was he well known by, I mean? *I* never heard of him.'

'No, you wouldn't have. Nor would I. Well known by the other clubmen, it means, of course.'

'Well, most people are well known by their friends, aren't they? Too well known, I dare say.'

'Dad's well known, aren't you, old man?' his wife added.

'Well known by me, anyhow. Now get off upstairs, the lot of you, and let Emily and I clear away. Daisy, you go right off to bed if you're tired, and Mother'll come and unpack for you later. You'll find the bath water hot, Emily's kept the fire up.'

3

Daisy did go to bed, following (as Ed would have put it) a hot bath. Mrs. Arthur managed, with the minimum of effort, to produce comfort in her ugly house. This was done in the only way in which comfort is ever produced in any house, by extravagance.

Daisy lay on a soft mattress in the familiar bedroom, and heard the loud-speaker in the drawing-room playing dance music, and felt that she was comfortable. Here, in her jolly, common, philistine family, she could be utterly herself. She needed not Daphne here to screen her from the world; in fact, Daphne, not being related to Mrs. Arthur, felt out of place in East Sheen. Daphne belonged to the Folyots, to that distant world of beauty and culture and breeding and grace. At the thought of Daphne, of the Folyots, of that other world, so remote now in its difficult charm, Daisy suddenly rolled over on her face and began softly and bitterly to cry, seized again with the acutest nostalgia, which is to say, pain connected with returning home.

Mrs. Arthur, coming into her daughter's room, found her crying, plumped down beside her on the bed, and gathered her into rocking arms, crooning: 'There, there, old lady, there now, stop. Tell mother about it, can you?'

'Oh, mother . . . oh, mother, I'm so miserable. . . . I didn't want to leave them, but I couldn't stay. . . . I ran away and left Charles to a wild boar, and they saw me. . . . They knew I was a coward, and I couldn't stay. Oh mother, mother . . .'

'Mother's own little pet girlie, don't cry. You'll feel better in the morning; you're just tired out travelling. Wild boar, did you say? Why, of course you ran away; anyone'd run from a wild boar, nasty brutes. Where'd they expect you to run? Into its mouth? Now, you go right off to sleep and don't worry. Mother's holding her girlie tight.'

Thus she had soothed the infant Daisy thirty years back, herself a round-faced mother of nineteen; thus had she soothed her ever since, at those crises when Daisy broke down and bewailed herself and wished to die. As she gently rocked and crooned, she thought 'Wild boar?' and hoped for an exciting story one day, when Daisy should feel able to tell it. 'Did those Folyots,' she further thought, 'give my girl the bird for running from a boar? Well, I never.' And, 'If I'd have known they were taking her to a place where boars run about loose I'd not have let her go. Boars, indeed!'

'Oh dear, oh dear,' Daisy sobbed, more gently and resignedly now. 'I've got through all my handkerchiefs but one.'

'I can give you plenty to go on with, my lamb. And Emily shall wash yours out for you to-morrow. No time at all it won't take her, just to wash them out.'

Why did washing them out sound easier and quicker than

washing them? It always did, Daisy thought. Yet the process must be the same. . . .

'Thank you, mother. G-good night. I think I feel a little better now.'

'Good night, mother's own. Well, we've all got our troubles; if it isn't one thing it's another. It's wonderful what we can suffer. But crying never mended anything yet, only spoils pretty eyes.'

It took a mother, Daisy thought, to find her eyes pretty. She did not suppose that anyone else had ever seen them as this, not even the occasional young men who had kissed them. The fact was, her eyelashes were too light.

'That,' remarked a vibrant and nasal voice over the ether, 'was the Blue-Eyed Baby Fox-trot, played by the Savoy Havana Band at Princes' Restaurant.'

Since her first-born child required her no longer, Mrs. Arthur joined the rest of the Arthur family in the sitting-room, where she sat and tapped her feet to the Savoy Havana Band.

CHAPTER 8

Daisy and Daphne in London

Next day Daisy returned to her flat in Maynard Buildings, Great Russell Street, and here Daphne presently joined her.

The relation between Daisy and Daphne was at this time a little strained. Daphne at all times had a faintly irritated contempt for Daisy, and this was now heightened by Daisy's disgrace in the matter of the wild boar. Daisy, who usually admired Daphne a good deal, just now felt annoyed with her for not having been on the spot that afternoon on the maquis. For a time Daisy felt quite sick at the thought of Daphne, and Daphne, herself in poor form and spirits, kept away. But, presently, old habit overcame them and Daphne joined Daisy once more in the Buildings, and they went about together, though, far more often than when abroad with the Folyots, Daisy would go by herself. But when she saw friends, such as Theo and Geranium in the flat overhead, Daphne was always there too. It was Daphne whom their friends knew; Daisy, more retiring, was almost a stranger to them. Daphne now shared in Daisy's journalistic work, and was amusing about her articles with Theo and the rest, often introducing the subject. She was less highbrow than she had been with the Folyots and more of a rake, and sometimes even quite vulgar in what Daisy thought an amusing way, particularly when she was with Theo Gerard, who was amusing and vulgar and a rake.

The flat of Theo and Geranium was the only other in Maynard Buildings that was not a poor person's flat. You could tell that from the street, because instead of lace window curtains, looped, these two flats had orange and blue curtains straight. Behind the orange curtains lived Theo Gerard and Geranium Brown, who were cousins. They were quite different. Theo was twenty-nine, tall and beautifully built, and wore very neat tailor-made suits, and

had very agreeable contours of face and form, and a soft half
dimpled classical kind of face, rather like that of a Madonna
gone slightly off the rails. She drank rather too much, was
cheerful, extravagant, dissipated, carelessly generous,
extremely lazy, and unburdened by moral principles. She
liked to earn her livelihood by intelligent gambling on
horses and the Stock Exchange, but this was not usually
what she did to her livelihood by these means. She had
intelligence, but did not, as a rule, apply it well, and her life
must be regarded as in many ways wasted. She had not a
bad influence over Geranium, for, though Geranium was
only twenty-two, no one had influence over her. Geranium
was dark-eyed, sturdy, clever, and rather grave, with a
square head and face and a sweet wide smile. She designed
wall-papers and fabric patterns, smoked scarcely at all and
drank even less. Theo said she was too young for vices. She
did not find Theo's broader stories amusing, and usually
showed no signs of having heard them; perhaps she really
did not. Neither did she read Daisy's and Daphne's articles
in the *Sunday Wire*. Theo, however, read these with
entertainment, and often provided suggestions for them.
Theo was a comfortable companion; it pleased and
stimulated Daisy and Daphne to be with her. She was a
good refuge from thought and memory, and provided an
outlet for reaction from the Folyots. It was, after all, a relief,
Daphne found, not to have to be so highbrow and so
refined. You could almost be yourself with Theo, Daisy
thought, but all the time she knew that you could not really
be yourself, not quite yourself, with anyone who mattered
to you, since yourself was so foolish and dull and low a
thing as surely to appal anyone of ordinary standards.

2

Daisy's life adjusted itself to London again; each day was a
little train running along well-known rails. Each morning
she woke to the cheepings and twitterings of sparrows, to
the stampeding of the loud feet of newspaper boys up and
down the iron stairs, to the clattering of milk cans, to all the

desolate and frantic cries of London dawn. Among these rose shrilly and regularly, on a lower stage of the outside stairway, 'Wee, wee, week! Did he love his mummy, then?' and it was apparent that one interrogated, vainly, a cat. When they inquire of animals and of infants the state of their affections, Daisy drowsily mused, they are apt to use both the third person and the past tense. Sometimes they inquire, with a large vagueness, as to the past life in general of the object of their solicitude, as 'Was he?' or 'Diddums?' It has been found to be of small use to ask such inquirers why it is of the past rather than of the present that they would particularly inform themselves, or, indeed, to which aspect, fact, or moment of the past they refer, for they seldom know, and here, as elsewhere, the interested investigator into phraseology and its causes meets with scant reward. One supposes that there is some connection between the past and love, so that affection induces this tense.

When Daisy had thus fruitlessly mused for a while (Daphne was never yet awake) she stumbled out of bed into the kitchenette, put on the kettle, fetched in the bottle of milk and wrestled with the cardboard disc in its mouth, stabbing it with tin-openers, knives, pencils, finger-nails, and latchkeys with the impatience for an improbably attainable liquid with which Moses struck the rock, or with which one wrestles with the udders of a cow. Still Daphne slept, and it was Daisy who made tea and cut bread and butter, lit the geyser and turned on the bath, picked up the newspaper from the iron balcony outside the door and the letters from the passage inside, and took both back to bed to read. When the telephone rang it was Daisy who first answered it, but it might be either Daisy or Daphne who continued the conversation, according to who had rung up. Daphne was often woken by the telephone. Daphne was the better tempered and more tranquil by telephone as in other intercourse; Daisy would sometimes succumb to nervous irritation, and when supplied with too many wrong numbers would become impatient or sarcastic, and would sometimes say, in response to the young lady who was sorry she had been troubled, that she too was sorry for this. Daphne's snare, on the other hand, was superfluous facetiousness; when people said to her: 'Look here, that magneto you overhauled for me has gone wrong again,' or 'I want a permanent wave at twelve o'clock today,' she would answer: 'Did I overhaul your magneto for you?' or 'Well, I hope it will look nice,' playing to an imaginary audience, like the facetious hero of a novel, instead of merely saying: 'Wrong number,' as business-like persons in real life do. When it was Theo telephoning from her bed overhead, it was always Daphne who answered, and then they would both be facetious for several minutes on end. Sometimes it was the *Sunday Wire,* which had been struck by a bright idea for the woman's page article.

'Look here, Miss Simpson. Can a woman run a baby and a business at the same time? Work out something on those lines. The editor wants it hot and live, to follow right on what Lady Lennox said about it at Derby yesterday afternoon. Yes, she did: it's all in this morning's papers, with special headlines. *Why?* I don't know why. I suppose because it's about women and babies. Read it up, and get out something along those lines. Make it human. It doesn't matter which side you take, but make it live and human. Talk about the little chap, you know, as if he was there. Make 'em hear him crow.'

'*Crow?* That's cocks, not little chaps. . . .'

But the *Wire* had rung off.

Daisy would sit down to the typewriter directly she was dressed and tap out a live human article along those lines. The typewriter somehow helped her. It always seemed to know its job. Under its taps the hypothetical infant became not merely a little chap but a tiny tot, and his crows rang out like Chanticleer's, distracting the unfortunate mother from any business whatever. It was a male tot, they go better with mothers; Daisy speculated as she tapped whether a female tot would, instead of crowing, cluck, even perhaps sometimes lay an egg. But the typewriter never permitted such speculations as these to reach the paper; it knew better. Instead, it broke into reflections on the lot of a mother o'

men. Well it knew the news value of an occasional curtailed
'of'. Another reason why the tot should be a male tot. A
mother o' women isn't, somehow, so good; one sees no
reason why the 'f' should have been removed. Ever since
Daisy had had in an early article the preposition in the
phrase 'Love of Life' abbreviated by a sub-editor, she had
seen that this was a good idea, and occasionally served it up,
to please the simple souls in the *Wire* office, though she was
a little vague as to the correct occasions for its use, beyond
the elementary fact that it must precede consonants only.
Son o' mine, for instance, sounded all right, so did friend o'
mine, but did aunt o' mine, or uncle o' yours? And God's
great out o' doors went well, but take the dog out o' doors
not so well. 'Hot pie and nice cup o' tea' you saw sometimes
over eating-shops in low streets, but less often 'Nice mug o'
beer.'

Anyhow, 'Whatever happens to our work,' tapped the
portable Remington, rapidly and firmly, 'the children must
come first. The kiddies have got to know that mother is
always by, to help and comfort when things go wrong, to
bind up that cut finger, to control that naughty little
temper, to soothe away that nightmare. That business must
do without mother if that baby needs her. . . .' Daisy read
this last sentence over, altered its first 'that' to 'the,' and
eliminated the second. The demonstrative article is a very
moving word in its place (as in that tired feeling, that boyish
figure, that fresh look, that schoolgirl complexion), but it
can be overworked, and, indeed, sometimes is.

Having typed her thousand words, Daisy would wander,
idly busy, round the flat, trying how various kinds of polish
looked on the floor, sorting her clothes, stemming
randomly, and on the whole vainly, the river-like
eloquence of the morning woman, who, if asked: 'Did you
see my pen lying about the bedroom?' replied: 'I've not
done the bedroom yet miss I set to work in the kitchen first
to-day while you was typing in the sitting-room so as not to
disturb you thinking to do the bedroom next while you was
still working then you left off of typing and went into the
bedroom and I went to do the sitting-room I always study

not to disturb you working I think it's only right miss to study the ladies you work for so I always does so arranging the work in the order that suits and fitting things in as it were. . . .'

'In short,' Daisy would break in, 'you have *not* seen my pen,' and would return to her occupations, but still the stream flowed, until, like the weariest river, it ran somewhere safe to sea.

It's like English rain, Daisy would think, listening, stunned but half fascinated, as the river ran on. You think there can't possibly be any more to come, and there always is. Morning women are marvellous. They must be among the world's nine wonders. Theo Gerard had a theory that they were the veritable Women, of which the popular press was so full.

'But,' Daphne would argue, 'morning women can't be all like one another. Going out to work in people's houses in the morning can't make thousands of women alike. Why should it? If we thought all morning women were like each other we should be as stupid as the people who think women in general are alike, or people born in the same decade alike.'

Theo said that morning women were alike; she could not help their being so, she had not made them. The Lord had seen fit to create his morning women after one image. Theo was dogmatic about life's riddles: she disposed of them as readily and as fluently as a Catholic priest of theological speculations, allowing nothing to trouble her.

3

Daphne and Daisy revolved together in two quite different milieus. They belonged to various literary clubs and circles where those who wrote and had a taste for meeting others who wrote often gathered together for discussions, lectures, and innocently happy evenings. Before these persons there was no necessity to conceal one's novel or one's journalism. They did not, for the most part, think scorn of either, for many of them had perpetrated worse novels themselves or would have liked to, and those who ridiculed such articles as Daisy's knew that one must live and that these were the topics appointed by editors to female writers. These literary circles were not, in the main, composed of intellectual or highbrow writers (who do not, for the most part, care very much for circles) – some were intelligent, some foolish, some successful, some failures, but the prevalent air was of a friendly, gay, and innocent kindness, before which any shame might be spread without embarrassment. Indeed, many of Daphne's and Daisy's literary friends thought *Youth at the Prow* an excellent novel, and spoke to them of it in kind voices.

Their other circle was very different; more raffish, less innocent, less reputable, and no members of it took the trouble or had the time to write anything beyond cheques, telegrams, and I.O.U.s. This was Theo Gerard's set. Daisy accompanied Daphne to the haunts where these took their pleasure, but she sat silent and unnoticed among the gay throng; it was Daphne who talked and danced and ate, and drank, yet Daisy's head would swim while Daphne appeared to Daisy to remain tranquil and sober.

Daisy's uncertainties as to what was the precise impression made by Daphne shook sometimes the stability and the poise of Daphne and caused her to incline now this way, now that, as if seeking different exemplars. She inclined greatly at this time towards Theo Gerard, so different from herself, and achieved, so Daisy thought, a wordly air, a rakish gaiety, a calm indifference that triumphed over life's mischances, over life itself. Such calm, such indifference were never Daisy's, who was woundingly moved to excitement, or impatience, or hilarity, by all that she encountered, so that her soul frequently howled within her like the wind, or like the little mycetes monkey of the South American jungle, her pulses throbbed like hammers, blood ran swiftly round and round her system like greyhounds after an electric hare, and she would be awakened in the small hours of the night by the most acute stabs from the darts of frustrated ambition or love. Indeed, life was all too terribly, prodigiously exciting to be taken tranquilly at all.

But Daphne, blasé, cynical, and amused, and so cosmopolitan that she preferred to say it in French, would remark: 'Demain, puis demain, puis demain, glisse ainsi à petits pas jusqu' à la dernière syllabe que le temps écrit dans son livre. Et tous nos hiers ont eclairé pour quelques fous le chemin de la mort poudreuse . . .' thus indicating her view of the infinitely monotonous unimportance of this surprising life.

4

Meanwhile, one had to work for one's bread.

'Listen, Theo. How soon does married love die and why?'

'Practically immediately. Why? Well, why not?'

'Oh, you're no use. No one would give you twopence for anything you wrote. Listen. What is the religion of women? Also, which way will the women vote?'

'They are Roman Catholics. No, Swedenborgians. They vote Liberal. Also, they are five-foot seven in height, their hair is black and straight, their eyes grey, their complexions pale, their lips red, their tempers bad, they prefer mutton to beef, dislike porridge, and weigh eight stone two. They enjoy the tastes of tobacco, coffee, tea, marzipan, and anchovy. Anything more about them?'

'Yes. Why do they commit murders? When they do, that is.'

'Why not? Oh, well then, because there is some fellow-creature whom they desire to remove from the world. Further, they can neither feel pain nor see jokes, but are subject to disturbed stomachs when at sea.'

'Are they good-looking?'

'Certainly not. Not much better-looking than men, if at all. No human creatures . . .'

'Should they tell?'

'Tell what?'

'Anything, I suppose.'

'Certainly not. Nothing in the world. However, they do.'

'Have they reason?'

'No, no reason. Not as a rule. Just because. Did I give their girths, by the way? Take them down. They measure twenty-seven round the waist, thirty round the hips, thirty-two round the chest. If they can get their heads and shoulders through a hole the rest of them can follow. They sing contralto and in their baths, the colour that suits them best is green, their teeth are numerous but bad, and give them much anguish – which, fortunately, they can't feel. They like fish, potatoes, and dogs. They are unmarried and have three children. Now I must have given you material for a month ahead, so cease this brooding and come to the Eiffel Tower.'

5

Daisy often wandered alone about London, seeing and hearing what was to be seen and heard, prowling and questing like a small beast of curiosity but mediocre intelligence in a jungle, her mind bewildered and dazed by uproar, clatter, and the peculiar behaviour and surprising utterances of others, yet frequently pleased by what she encountered. She would sometimes join the female herd that wound slowly past the shops which sold female clothes, eyes covetously agape, mouths dubiously primmed, legs and spines curiously cast awry by high-heeled shoes, and she would think, That would suit me. That's new. A nice colour, too. I'd like to have that. Reduced to three guineas. . . . And her eyes would stare and her mouth prim like the others. Then she would think, how odd. All this to-do about what we put on. What does it all mean? Is one thing actually better than another to wear, and if so, why? That might be a subject for an article. But she would not be allowed to write it along the lines it took in her mind, but quite the contrary, as 'Smart women just now are all wearing . . . Every woman who wants to look her best must consider not only fashion, but her own special style and shape . . .' Never must the question be raised, why the devil should women or men consider anything about it at all, instead of just throwing on the first thing handy?

Instead the world had agreed to make a science, or an art, of this business of putting on clothes, arranging a different costume for every division of the day, every occupation. Daisy had very few of these costumes, unlike Theo Gerard, who appeared to have them all. When Daisy was bidden to some entertainment for which she was tersely requested on her invitation card to don Morning Dress, she discovered, on considering her wardrobe, that she possessed no Morning Dress, or rather that the jersey and skirt in which she worked in the mornings had an air of being unworthy of the name. When she looked at those illustrated advertisements and catalogues of their wares which shops so kindly and gratuitously send forth to all and sundry, the gaps in her wardrobe depressingly yawned. She did not think that she even had an afternoon dress; the pictures of this garment looked, anyhow, quite different from the coat and skirt in which she sallied forth in the afternoons. She certainly had not a rest gown (apart from her nightgown) or a tea gown. Her tea gown was the same as her lunch and afternoon gown; the only meal which elicited from her its appropriate costume was dinner. And, in the event of her being asked to join, after dinner, in a game of bridge, she perceived that she would have to decline, as she had no bridge coat, a mysterious garment apparently donned by bridge-players as tennis, golf, and cricket costumes are by the practitioners of these sports. 'No, thank you, I'm afraid I've not brought my bridge coat,' she would be obliged to say. Life must be, to those who lived sartorially, a complex and many-changing business; they must be at it from morning until night, in order not to risk being caught in the wrong clothes. Daisy knew that she would never be any good at this game.

Neither was she any good at shopping. Sometimes she would venture, in search of some object she would fain acquire, into a huge shop, honeycombed into a hundred cells, each cell purveying different goods. When she inquired the way to the department she sought, they always said, they quite invariably told her, 'Straight through.' Through where, what, in which direction? Confronted with a thousand avenues that branched like a catacomb, like a millipede, like a honeycomb, even soaring upwards like a tree, she stood revolving helplessly, a bewildered teetotum. If she asked 'Through what?' they told her 'Straight through the arch,' and she felt like an Edward Lear young lady, foolish, helpless and browbeaten before their enigmatic instructions, and would go straight through the door into the street, for Daisy was no good with life; it could so easily and so lightly dominate and bemuse her. In her life, so weak, straying, and confused, there was nothing certain but death. She read this truth on the pavement on the Embankment one afternoon, very beautifully written in mauve chalk. 'In this life there is nothing certain but death.' He who had written it had also written, in pink, blue, white, green, and cerise chalk, other truths, such as: 'He who walks on tiptoe will never be down at heel. Life without a friend is death without a witness. Think of ease, but work on. It is more pain to do nothing than something. Home is the place where you grumble most and are treated best. Books, like friends, should be few and well chosen.' This last struck Daisy as very true. Books should be few. Certainly books should be few. But are they few? They are not; they are many. Publishers and writers ought to hang that remark on their walls and try hard to profit by it. Possibly friends, too, should be few, but one sees no such cogent reason for that. Daisy gave the scribe two-pence. In gratitude he showed her how he had also written (in cobalt blue):

> *'A little more kindness, a little less creed,*
> *A little more giving, a little less greed,*
> *A little more smile, a little less frown,*
> *A little less kicking a man when he's down,*
> *A few more flowers as we pass through life,*
> *And fewer on graves at the end of the strife.'*

He was full of such happy and simple thoughts. But this poem faintly worried Daisy, because it seemed to lack a main predicate, and remain rather an ejaculation than a statement.

She wandered on her way towards Fleet Street, still

looking right and left from under light, drawn-down brows for whatever might encounter and please her eyes and what she held to be her mind.

A crazy life! A disordered, brainless life! It had no symmetry, no significance, no plan, it was vulgar, it was lost and blind, but lit nevertheless at times by gleams of soft sunlight on grey ebbing water, and penetrated, through the wild stream of traffic, by the wistful and melancholy crying of sea-birds, and by the monotonous rise and fall of plain-song, for Daisy would sometimes slip into a church, and allow the drifting clouds of incense and chanted psalms and prayers to weave about her a spell, till she felt herself in some other universe, enchanted, perfumed, and remote. But if she was by chance walking with Daphne, she did not enter churches; they were her own private adventure on which she put out like a solitary mariner on a misty sea, and when she returned she did not mention it.

6

Daisy would occasionally, when she had been to her newspaper-office in the morning, lunch with her half-brother Edward. Daphne, too, would go with Daisy to the office, and be nonchalant, clever, tranquil, and gay, and the staff knew that, though she was doing this strange work (the same work as Daisy), she was above it in her intelligence, and smiled down at it, derisive and amused. No one would have imagined that Daphne took her work seriously.

But Daphne never came out to lunch with Daisy and Edward. She was not, of course, Edward's relation.

Edward and Daisy would go off alone together, sometimes to Simpson's, sometimes to the Strand Corner House, or to any other eating-place that presented itself, for these young people were not proud.

Edward was good company, for he had often just come back from, or was shortly to set forth in search of, some amazing story. Before Edward's feet amazing scenes blossomed as flowers do before the feet of fairy princesses. Talking with him one suddenly saw the world as an amazing place; events the most ordinary – as that this or that royal personage had left the appropriate station for some destination elsewhere, that a number of persons had assembled to see him or her do so, that there had been quite a crowd going off to seaside resorts before a holiday, that this or that hitherto unknown young woman had wed this or that young man, that someone had, in an access of covetousness, of rage, or of those other human passions that stir murderers to their crimes, taken the life of another, that thieves had plundered a shop-window of its contents, that a cleric had stated that he did not believe the Book of Genesis to be the literally true explanation of the origin of man – all these quite usual happenings assumed, under Edward's amazed manipulations, the character of Incidents.

'I don't know what you think you're going to make of *that*,' Daisy said at lunch, à propos of the clergyman and Genesis. 'If you could find a clergyman who *did* believe Genesis, you might make a story of it.'

Edward's eyes became speculative. He was seeing the heading.

'ADAM AND EVE TRUE
AMAZING BELIEF OF BISHOP.'

'Perhaps you're right,' he admitted. 'It *would* be better, so far as the public go. But what they like in the news room is the other. Monkeys, you know, and sponges, and all that.'

'What's the matter with them,' said Daisy, 'is that they're about seventy years behind the time. They've probably never met any parsons.'

'Dunno.' Edward was indifferent as to that. 'You don't need to meet them. Everyone knows what parsons have to believe. Look at the row there was in the churchy sets when old Darwin launched his monkey business. Oh, yes, I know when it was, but it's good enough for us. A stunt like that is good for seventy years or so.'

'I wonder,' said Daisy, 'that the press doesn't make out that the clergy still believe that the sun goes round the earth. I can't think why they've let the Copernican sensation die out.'

Edward reflected on that. 'No, it *was* a mistake. The fact
is, we weren't enough on the spot in those days. The press
has come on a good bit in smartness the last fifty years or so.
But we might get back to that sun business, even now.
Does Sun Revolve Round Earth? Amazing Claim by
Dean.'

'What Women Think About It,' Daisy supplemented.

'That's the stuff. And we'd work it up along religious
lines. Religion's a hot penny just now.'

'Always has been, I think.'

'That's right. Always has been. Funny thing. The *Wire*
comes out with some religious stunt every August. Religion and the Channel. Religion's beaten the Channel this
summer, due to the rotten weather. Then, of course,
flying's had a good show lately. Specially women flyers.
Murder's been a bit of a slump. There's not been a good one
for weeks. I must say I enjoy getting after a good crime
story. There's some guts in that. I always feel a bit of an ass
sidling up to a dean or an actress with a pencil and asking
them if we're descended from sponges. The deans look as if
they thought I'd got loose from somewhere. The actresses
are better; at least they're not surprised, and don't bite a
chap's head off, and they don't cut up rough if I make them
say: "When I see the flowers or the little children I feel
convinced that life holds more meaning than ever came out
of a sponge." They think it's a jolly smart remark, and wish
they'd thought of it.'

'What do they really say?' Daisy was interested.

'Oh, nothing much. Not about that, anyhow. They leave
it to me. They know I'll do it a long sight better than they
can, and, anyway, they never thought about it. They begin
to talk about their parts and prospects, and how many
managers are after them, hoping I'll work it in somehow. I
do my best for them. I like 'em a lot better than the parsons.
They know a fellow has his job, and has to live, and aren't
always complaining they've been made to look fools. It's
not all syrup, a reporter's job. It's all very well for you; you
can just pour out the goods sitting in your room, and
needn't go hopping round asking people fool questions –

or, anything, not much.'

'I have to write fool stuff, just the same. And I could be writing something decent – I know I could. That's the damned part about it.'

'Your stuff's all right. As a matter of fact it's jolly good. They were saying so in the news room the other day. You hit the nail right on the head just where they want it hit. They think quite a lot of you. I don't mind telling you.'

'God, it's awful.' Daisy cupped her chin in her hands and sank profoundly into melancholy.

'Listen, Ed. Do you ever want to get so drunk you can't think or see?'

'Don't know that I *want* to. I do sometimes, of course. Not often, though. Bad for work. . . . Why?'

'Nothing. Why Women Drink. I could write on that.'

'That's right. That'd go. Now I've got to be off to Kentish Town. Miss! The bill, please.'

Daisy watched him collecting his hat, his dispatch case, Miss, and the bill. An alert, business-like young man, with kind and merry brown eyes and a sharp nose. She liked Ed. He was not related to Daphne, but he was profoundly and essentially related to her. She really *could* write on Why Women Drink, or Can Women Think; she might and did damn these subjects, but she could write on them something which Edward and his colleagues held to be the goods. She was not like the Folyots, who could not have thought of anything to say about them. Oh, yes, she was truly and intimately related to the Arthurs of East Sheen.

She sat on vaguely after Ed had gone, mournful with regard to her next destination, which was, in fact, a dentist. In that mood of acute sensibility which precedes these visits, she heard with pleasure and surprise all those light human cries which seem to link us with our fellow-creatures and attach us to this planetary life, reminding us of our daily wants between which and ourselves, Miss, running hither and thither like a kindly ant, ministers.

'Sausages and mash twice,' Miss cried. 'Two veg, toad twice, and three portions of jam.' What a thing is a human meal! What an exquisite miscellany, what surprising sequences, as in the music to the sound of which it was devoured, Messrs. Lyons' musicians passing from 'Pinafore' to 'Tannhauser,' from Rachmaninoff to 'Brown Eyes, Why are you Blue?'

'I shan't come here again; I mean, I haven't an hour to spend waiting to be served. Life isn't long enough, I mean.'

'That's right. I mean, we got in here at one-thirty sharp, and it's ten to two now. And there's several come in after us been served first. It's not right, I mean.'

In her mood of sensibility, in which all life unrolled its tragic drama before her eyes, Daisy felt profound pity for these poor girls, who meant so much and had lunched so little.

'A brandy liqueur settles your lunch. I mean, if you've had lobster or anything it does. I always say it settles your lunch.'

This was a man. He was so deeply in earnest that his saying took on the dignity of one of those philosophic maxims that are written on pavements in chalk. *Look up not down. Books should be few. A brandy liqueur settles your lunch.*

The hour of the dentist approached. Daisy sought the boudoir where ladies who have eaten at Lyons' restore themselves to beauty, finding taps of running water, mirrors before which to comb the hair disordered by swallowing and to powder the face disarranged by biting. Also, since it was the dentist, she brushed the teeth.

Having by these attentions made of herself a better figure in the world's eyes and in her own, she ventured once more into the streets, plunging into a world which, in her mood of sharp receptivity, seemed to be intolerably dominant, harsh, and neglectful. What was it to the world that screamed and clattered by her, like a herd of stampeding wild elephants, that she would presently, seated in a chair, endure, superimposed on the pains of frustrated love, the anguish of drilled teeth? It was too much. No one, Daisy reflected, anyhow no woman, should be called on for so much endurance. No woman, she thought, for women suffer excessively. Everything, she thought, is against women. They live in their emotions; they have, as a rule, too few intellectual or physical distractions. Look, she thought, at wives. Husbands go out to work, to companionship and sanity, leaving behind their women (so often) to do that work inside houses which becomes mechanical and is also lonely, leaving their minds free to turn to and fro on themselves, their personal relationships, personal griefs. The more nervous, emotional, excitable, and passible sex should be given more consolation and distractions, not fewer, than the other, so much firmer, steadier, and stronger in body and mind, so much better fitted to endure. Women, Daisy thought, have no armour. Was it her fault if she had learnt, through her so degraded calling, to say 'Women,' to say 'Men,' to trample down the purely individual distinctions of the human mind and soul? Was it her fault if she, who had it in her (thought Daisy) to write and think intelligently, did, in effect, think and write like that, caught up in the maelstrom of human imbecility, her intelligence functioning only as disgust?

Assailed suddenly by desire to make her mark in the world, to emerge from the welter of the inconspicuous and foolish herd in which she ran, emitting its tedious cries as her own, Daisy leapt into a hansom cab, which ambled gracefully along the Strand, retarding and hindering in its dignified way such traffic as was not drawn by the animal creation.

'Five, Upper Wimpole Street,' Daisy cried through the trap in the roof, and settled down behind the open doors to receive any plaudits that the populace might be minded to give her as she jingled up Chandos Street.

It is a proud thing and a noble thing to be riding behind a horse, and more than one group of young men or children gave Daisy's hansom an applauding hand as it jingled northward. The expense proved great, for it became apparent before Oxford Circus that this was no way in which to arrive at the dentist's in any sort of time, so the hansom had to be exchanged for a taxi, and even so the appointment was overshot by twelve minutes; but at least Daisy had her brief moment of notoriety, was for a little time lifted from the rut, like an actress, a suicide, a channel swimmer, or a human creature who has flown across the Atlantic. Or so, anyhow, she felt.

CHAPTER 9

Mrs. Arthur's Day in Town

Mrs. Arthur travelled up to town for the Sales, and she would see, also, a matinée. From Knightsbridge Station (she had bought celanese cami-knickers at Harvey Nichols', reduced) she telephoned to her daughter Ada, at the Oxford Circus branch of Keith's Cheap Books Store, that she would visit her there and that Ada was to find her a nice book. From Piccadilly Circus (she had bought gents' silk ties, a lady's purple hat, a yellow woollen jumper suit, out-size, three silk jerseys, stock size, and more than one cotton sheet, reduced, at Swan and Edgar's) she telephoned to the *Evening Wire* and inquired for her son Edward, but Edward was out on a job, so she said 'Tell him it's his mother, and he's to meet me for lunch at Peter Jones' and come to the *Farmer's Wife* after.' From Bond Street Station (she had bought gramophone records at His Master's Voice, and a veal pie, a plum cake, six pairs of silk stockings, three shingle nets, a grey leather vanity bag, a bottle of scent, a pink silk nightdress, more than one pillow case, and some reducing bath salts at Selfridge's) she telephoned to Daisy in Maynard Buildings, but got no satisfaction beyond a kind 'I'm trying to get them for you,' from Exchange. 'That's a good girl,' Mrs. Arthur responded, feeling maternal towards telephone girls because of Amy. But presently, 'Don't you worry, dear. I shouldn't wonder if she wasn't gone out. I shall just pop round there and see,' she said, and rang off. However, when she got into the street she saw that it was time to go to Peter Jones', so she gave Daisy up and popped instead into a bus which took her to Sloane Square. From Sloane Square Station she telephoned to her husband in Baker Street, bidding him join her at lunch and at the Court Theatre, but it appeared that he had engagements with regard to the decoration of houses that would occupy his afternoon. Mrs. Arthur lunched very cheerfully at Peter Jones' by herself, on lamb, peas, a glass of lager, and a fruit sundae, expecting at any moment to be joined by her husband or one or another of her four children, especially by Daisy, with whom, however, she had failed to establish any communication beyond that conveyed by thought and by the ringing of a telephone in an empty room. None of her family appeared, so she had coffee, smoked a cigarette, and went across to join the pit queue at the Court.

Her reactions differed from those of most queue-standers, for she extracted from those who lined the pavement in front of her the pleasure that tourists feel while viewing the entertaining creatures which dwell in countries, other than their own, and that Londoners feel, as a rule, mainly at the Zoo. She was so pleased with looking at them that she did not grudge them their victory over her in the contest for places, but watched them with the derision and kindly applause which one accords to the occupants of the small monkey house or to the yellow-backed whydah bird, that little golden creature who surely had for father a canary and for mother a cock-chafer, and who hurls himself to and fro across his enclosure with such lepidopterous, or is it orthopterous, élan. Such pleasure as these and similarly comic beings afford to simple souls was given to Mrs. Arthur by the contemplation of her neighbours, while she stood, a little tired, her out-size body in its knee-length purple dress and coat poised heavily on stout artificial silk legs and Louis XV heels, her new purple hat (she had left her old one at Swan and Edgar's to be sent on with the sheets) cocked gaily on her shingled and marcelled and brass-hued head, her hands draped, like the boughs of a Christmas tree, with her smaller parcels, most of which were for the husband and the children.

Fate, bountiful as always to Mrs. Arthur in the matter of humorous provender, presently supplied further to comedy in the queue, farce in the road beside it, for here a comedian went through his repertory for her benefit, the while she shook with mirth and observed ever and anon to her neighbours, 'Well, I never! Have to laugh, don't you?

Silly fellow!' When the entertainer, his task finished, soli-
cited the reward of merit, she dropped sixpence into his cap,
said, 'Does you good to laugh, I always say,' and pressed in
her turn through the opened door.

'Well, I never!' she ejaculated many times during the
afternoon. 'Have to laugh, don't you?' And her neighbours
agreed that you had. She missed having someone with her,
someone to whom she could say over aloud the funny bits
which the actors had just uttered; but after the first act she
got familiar enough with her left-hand neighbours to prac-
tise on them this recitation, which, however, they
sometimes got in first on her. Mrs. Arthur laughed a great
deal, as did everyone else. 'Can't keep a straight face, can
you?' she said, after the first act. 'Laugh and grow fat, they
say. I don't need that, do I; I ought to go and see
Shakespeare and do some crying! I do cry at the play, too;
the husband says next time he takes me to a tragic piece he's
going to bring his mack and big umbrella. I'd rather laugh,
though, any day; helps the digestion more. I always say
there'll be lots of time for crying when we go where we
deserve at the end, so we may's well put it off till then. Oh,
dear, the curtain's going up again. I'll say I'm enjoying this
piece!'

To the end she enjoyed it; when she came out into Sloane
Square again, at nearly five o'clock, the risible muscles of
her face were sore with exertion. Now, she thought, I'll go
to Keith's after that book, and took the tube to Oxford
Circus. At the Cheap Books Store she had a nice little chat
with Ada, who was seated behind the counter with other
young ladies, very busy among cheap books. To her
mother their sudden meeting like this in the heart of
London, when if she had not come to town they would not
have met until an hour and a half later, had the joyful quality
of an assignation. She sold the book she had bought last
week, which was by Mr. P. G. Wodehouse, and which she
had enjoyed very much, and said, 'I'll have something deep
this time. Time I improved my mind. What have you that's
deep, Ada?'

Ada jeered at her. 'You don't want anything deep, Ma!

Better have the new Wallace, really you had. Then Dad can read it, too. Dad won't be pleased if you bring him back a heavy book.'

'Well, Dad and I ought to improve ourselves, that's a fact.' She turned to another young lady. 'You tell me a nice book, dear, as Ada won't.'

'Something deep, Mrs. Arthur? Why, of course. Would you like to try *Mother India*? We've a few review copies cheap, and they're being sold out awfully quick.'

'Plenty of it, anyhow.' Mrs. Arthur fingered *Mother India* with caution.

'Dad wouldn't like it much, Ma,' Ada intervened. 'It's not deep so much as – well, *you* know. Hot.'

'Oh, hot.' Mrs. Arthur brightened a little. 'That'd help Dad and me through a bit, wouldn't it? Still, what's the use of being nasty in a book, I say; there's enough of that in real life. A little fun I don't mind, but these writer chaps, they don't always know where to draw the line. No, Ada, I won't take it, it wouldn't improve my mind. If you girls can't give me any real good book, I'll just have to take another Wallace.'

'I put it by for you when you first came in, Ma.' Ada handed her *The Claws of Fate*. 'Now you'd better move along, you giddy old thing, instead of wasting my time chattering. Got my work to do. Ta-ta, be good.'

'Don't you be late home, Ada. I'm off to see Daisy before my train. Seen her to-day?'

'No. Why?'

'Oh, nothing. You girls ought to meet more and have fun together. Well, tootle-oo, dear.'

'I like your mother, Ada,' said Ada's friend. 'She always has a laugh ready.'

'She's not a bad old dear,' Ada absently but affectionately returned.

2

They opened just as Mrs. Arthur emerged from Great Russell Street tube, and, feeling tired and in need of restoration, she entered the Hay Wagon, and had a small port.

That's better, she agreed with herself, as she came out. Makes you feel quite made over. They keep shut too long, and that's a fact. She felt more fit now to cope with her parcels and with the Maynard Buildings iron stairway that spiralled up outside the flats like one of those toy snakes, so full of gaps, that one buys in the street. She was accosted at its foot by one who sold bunches of white heather, and who remarked that, if she should purchase one of them, he would be enabled to buy a cup of tea.

'All this tea,' she commented, unfavourably, 'that you street sellers drink, it can't be good for you. It's what you all say, you'll buy a cup of tea. You must spend all your time drinking the stuff; you shouldn't, it upsets the stomach. Now you go right in there and get a nice glass of stout, it'll do you far more good.'

Arrived at Daisy's door, Mrs. Arthur loudly knocked in case the bell should be out of order, as bells so often are. Daisy, who was within, sitting quietly and listening to the talk between Daphne, Theo Gerard, and a young man friend of Theo's, went into the passage to open the door. Outside it stood Mrs. Arthur, stout, purple-clad, smiling, hung with parcels, the better for her glass of port, whose aroma stole fragrantly from her lips.

'Why, mother!' Daisy said beneath her breath.

'Well, miss. Here I am, like a bad penny. Give me a kiss; there. Didn't expect me, did you? I phoned, but you never answered, so I went to the play alone. It was rare fun. I couldn't help but laugh. If I'd have thought of it yesterday, I'd have dropped you a line to come, but it came into my head quite suddenly when I was out shopping to-day. 'Well, aren't you going to ask me inside? I've something for you here.'

'No – wait, mother.' Daisy stood between her and the room door, and spoke in a whisper. 'Listen, mother. It's no good going in there yet, there are people there. . . .'

'Well, who cares? They won't eat me, I suppose. Nor I them,' Mrs. Arthur added after a moment.

'No, but listen. They're tiresome people; stupid people;

we'll wait till they're gone. I'll send them away. They belong upstairs, in the flat above. You come into my bedroom while I get rid of them.'

'Oh, well.' Mrs. Arthur followed Daisy into her bedroom, plumped her parcels on the bed, and removed her hat.

'There. There's a silk jumper I got for you somewhere among them; want to see? Swan's I got it. Jade. I thought to myself, that will go with the girl's eyes. Got myself a jumper-suit, too. Yellow wool. Out-size, but still wants altering. It suits me pretty well. Let's see now, where's that silk jumper. . . .'

Daisy, however, had gone into the sitting-room, shutting the bedroom door behind her. Mrs. Arthur, opening it to speak to her, heard: 'Listen, Theo. There's someone come to see me. She's in the bedroom. You must go.'

'My dear,' a pleasant rather deep girl's voice answered, 'why should we go? We'll wait in here till you've done.'

'But I must bring her in here.'

'Oh, must you? Who is she? She sounded as if she was your old nurse. Rather nice, I thought.'

'No, she's just someone I've always known. And she may stay some time, so you'd better go on without me.'

'You'd better let us stay. We could get rid of her for you. You're helpless by yourself.'

'No, no, I want to see her; it's really all right. Only you must go now.'

'All right, you ass. Come along, Tony. We must leave her behind if she won't come. Why not come and bring Nursie, too, though? I liked the sound of her; I'd like to know her. She sounded jolly and gay.'

'Oh, yes, she's nice. But she wouldn't come. Goodbye.'

Footsteps in the passage; the front door opened and shut. The visitors had gone, and Daphne, too. Daisy turned to the bedroom door; it was open, and her mother stood inside it; her fair, merry face looked odd, puzzled, flushed. Seeing her standing there at the open door, Daisy turned scarlet. Her mother's shrewd blue eyes watched the rush of colour and the quivering lip.

'All right, girl,' she said, in a new, flat kind of voice. 'Don't you mind me. I'll be your nursie, if you'd rather. Not quite the class for mother, am I?'

'I never said. . . . It was Theo who said you were that. I said you weren't.'

'Yes, I heard. But it didn't seem to come out that I was your mother, somehow. Never mind. Might get in your way, having a mother like me, mightn't it?' Mrs. Arthur looked at her image in Daisy's mirror, dubiously, questioningly, as if she sought to discover precisely what was wrong, how she fell short.

'Your aunt never thought I was much, I know,' she said. 'Comes of my being lower born than your father was. Well, there it is; it can't be helped. I'll try and not disgrace you, girl, by butting in.'

Daisy was in tears.

'Mother – oh, mother. *Darling* mother. Oh, I do love you so!'

She was borne down by the storm of her love and her remorse; she clung to the firm purple figure as to a stake in an engulfing sea. Mrs. Arthur patted her shoulder. 'There, there, old lady, don't take on. I'm sure no harm's done. You look at the jade jumper I got you, and see if it fits.' She extricated it from its wrappings, and held it up, a shiny thing of synthetic silk, less the hue of jade than of emeralds. Daisy blew her pink nose and took it.

'Lovely, mother. Just my size, I can see. Thank you, ever so much darling.'

'Well, I think the colour suits you. Now I must be getting along. No, I can't stop; I must get back for dad's and the girls' supper. Can't you go out with your friends still, or are they gone?'

'I don't want to. I'll come to the station with you. What a smart hat, mother.'

She wanted to praise everything her mother wore, or had ever worn; she was aflame with extravagant but unimportant desires towards her; such as to pour out for her flagons of spiced wine, spread trays of *marrons glacés* in her sight, spray her with luscious scent, put hot bottles to her feet and wreaths of roses on her head, gratifying her by those elegant attentions which have from all time been offered by lovers to those whom they would please. She would fain have been Aladdin, to turn a ring and summon black slaves who should run hither and thither at her mother's behest, or Medea, to assist her to a golden fleece, or Paris, to press upon her the golden apple which is presented to the fairest among women, or a pirate chief, to festoon her with silk purses full of golden guineas, or some beneficent god, such as Priapus, to offer her his garden fruits – gaping pomegranates, purple figs, ripe yellow medlars, golden and indigo grapes – or Jehovah, to make her corn and wine and oil increase.

Instead of which, her mother laid smaragdine jumpers before her (of vegetable, not animal, silk, but was not silk the purer for this origin, no animals being so pure as the grossest plants, and worms being among the more gross of animals), gave her white heather, and even sprayed scent over her, producing from another parcel a bottle with a syringe that filled the air with liquid perfume.

'You can keep that, Daisy. I got it for you.'

'Oh, mother, you shouldn't! Oh, you are nice to me!' Daisy kissed her mother again. She thought, how my father must have loved her, and what a damned snob I am. To Daphne, snobbery would have been impossible. She would never have disowned any mother, however common. But Daphne's mother, whom no one ever saw (she had married again, like Daisy's), was a cultured woman, of the same class as the long dead father and the recently dead aunt whom Daphne and Daisy shared. Daphne had what is called good blood on both sides, and possessed those careless faults, those easy, generous, gallant virtues that decorate (or should decorate) gentlewomen. To Daisy belonged that last meanness which has warped so many bourgeois natures from Beau Brummell's to George Meredith's. Did either of those two gentlemen, or any other of the world's snobs, know the anguish of compunction that struck Daisy to the soul like poisoned barbs? Daisy believed not.

'Darling, I wish you'd stay till the late train, and come with me to another play. . . .'

Mrs. Arthur's eyes glistened; she was tempted. Dearly she loved two plays on top of each other; it seemed to round off the day. But no, she mustn't. She must really get home; she'd promised dad. Besides, Daisy, if she didn't stay, could go off and join those friends of hers.

'No, girlie, I can't. Don't tempt me, or I shall. I must get right back now.'

'I'll come with you to the station, then.'

'Well, if you must. . . . Kiss your old nursie. There. When are you coming down for a Sunday?'

'Quite soon. This Sunday, perhaps.'

'Time you had some good Sunday beef. You're thin, child; you want to eat up.'

'Oh, I eat enormously, mother. I'm fat.'

'Don't you tell me that. Look at you and me. Seven of you, I'd make. It's all this scribbling you do, I shouldn't wonder. I remember . . .'

What she remembered was a thin young man thirty years ago, scribbling and scribbling, and staying thin, for all the good butter and cream he ate up at the farm.

'Well, I suppose the Lord made us fat and thin according to His pleasure.'

She looked at Daisy with the attenuating eye of a mother who sees her most prized children as thin, tired, wasting away, when really they are plump as young partridges. She desired to feed Sunday beef to Daisy as one feeds meal to table fowls, to replenish her with suet pudding, with treacle, with dumplings, until her eyes should run over with fatness and her bones should melt away, until she should take to rubber corsets and reducing salts in the bath, which, however, would not reduce but increase.

'There, get along with you,' said Mrs. Arthur.

CHAPTER 10

The Folyots

The Folyot family were back in London. This, though they did not care for London, they had considered necessary, since Mr. Folyot had a cure of classical antiquities in the British Museum, Mrs. Folyot was a member of many committees which did good work all the winter time, Raymond Folyot delivered lectures of some biological kind to students from overseas at the Empire University, and Cary and Charles Folyot attended day schools. That is, of course, the trouble about this city, which so lacks elegance, brightness, foreignness, cafés on the pavement, and charm – so many persons are tethered to it by some curious links which they do not, for one reason or another, see fit to break. Cary Folyot, who already was a good European, and preferred abroad, thought it a great pity. School bored and fatigued this poor child.

Raymond, too, thought it a pity, but he did not seriously object to his work. He was just now interested in the autumnal habits of British birds, and spent fine week-ends in British woods, investigating these. He liked to encounter the winter visitors in act of arriving, the summer visitors in act of departing, the birds of passage in act of transit; he desired to find a bearded reedling in Hampshire, to establish definitely that this little bird is not, as is so often said, extinct in this county; he enjoyed the curious ways of the mealy redpole, pine grosbeak, waxwing, and great grey shrike, and liked to watch the hoopoe at its habits.

He said to his parents one Saturday at breakfast, 'I have rung up Geranium. Geranium and I are going to Ashstead for the day. I shall probably not be back to dinner.'

Mrs. Folyot said (she was opening a great many letters with great speed and firmness), 'The *Times* won't print my letter on the *confinati* as it stands. They say it must be toned

down, it comments too indignantly on a friendly government. Friendly fiddlesticks. Are either of you going to be in
for lunch? I am lunching with the Six Points.'

Mr. Folyot said that the unduly prolonged rains in
Calcutta were spoiling, if they had not already spoilt, the
rice.

Cary and Charles, whose reaction to spoilt rice was one
of gratification, and whose holiday it moreover was, looked
affable, and Cary inquired, what about porridge, how
much rain was needed to spoil that?

Raymond said, 'I hope no one wants to use my car,
because I am taking it.'

Charles, ever hopeful, said, 'Should me and Cary come
with you?'

Raymond said that they should not, for he intended to
look at birds, and the effect of Cary and Charles on birds
was that which farmers erroneously hoped that scarecrows
had.

Mrs. Folyot said, 'And the Deported Armenian Women
Committee has put its meeting at twelve to-day. *Most*
tiresome. By the by, two new refugee Italian professors are
coming to dinner – Turati and Silvio. They are seventy-six
and seventy-nine. What should they eat? No soup, I
thought . Those great Italian beards . . .'

'You've taken too much marmalade,' said Cary to
Charles.

'Daddy, can I have a water tortoise?' said Charles, changing the conversation.

'And a few people coming in after dinner,' said Mrs.
Folyot. 'I thought the professors should say a few words.'

A pre-occupied family; they none of them threw themselves into the interests of the rest, but each ploughed his or
her own furrow. Their thoughts, their little passions and
hopes and desires, all ran along separate lines. Family life is
like this – animated, but collateral.

2

Raymond went back with Geranium to Maynard Buildings, after they had spent the day in Ashstead Forest and dined later in town. They had had a good day, decorated with birds as is the night of an astronomer with stars, and had observed the snow bunting just arrived, travel-worn and flustered, from those austerer climes where he had spent his summer.

In the flat were Theo and a young woman of middle height and small pale, freckled face, her short, straight hair ruffled over her head.

'*Daphne*! Hullo, Daphne. Geranium, you never told me you knew Daphne.'

'No. I didn't know you did.'

'Of course I do. She was with us abroad. . . .' He paused on that, remembering various things that had occurred abroad.

'Have a drink,' said Theo.

'Thanks. Where are you living, Daphne?'

'The flat below this. How are they all?'

'Oh, all right. Look here, you must come and see them. Mother'd love to see you. What are you doing in these days?'

'Earning a little. Spending a lot.'

'What are you working at?'

'Oh, writing, mainly. Articles, Raymond, of great insight and beauty, for our press.'

'Articles? What about?'

'Anything. I am like the Bishop of London; when I think of a thing I write it down.'

'I never knew you journalised. What about your poetry?' For poetry had been what Daphne used to write, and had spoken to him about sometimes, but he had contrived never to see any of it, as he did not care about verse. He changed the subject from poetry, saying, 'Well, this is fine, meeting you here. . . . What are you doing to-morrow?'

'Nothing particular.'

'Well, will you come out with me and see birds? I want to go back to Ashstead; I hadn't nearly done when it got dark. Will you come?'

'All right. Will it amuse me?'

'It will, won't it, Geranium? It's most exciting – if you like the sort of thing, and I remember you do, don't you? Good, then. I'll call for you about ten. Come back to supper and see the family.'

There was about Raymond that fraternal warmth which makes some zoologists such agreeable company, like little boys who take your hand and say, 'Come and play with me.' It comes, perhaps, from much association with animals, who do not stand upon ceremony with one another. He was pleased to see Daphne again; they had shared many adventures together, and he had half forgotten how attractive she often was, with her gay derisiveness and her impudent kind of gamin face, that was now faintly flushed with conversation and the fire.

Raymond settled down, and he and Theo and Daphne talked. Geranium never talked much; that was partly why she was good on bird walks. Raymond thought, he must tell Daphne to-morrow not to chatter like a magpie in the woods. She was chattering a good deal this evening, and being rather amusing. She had, it seemed to Raymond, changed a little, become more of the world, more derisive and assured. He looked forward to resuming their friendship.

3

Raymond found his home full of persecuted Italian professors, large grey beards, and sympathetic people who had come in after dinner to hear the professors say a few words. One of them, the professor of seventy-six, was saying them as Raymond slipped into the room, speaking French with the accent and idiom of Lombardy. He seemed to be approaching the end.

'Et comment sont punis ceux qui essaient de fuir ce régime devenu intolerable à tout homme de raison et d'esprit? Si l'evadé est repris, suit un procès à faire rire, un procès moins juste que celui accordé aux criminels les plus vils, et un jugement le condamnant à un long terme d'emprisonnement, soit dans une de nos prisons regionales, soit sur une des îles arides et execrés qui se trouvent au large de nos côtes. De ces îles je ne parlerai pas.' (Raymond, who disliked the form of speech called paraleipsis, perceived that the professor was indulging in it.) 'Je ne veux pas, parce que je ne le puis pas, vous raconter comment nous sommes obligés d'y vivre dans les conditions les plus cruelles, parmi des assassins, des faussaires, des ravisseurs. Je vous demande, mes amis, pour combien de temps doit on supporter cela? Quand l'opinion publique du monde demandera-t-elle que ces choses-là finissent? Mon pays malheureux est affaibli par la lutte et la douleur; le jour viendra ou la Jeune Italie, une Italie réanimée et debarrassée de ce cauchemar affreux, se levera et mettra un terme à cette tyrannie, mais, en attendant, ces pays d'Europe qui sont encore libres doivent réagir – la Francia e sopra tutto l'Inghilterra, sempre sempre l'amica della libertà, e sempre l'amica dell' Italia. . . . Scusino, signori . . . je vous demande pardon, Messieurs et Mesdames, si je me laisse entraîner par mon sujet si malheureux.'

They excused him and clapped him and pitied him and praised him, and in some eyes tears stood. Mrs. Folyot, stout and moved and efficient, seated him, the unhappy old professor, in an arm-chair, and beckoned Raymond to feed sandwiches to him and to his still older friend; while Mr. Struther, the clergyman, rose, and said such words as one can well imagine for oneself, speaking French with the accent and idiom of Marlborough.

Mr. Folyot, meanwhile, was conversing with the still older professor. It seemed that an important Roman remain had been dug up on one of the penal islands whereon the political good were herded together with the non-political bad. The Italian professor was something of an archaeologist, and conversed on the matter of the remain with all the intelligence of his race, so that in Mr. Folyot's eyes this poor man's sojourn on the island had not been unmitigated misfortune.

Raymond, whom unhappy foreigners moved less than if his childhood and youth had not been largely spent in consoling, with plates of food and glasses of drink, their sorrows, drifted from the room. A characteristic home evening, he felt it to be, of the kind his mother preferred. Raymond knew it to be important to mass public opinion against the iniquities of other countries; vaguely he knew his own attitude of 'let people alone and get on with your own job' to be selfish and lazy. He admired his mother for being so public-spirited and compassionate, his father for abetting her. All he felt against it was that it was rather a bore finding a crowd in the drawing-room when one came in.

Cary, in pink pyjamas, sat on the stairs, her arms hugging her knees, her eyes bright and awake.

'Hullo, what are you doing there?'

'Listening to the party,' Cary replied. 'It makes a noise like the Zoo. I heard the man talking, but I couldn't hear what he said. Now they'll all talking at once. That's how I like it. What was for dinner?'

'Don't know; wasn't in.'

'Oh. Well, what did *you* have for dinner?'

'Hors d'oeuvres, clear soup, sole Morny, vol-au-vent of chicken.'

'Yes? What else?'

'Brussels sprouts, I think.'

'I mean, what pudding?'

'I can't remember.'

'Fancy forgetting the pudding. It's the important part. Was it apple-tart?'

'Shouldn't think so. Glace, I think.'

'Oh.'

'Look here, isn't it time you were asleep? Cut up to bed, or you'll catch it.'

But Cary engaged him in conversation.

'Did you have a lovely day? What did you do?'

'Looked at birds in a wood. Yes, quite a good day. And afterwards I saw a friend of yours. I went back with Geranium and met Daphne.'

'Oh.' Cary's voice was politely non-committal.

'She's coming here to-morrow night to see us all.'

'Oh.'

'You'd really better get to bed, you know, before anyone finds you here. You're half asleep already.'

'All right. Did you think to bring a sandwich or a chocolate out of the drawing-room in your pocket? Charles and me get rather hungry late at night when there's a party. It's thinking of the people eating, I expect.'

'I didn't. But I'll get you some biscuits from the dining-room if you like.'

'No, thank you. Biscuits aren't ackshully what we want. Well, I think I'll go to bed now.'

4

Raymond sat in the library and scribbled notes about crustacea, on which creatures he would lecture on Monday, until he heard sounds of going. These sounds being completed, he sought the dining-room, where his parents sat exhausted among the débris of their little philanthropic party. Mrs. Folyot was eating sandwiches, and Raymond assisted in this occupation.

'Raymond, you should have stayed. It was all most interesting. . . . Those poor old professors; how well Turati spoke! Incredible, what he's been through. He enjoyed the foie sandwiches, they seemed to comfort him. Silvio preferred the relish. It was a good audience, didn't you think, Hugh? They asked the right questions. Audiences are so silly sometimes; they don't seem to get the point. Though Sir John did go fast asleep in the front armchair. Now, Raymond, why *did* you go away like that, only looking in for a moment?'

'For one thing I was filthy, mother. My woodland clothes. For another, I had some work to do. For a third, I wasn't feeling gregarious. And I knew all about the poor professors' troubles already.'

'Have a good day?' Mr. Folyot asked, intervening.

'Quite good. Then I went back to Geranium's flat and met Daphne Simpson. It seems she lives in the same buildings, and Geranium knows her quite well. She's coming out with me to-morrow, and I asked her to come back to supper here. Is that all right?'

'Very nice, dear. Remind me in the morning, will you. Yes; I shall like to see Daphne again. I wonder what she's interested in now. If she's not too busy she might care to help me with the Armenian Refugee sale next month. . . . Well, I'm off to bed.' Mrs. Folyot, a good mother, selected two sandwiches, which she would place beside the bedsides of her younger children, in case Cary should be lying awake or Charles should wake in the morning.

'I really have enjoyed this evening,' she meanwhile said. 'We had some *good* talk at dinner. Didn't we, Hugh? And everyone got so interested. I think it's been really useful, don't you, Hugh?'

'You never know.' Mr. Folyot was a cautious man. 'Anyhow, the old professors enjoyed themselves.'

CHAPTER 11

Sunday Out

In a yellowing wood Raymond Folyot prowled, like a cat seeking birds, with the Miss Simpsons, for Daisy, too, was of the party. Daisy, whose reactions to birds were all incorrect, was silent, leaving the conversation to Daphne, who was able to sustain it tolerably, even where birds were concerned. That is to say, Daphne took intelligent notice, and agreed or differed with what Raymond thought he perceived. But when Raymond said, handing Daphne his bird-glasses, 'It *is* a goldcrest. See? He's hanging upside down on the top right-hand branch, near those tits,' and Daphne replied, 'Yes, I've got him. But isn't it a hen?' Daisy thought, a harlequin in a yellow cap, performing turns in a pantomime. When Raymond said, 'A Dartford warbler – see? Skulking in that furze bush – shy little devil. He's very rare round here,' and Daphne said, 'Oh, look at his red waistcoat. Now he's hidden himself,' Daisy thought, a deserting grenadier. When Raymond said, 'A cock stone-chat,' and Daphne 'On the top twig?' Daisy thought, Napoleon, or Lord Grey. And when Raymond and Daphne agreed (but Raymond thought of it first) that the flock wheeling over the plough-land beyond the wood must be the first fieldfares, and that they had arrived early, Daisy thought of those droves of motor-cyclists who flock together on Sundays and settle at lunch-time outside inns in country towns. When Raymond said, sniffing, 'A distinct smell of woodpecker,' and Daphne sniffed, too, saying, 'Rather like it, certainly,' Daisy thought of American bisons, and trappers who snuff the wind for them ten miles away.

The wind got up, a scatter of rain came down, and to Daisy there seemed in the October woods to be a concert, the pine trees playing the violin, the robins the flute, the thrushes the whistle, while the rain drumming lightly on the woods was like the brisk, tripping, tapping notes made by pianos. There was even in the band that worst of instruments, the human voice, for somewhere in the lane beyond the wood a young man sang, inquiring how in the world the old folks knew it was not going to rain no more. A young woman's voice joined in, so that the concert became more of an opera, and Daisy lost interest in it. Instead, she looked at Raymond, who was talking to Daphne, and saw the way his dark hair grew on his neck, and the long, lounging steps he took, and how his black eyebrows turned up a little at their outer ends and sloped down to his nose, and how from beneath them his eyes peered, bright and brown, with frogs' eggs in the brown; and looking on Raymond she loved him, as if no one yet in the world had loved another before.

Raymond, however, was not noticing Daisy at all, he was talking to Daphne, who walked at his side through the wood, her small and impudent face wet with the rain beneath her brown leather hat, her hands thrust deep into her coat-pockets. They talked of birds, of the habits of weasels and squirrels, of foxes and badgers and voles. Leaving then the wood for the field-path to the station, where they would take a train for Victoria, they spoke, by a natural transition, of abroad, and of that island whereon they had stayed. His mother, said Raymond, had brought back from it a cook, a poor girl who had offended local prejudice and whose life had not, therefore, been comfortable on the island, but who could cook very well, though English food surprised and shocked her a good deal. They reached their station and mounted their train, and in their compartment someone had left the *Sunday Wire,* and it lay open at an article called: 'Is the modern girl religious?' by Marjorie Wynne. Daisy, whose first impulse was to sit on it, thought that instead she would, for once, test the reaction of Raymond to Miss Wynne, and said, picking it up and showing it him derisively, 'Is the modern girl religious?'

Raymond, glancing at the heading, indifferently asked,

not even amused, 'What modern girl is it talking about?'

'I suppose,' said Daisy, 'the modern girl that the press do talk about. Just modern girls in general.'

Raymond said, 'Do they talk about modern girls? Why?' and lit his pipe.

'No one knows why,' said Daphne, intervening. She added: 'Ever heard of one Marjorie Wynne, Raymond?'

'Marjorie what? No, not that I remember. Who is she?'

'Oh, a writer of sorts. She wrote a novel called *Youth at the Prow,* and she writes articles in the newspapers.'

'Never heard of her. But I very seldom read novels or articles.'

Daisy thought, she might write for fifty years, and still he wouldn't hear of her. Marjorie is quite safe from him, and was relieved. The impregnable security of one class of writer from another class of reader is more than the security of snails from British cooks, of pigs from Jewish butchers, of the skunk from the squeamish hunter.

2

They reached the Folyots' house at seven o'clock. In the drawing-room Cary and Charles lay on the floor, where Cary wrote a novel and Charles did meccano. Both politely rose. Daphne, kissing them, inquired how they both did.

Cary replied, literally, 'Charles has a cold and I have a bad knee from hockey.'

'Yesterday,' Charles amplified, 'I used five handkerchiefs. To-day I've had four, up to now. But I think I shall begin my fifth soon.'

'I don't call that many,' said Daphne. 'I can use ten a day easily when I have a cold.'

'And I could,' Charles explained. 'But I don't get so many. Florence says five are enough for one day.' He returned to his meccano, though still looking hospitable and polite.

'Writing a story, Cary?' Daphne asked, knowing Cary's habits.

'Yes. A long book.'

'Good. What about?'

'About adventures. It has no love or men in it, it's all adventures.'

'Where do they happen?'

'Round the world. They have an adventure in a place, then they take a train or a ship for another place, and have more adventures.'

'I see. But why no men?'

'Well, when men come in there's love. If it's all girls there can't be love, only adventures. But I have monsters, and sea leopards, and sea lions.'

'Sea leopards and sea lions are mere seals, you know,' Raymond informed her.

Cary looked at him with the contempt of the novelist for the scientist.

'Not the ones in my book,' she said. 'They come up out of the sea and eat people.'

Perhaps fearing further minishment of her more ferocious characters, she returned to her manuscript, remarking, 'I must finish this chapter.'

There was a noise in the hall as of people departing, and then Mrs. Folyot entered, cordial and cheerful and kind. Daisy felt that the boar, though scarcely forgotten, did not really much matter any more, that life had hurried on, that a great deal had occurred since, and that among the clamouring needs of a thousand touching malcontents, the savage pig and her own reaction to it constituted a tiny episode in a past grown already remote.

Mrs. Folyot greeted the young ladies with affection.

'You've not been in long, I hope? I had some Armenian bazaar stall-keepers in; there's so much to arrange. Daphne, I wish you'd come and help with the book-stall. It's on November the first. You've heard about it, I expect? To raise money for the irrigation of Erivan. All those poor Armenians; there's Erivan appointed for them and they waiting to settle in it, but it seems it has to be watered first, and the money to water it can't be raised. Nansen's heartbroken; he can't make the nations give the money; nations do hate giving money always, naturally, and particularly to

Armenians, whom none of them like. So we must all do our
bits. Can you spare a little time to help with the book-stall,
Daphne?'

Daphne thought she could.

'That's splendid. Good girl. I'll let you know when our
next meeting about it is, and you can come along and meet
Miss Plunkett, the stall-keeper. What are you busy with
now, by the way?'

'I'm writing a little.'

'That's nice. What?'

'Oh, different things. Articles sometimes. . . .'

'What do you write for?'

'Different papers. I don't sign them. They're about
anything that turns up.'

'Well, I wish you'd write one about Erivan. The more we
can keep it before the public the better. I write letters, but
they're not always published, I suppose they're too strong.'

Middle-aged and elderly people, thought Daisy, often
think that when the letters they address to newspapers are
not printed it is because they are too strong.

'I'll try,' said Daphne, who knew that the *Sunday Wire*
would reject an article by her about Erivan, for Erivan was
not at all the goods. People like Mrs. Folyot never learn that
the press does not exist in order to do good to their
protégés.

'I must give you some facts, and you can work them up
into a little article.'

That wave of generous energy that swept all her acquaintances out into a sea of dire activities! It was noble, yet
terrifying, thought Daisy. Fortunately Mr. Folyot here
entered. He was cordial and friendly, and smiled the smile
that had always captured Daisy's heart.

'I missed you,' he said, 'after you left us. Our niece who
came out was a very nice girl, but no help to me. I had to get
along by myself, and the book suffered. You shouldn't have
run away from us like that, you know.'

He was a pleasant hypocrite; even in his thoughts he
ignored awkward and embarrassing circumstances,
remembering that Daphne had run away from him and his

book, pretending that Daisy had by no means run away
from a boar.

'Now, children,' said Mrs. Folyot, 'put your things away
and go up and get ready for supper. Yes, every piece into
the box, Charles; don't leave any about. They're having
supper downstairs with us to-night for a treat because
you're here,' she explained, and rang for a maid, who
conducted the young ladies upstairs to get ready for supper.

3

Throughout supper Daisy experienced those sad and sweet
pangs with which one reacts to reminders of past joy.
Finding herself once more within this adorable circle, she
wondered what folly could have expelled her from it before
the appointed time of severance, what fantasy of hurt pride
had driven her from its sunshine. She had half forgotten in
the last months, as memory had lost its edge, how blessed
had been her state, seated every day, at every meal, among
these people. The children's little freckled faces seemed
beautiful to her. Mrs. Folyot's rapid, deep-voiced talk of
Erivan, of irrigation, of bazaars, had the purposeful charm
and cadence of waterfalls that turn mills and light villages;
Mr. Folyot was amused and kindly, like a god on Olympus,
and made little agreeable jokes; while as to Raymond, who
had been all day like a boy, business-like and charmingly
intent on practical matters, he was now gentle, courteous,
and entertaining, like a host, like a man.

Little arrangements were made between Mrs. Folyot and
Daphne concerning the irrigation of Erivan, and it was
established that she would attend next Wednesday afternoon a meeting of stall-keepers and learn from Miss
Plunkett how she should function in the matter of the book-
stall. Daphne was not at all used to bazaars, but still, she was
used to books, and liked to help Mrs. Folyot and the poor
Armenians, liking the former and feeling generous com-
passion for the troubles of the latter, which, however, left
Daisy cold.

'No one,' said Mr. Folyot, 'can get safely away from this

house without some burden being tied on their backs. It's
scandalous!' But he smiled, in love with his wife's energy,
though it upset his house, filling it, day and night, with
philanthropists and philanthropees.

Raymond, watching Daphne's impudent yet sensitive
face, with its snub nose and pale-green, far-back eyes under
light brows, thought, she at a bazaar! What nonsense. She
belongs to woods; she's like a faun, a little snub-nosed,
freckly, green-eyed faun. He had forgotten all this time
how Daphne had been like a faun, and therefore delightful
in woods and on the seashore. He would make her come
with him a lot into the country.

He told her so, as he accompanied her and Daisy back to
Maynard Buildings afterwards. She said, 'Rather. I love it.'

4

Meanwhile Mr. Folyot, who was something of a gossip,
was saying to his wife: 'Daphne seems quite to have become
Raymond's girl friend again.'

'Oh,' said Mrs. Folyot vaguely, 'Raymond's girl friends.
. . .' And her gesture implied that these were not a few.

Presently she added: 'I think I must ask that nice child,
Geranium Brown, to dinner one night.'

'She's not,' said Mr. Folyot, 'got Daphne's kind of gamin
charm, that attractive impudence . . .'

'There's more to her,' his wife said. 'An able child, as well
as nice. And the sweetest crooked smile. Oh yes,
Geranium's attractive. Raymond finds her so, you know.'

'Well, I don't blame him. He has a talent for girl friendships, Raymond has.'

'I'm fond of Daphne,' Mrs. Folyot pursued. 'But she's
like water – takes any colour, slips away, changes her shape.
Fluid.'

'Aren't we all?' Mr. Folyot speculated. 'I'm blest if I
know where to have anybody – or myself, for that matter.
We're all slippery.'

'Not Geranium. She's a firm little rock; she's got character and grit. I never feel *sure* of Daphne – what she's really

like, I mean, or how sincere she's being. Never mind; I'm
sure I don't know why I should sit here and pull her to
pieces, when she's just been our guest and is going to help
with the Armenians. We're a couple of old gossips, and it's
time we were in bed.'

5

Daisy wrote to her mother, next day:

'DEAREST MOTHER, I was sorry I couldn't come over
yesterday, but I was out all day in the country with a friend.
I'm afraid next week-end I can't come, as I've got tied up
with a lot of necessary engagements, I'm so sorry. If I find I
can get time to come down during the week, I shall. I've an
awful lot of work just now, though. Lots of love, darling,
in haste,

DAISY.

P.S. The green jumper is lovely, I wear it a lot.'

CHAPTER 12

Love

The weather proved agreeable that autumn, and Raymond spent many of his spare hours in animal research in the country. Indiscriminately biotic, he would alternate ornithoscopy with entomology, and spy out the autumnal habits of the tiny enemies of man, often speaking to his companion of their larvae, their metamorphoses, the drab, unsatisfactory careers of the aphides, the intrusive lives and deservedly unhappy deaths of the more philanthropic orthoptera, the pleasant epicenity of bacteria, the good sense of vanessa, who sleeps the winter through, the simple gluttony of the thrips, who takes his pleasure among corn and grape-vine, and the many bizarre complications of entomoid life.

Alternatively, he would seek reptiles, and, valuing snakes, lizards, and batrachians as among the few British beings which at once possess teeth and lay eggs, he would emulate Melampus by bringing them back into his home. After all, did not his mother bring refugees, who, though they for the most part possessed teeth, could not between them lay one small egg?

To Daphne Raymond gave – offering of love – an infant saurian creature new from its egg, and apparently descended from the union of a lizard and a snake, but already, it seemed, orphaned. She took it, little dragon, back to Maynard Buildings, where it stole milk, terrified the morning woman, peering at her like a chameleon or an elf from the tops of bookcases and from the folds of curtains, and finally, so Daphne informed Raymond, it ran away.

'A tortoise might be better,' said Raymond, quite decided that Daphne should support in Maynard Buildings some little saurian. For he believed the society of these little beings to be beneficial to Daphne, reminding her of country

life, of God's minor creatures, and of himself, and of how
far more congenial to her all these pleasures actually were
than the joys of London, of street life, of dining, dancing,
conversing, and seeing the play, to which he found that she
was too assiduously addicted. He took pleasure in counter-
acting the urban influence upon Daphne of Theo Gerard
and her set.

Daisy perceived that Daphne was dropping many of her
simple urban pleasures, and becoming quite countrified. As
to Daisy, she often visited alone the Zoological Gardens,
where she studied creature life as caged and tagged, absorbing little facts concerning the stump-tailed skink and other
batrachians, the fishes, and the small and large birds. But,
though it was Daisy who absorbed these facts, it was
Daphne who mentioned them afterwards to Raymond.

2

Meanwhile, Daphne visited sometimes the home of the
Folyots, and contributed towards the irrigation of Erivan
her services as a book-stall assistant at the Armenians'
bazaar. The stall-keeper asked her if she could collect from
literary acquaintances free and signed copies of their works.
Daphne did collect some, including two copies of *Youth at
the Prow* signed by Marjorie Wynne. These Mrs. Folyot
turned over with the other books as they lay waiting
arrangement in her house.

'Marjorie Wynne? Who's she? Never heard of her.
What's she written?'

'Just that, I think,' said Daphne.

'I see. One of these first novels girls keep writing. There
are so many of them. It seems to be the first thing girls turn
to on leaving school or college. Terrible waste of time, I
think, but they will do it. I wish some of them would take
some interest in public affairs instead.'

'Interest in public affairs doesn't pay royalties,' Daphne
reasonably pointed out. 'A girl has to live.'

'Besides,' Mrs. Folyot scornfully returned, 'they *like*
writing. It's a nice, soft, selfish job, that can be done

without training. If Cary ever thinks she's going to be allowed to publish novels before she's learnt another trade, she'll find she's mistaken. A girl's got to learn to pull her weight before she does the soft job.'

'A girl's got to live,' Daphne repeated, thinking that Mrs. Folyot had missed this point, which, whether accurate or not, at least represented a view.

'All this living . . .' Mrs. Folyot dismissed it with a gesture as superfluous, and bustled off.

Yet she was engaged in making arrangements whereby Armenians might live, unmolested by Turks and irrigated by Europeans, and if Armenians why not girls? Did girls, then, have to be deported, trafficked in, made white slaves of, before one took an interest in the little arrangements whereby they might live? How different was Mrs. Folyot from the press, which found itself interested not merely in the means by which girls lived, but in every detail of their living!

3

Several days at a time would pass during which Raymond and Daphne, each absorbed in their own pursuits, would stay away from one another, not even telephoning. This gave Raymond time to think. What is it, he speculated, about Daphne that is so attractive? Plenty of the girls I know are prettier, lots are cleverer, lots are more amusing. Yet there is something about Daphne that makes me keep ringing her up. . . . I wonder if she feels the same about me. I wonder what she *does* feel about me . . . and how much of what I feel about her is personal and individual and how much is just because she's female. . . .

For Raymond, being a scientifically minded young man, liked to have things clear, though it is usually only women who trouble thus to analyse emotion, men taking it more for granted. But, not being sexless, like bacteria, Raymond could not hope to detach and label his feelings about Daphne apart from the bias given it by the sex of both. His thoughts on it suffered from confusion. He desired to kiss her, to offer her little tortoises, to tell her a thousand trifling details of the universe and of himself and to hear her make reply. He liked to watch her mouth tilt up at the corners when she smiled, to watch her screw her eyes when she laughed. He was happy to see her taking her small strides at his side when they walked out, her hands in her coat pockets, her impudent head in its felt hat tipped backwards as she flung up at him some remark. For him, what she did and said and was had a faun-like charm, something apart from beauty, apart from brilliance, apart from grace. She was, he believed, twenty-five, but she was candid and gay and happy-go-lucky like a schoolgirl, though with a sophistication quite adult.

One evening in her flat he began kissing her, emitting meanwhile the appropriate sounds and utterances. She responded in kind, and the evening went well.

Daisy wondered next day (for she knew all that occurred to Daphne) whether he kissed Geranium too. But she would never know, for it was not Geranium's habit to make confidences.

It was apparent anyhow that just now it was Daphne whom he desired to kiss. So apparent did this become also to Raymond that in quite a few days he laid prudence and questioning aside and suggested, practical man of action, the adventure of marriage.

Daphne said, 'Why be so energetic? Aren't we very well as we are?'

Raymond said they were not, now that he had begun to think of marriage for them.

Daphne said, 'Let's think it over, and talk about it later. It would be lovely, Raymond, in lots of ways.'

Raymond explained that this was all *he* expected of it, too. He wasn't so stupid as to expect marriage to be all jam. But, in his view, it was worth it. Did not Daphne think so too?

Daphne considered it, her head on one side, her small forefinger tracing patterns on his coat. She had, in point of fact, far more to consider than he had.

They adjourned the discussion until next day.

4

When Raymond left Maynard Buildings that evening, Daphne left them too, and it was Daisy alone who sat on in the flat, considering the situation.

And it is apparent that the time has arrived when a small explanation (in case it has not all along been obvious) should be made in these pages – namely, that Daisy and Daphne, these apparently two young women, were actually one and the same young woman, Daphne being Daisy's present-ment, or fantasy (as the psychologists call it), of herself as she hoped that she appeared to others. Daphne Daisy her mother had named her, obedient to her father's odd whim in the matter of a name, but retrieving it by a second name by which a girl might actually be *called*. And Daisy she had always been called at home, but Daphne by her father's sister, with whom she had spent much of her youth, and Daphne at school and by her friends at large. Daphne was the educated, intelligent young person of cultured ante-cedents, Daisy the daughter of Mrs. Arthur of East Sheen, about whom Daphne's friends knew nothing. Daphne, who changed her character considerably according to her company, was with Raymond Folyot what Raymond Folyot liked to find her. The Folyot's Daphne had nothing, for instance, to do with the authoress Marjorie Wynne, though the Daphne known to many of her friends did not scruple to avow and jest about this connection. Also, the Folyots' Daphne was twenty-five, whereas Daisy was thirty.

It will be seen, therefore, that Daisy had food for thought, when considering this matter of getting married to Ray-mond. For, if Daphne should marry Raymond, even become affianced to Raymond, Raymond must, sooner or later, perceive Daisy skulking behind Daphne, learn Daisy's age, be apprised of Daisy's literary and journalistic habits, worst of all, meet Daisy's mother and become aware of her lowly birth and background and of Daphne's deceits in this matter. And that, so far as Raymond was concerned, would be the end of Daphne. Daisy, when he should become acquainted with her, he might or might not love, but it was, so far, Daphne whom he loved and desired to make his wife. How would he regard Daisy? She would emerge, in the first place, when she should emerge at all, as a liar, a snob, and a cad. Months ago, on an island mountain-side, she had, in a brief and fatal hour, emerged as a coward; the Folyots had seen a glimpse of Daisy then, and had liked it so little that Daisy had left them in shame, taking with her perforce the damaged, punctured Daphne. In a crisis of danger Daphne was always apt to vanish, leaving an unsheltered Daisy to handle the situation; for a moment once, when bathing, the time Charles had been caught by weeds, Daphne had fled, and Daisy, frightened and help-less, had cried, 'I can't get him up.' But only Cary had seen Daisy then, for the next moment Raymond was swimming towards them, and with Raymond's approach Daphne had returned and rescued Charles with her usual plucky cool-ness. So the only occasion when Raymond had seen Daisy face to face was the occasion of the wild boar. He had not liked that. Still less would he like Daisy the snob, Daisy the vulgar journalist and novelist, Daisy the liar.

What, then, to do? Daisy, crouched by her gas-fire, her chin on her knees, considered it, shivering with nervous apprehension and joy. What, then, to do?

There was one procedure which, having faced it for a minute, she perceived to be quite impossible. She could not renounce Raymond, send him away, tell him she would not be his lover or his wife. That was impossible, since she loved him with an adoration that sent every word he uttered thrilling through her body and soul like arrows dipped in ichor, since she lived now only for the hours she spent in his company, since he was to her, however much Daphne might disguise the fact with her cool and derisive camaraderie, a god.

There was, therefore, one course which was not to be contemplated at all. Since Raymond loved her, since she loved Raymond, they must proceed on that basis.

But marriage was another question. Daisy would have liked to linger on, indefinitely lovers, amorous friends and comrades, brightening one another's days with the small enchantments of affection that yet looked forward to no climax.

How could she contemplate marriage – that ceremony, however simple and secular, which mothers feel they have a right to attend? Mrs. Folyot and Mr. Arthur, side by side, conversing . . . Daisy's antecedents emerging . . . a thousand little details of her family life, her age, how she was called Daisy at home, how Mr. Arthur was in the building and decorating business, how Daisy wrote pieces for the papers. . . .

It would be Daisy, not Daphne, who would get married to Raymond. In fact, the ceremony, so conducted, would put poor Daphne for ever to death.

And even should they be married very quietly, as the saying goes – so quietly, so secretly that not even mothers need be there – one cannot for ever prevent one's loving mother from meeting one's husband. Even engagements lead, as a rule, to *rapprochements* between mothers and prospective husbands.

It was not that Daisy believed that Raymond was a snob. Raymond never cared twopence what class people were of; class said nothing to him. But his Daphne came of cultured people, and his Daphne, frail phantom, was fighting desperately for her life.

Daisy resolved that Daphne should put aside the marriage proposition for the present, should say: 'Aren't we happy as we are?'

Having resolved thus, she abruptly suffered revulsion. Heavens, she thought, here am I with a chance to marry Raymond, to live with Raymond in a house of our own, to have Raymond with me every morning, every evening, every night, all Saturday and Sunday, to go abroad with Raymond every holidays, to be, in brief, Raymond's wife; here am I, offered the chance of being the happiest woman in the world, and I am afraid of it, because of what? A fancy, a few small embarrassments that will readily be overcome, that will, surely, somehow melt away and become as nothing.

Very good, thought Daisy, rising to her feet and turning off the fire, Raymond and I will marry. Happy and elated in this prospect, she hurried into bed.

But in the night she awoke and thought, if Raymond should find me out, I should want to die. If Raymond should despise me, nothing would be left to live for. Sooner or later, Raymond *will* find me out. . . .

And in the morning she awoke again, and thought, it shall be a very secret engagement. Perhaps later on Raymond will get some work abroad, and we shall live there. Some South American university. . . . .

Whenever Daisy thought 'South America,' her heart was accustomed to miss a beat and then to race ahead, and she blushed, as if she heard the name of a lover mentioned. For this continent had always seemed to her infinitely desirable, romantic, and good. To think of the Amazon or of the Chico, to see on maps the range of mountains that compress Chile between Argentine and the Pacific, or the scatter of islands in the Chronos Archipelago, to encounter in cross-word puzzles such clues as 'A town in Ecuador,' to read in the newspapers of the League of Nations Assembly in Geneva, of whom so many are South American delegates, who yet do not seem to have their proportionate share of influence in the Assembly's counsels (here, perhaps, was a foreign wrong for Mrs. Folyot to redress), to think of Patagonian Indians, of Portuguese half-breeds, of Argentine señores, of Aztec remains, to devour Chile pepper, Cuba sugar, Bolivian salt, and Brazil nuts, gave to Daisy a reaction of romantic joy that not all the pagodas of China, the cherry blossom of Japan, the spiced winds from Ceylon, the bells of Mandalay, or any of the glamorous calls from east and south could afford.

So, 'Some South American university,' she thought, without even knowing if there were any South American universities. Even if there were none, there were plenty of South American animals, and Raymond could pass his time investigating the habits of the gila monster, and studying the ocelot and the tapir in their forest lairs. Surrounded by armadilloes and great ant-eaters, seeing toucans, tanagers, and sugar-birds singing on every tree, stroking the heads of peccaries, how should Raymond not be happy in his married life? Then doubtless little ones would arrive, and they too would repay biological study. Raymond in South America need never have an idle moment.

Already the problem seemed simple, and last night's nightmare fears were broken and dispersed like clouds before a morning wind.

5

Raymond came that evening to the flat.

'You know,' he said, after suitable greetings, 'that we are engaged, don't you.'

'Very good,' said Daphne, 'we are engaged. But quite privately.'

'Why privately? I can't see that it's private.'

'Well, I like private engagements best. They're more exciting.'

'We shan't get any wedding presents that way.'

'Darling, we shan't be getting wed for ages, anyhow.'

'Darling, we shall get wed directly we can find a house or flat to live in. Why not?'

'Can't we live abroad, Raymond?'

'What on?'

'You could lecture somewhere – some university. I thought of South America.'

'?'

'Well, Tokyo, then. That's where Englishmen always go to be professors.'

'Only poets. You seem to be having an attack of xenomania. You must fight it.'

'I certainly shan't. It's noble. It distinguishes man from the animals.'

'On the contrary, it is the most unreasoning instinct of birds and many reptiles. It's merely a symptom of the discontent of a trivial mind. . . . But what exactly do you mean by private? Private from whom? You don't mind my people knowing?'

'N-no. Not if they don't let it get about.'

'You are secretive, aren't you. I suppose you'll tell your family? Where does your mother live, by the way?'

'Oh, a long way off. . . . The Hebrides. The Outer Hebrides.'

'Does she? How odd. Rather fun, though. I want to go up there some time, after birds. Which of the islands?'

'I forget – oh, Uist.'

'That's where the tweed for my new overcoat came from. What does your stepfather do there?'

'Nothing much. He paints a little. . . . You know, Raymond, I don't get on awfully well with him, nor, really, with mother. I don't often see them.'

'I suppose not, if they live in Uist. Well, why should you? There's not much in being related, unless you happen to get on. Never mind our families now.'

Daisy, her face pressed against his, thought, 'Why Uist? Another lie to be found out. Oh, we must go abroad. . . .'

Little as Daisy was drawn to Asia, unpleasing as she found the contemplation of tea, rice, cherry blossom, and the yellow peril, she felt even Tokyo, being some distance from East Sheen and from Uist, to be a refuge.

You might have thought that Uist would be safe, but no. Raymond, with his birds and his new tweed coat, saw possible connections between himself and every place one could mention, forging imaginary links with the whole universe. If one should place one's family in Mars, Raymond would say, 'There's to be an expedition there next summer. We might go.'

CHAPTER 13

Vanity

Three days later Daisy went to East Sheen for the evening, wrapped in her secret engagement as in a golden but invisible cloak. She desired to tell her mother, but would not do so. Later she would tell; later, when the situation had developed, when either she had prepared the way for the little family encounters that must ensue, by revealing to Raymond something of her mother's status, or when (as she hoped) there would be, owing to this or that, no necessity for encounters. Things turn up, ways of escape arrive, as Daisy knew, or, if nothing better arrives, courage has been known to do so. Possibly Daphne would one day say boldly to Raymond, 'You must meet my mother. She's not the kind you expect mothers to be – she's quite different from my aunt, and from what my father was – but she's a darling.' Raymond wouldn't care, though he would be puzzled about Uist and the other odd things she had told him. But Mrs. Folyot would care rather, unless one could pretend Mrs. Arthur to be a refugee from Russia or somewhere, who had suffered misfortune.

Meanwhile there was no call for indiscretion.

When Daisy arrived at Thekla, Mrs. Arthur was alone. Having combed the cat, she was practising playing tunes on the comb, as she had seen men do in the streets to please (as they hoped) the passers-by. Mrs. Arthur one day had given such a one a shilling to show her how it was done. She was by no means yet expert, but could produce some species of comblike sound that pleased her ear.

'Why, Daisy.' Mrs. Arthur, comb in hand, embraced her daughter. 'Just you listen to this. I learnt it off a poor young fellow in the street. Blind he was, due to the War. And nine children – due to dear knows what; carelessness, I suppose.

Anyhow, he was playing the comb ever so sweetly. Now just you listen to mother.'

Comb splutters ensued.

'Lovely, mother. Was it a tune?'

'Was it a tune! Listen to the girl. Course it was a tune. Have you never heard "Lady be Good"?'

'Oh, was that what it was? Clever you are, mother.'

'Course I'm clever; always was. Now, pet, we've time for a nice talk before the others come in. How's everything? Not had a cold, have you? I enjoyed that piece you had on Sunday, "Do Thin Men Admire Fat Women?" It made Dad and I laugh. Dad says he don't know anything about thin men, but *fat* men like fat women all right. But bless me, girl, what do *you* know about it, I'd like to know? The stuff you write! What's it to be about this Sunday?'

' "The New Freedom and the Old Taboos," it's called, I'm sorry to say. Not my fault.'

'What old taboos? What's a taboo, anyway?'

'Oh, nothing you know about, darling. Just the things you mayn't do and say.'

'Oh.' Mrs. Arthur looked vague, and if she did not call any of these to mind at the moment. 'Well, I dare say it's a nice topic. You look well, girl; kind of bright. Happy, are you?'

'Very happy.' Daisy's secret joy rose in her like a song, and she thought that her mother must hear it.

'That's mother's girl.' A man somewhere about, thought Mrs. Arthur. I've guessed it for some time. Wonder who the chap is, and if he wants her. A west-end fellow, I suppose. I hope no harm'll come of it. So long as the girl's happy. . . . But it's funny her keeping so dark about it. She don't tell me things much; I wish she did. Ada and Amy now, they do.

Mr. Arthur came in and greeted his wife's daughter facetiously.

'Hullo, Miss Fleet Street! Brought us all the news? Between you and Ed, we keep going fine. Look here, Daisy, you mustn't encourage your poor mother in that comb game of hers.' He tapped his forehead and winked.

'She's getting on in life, poor old lady, and gets a bit potty. Thinks she plays tunes – would you believe it?'

'Get along with you, you silly, you're jealous.'

To chaff like that, with such gusto, such love, after five-and-twenty years, after a quarter of a century of marriage between a burly man who decorated houses and wiped his moustache when it got into the tea, and a plump woman who went out to the pictures and drank nips of port. . . .

Before Daisy's eyes all the love of the world suddenly sprang up, a soaring edifice, with pinnacles and impregnable towers. Psyche and Eros, Alcestis and Admetus, Paolo and Francesca, Antony and Cleopatra, Jacob and Rachel, Mr. and Mrs. Robert Browning, Mr. and Mrs. Arthur – all the fervent and constant lovers of history cried aloud that love was immortal. Those other lovers, as fervent, doubtless, but less constant, who cried that it was not, were shouted down by this cloud of witnesses. The sad and frail mortality of love was triumphantly, in the sitting-room of Thekla, denied.

2

At supper there was more concerning love, for it emerged, amid laughter from Edward, Ada, and Amy, that Ada had that very day betrothed herself (in her lunch hour) to a young man with whom she had been for some months very friendly. He was a reporter, one of Edward's colleagues on the Evening Wire.

'And I can tell you he's going to get somewhere, old Percy is. He's a right smart chap. No flies on old Percy. Not as a rule, that is; must have been a few to-day at lunch-time, letting himself be roped in like that. I didn't half rag him when he told me. Poor old Perce, he's done for himself all right. I told him we must try and get in a par about him: "Wire Man's Romance. To Wed Sister of Wire's Star Reporter." We must all do what we can to cheer the poor old egg up.'

Mr. Arthur, having wiped his moustaches, said, 'Come here, Adar, and give your old Dad a kiss.'

Ada did so, having already embraced her mother. Daisy touched her hand as she passed, and said, 'Good luck, Ada.'

As to Amy, she giggled throughout the meal, this being her natural reaction, after her hard telephonic day, to an engagement. Indeed, thought Daisy, she was quite right; it *is* amusing when two human beings arrange to pass together, on such intimate terms, their lives.

Mrs. Arthur ejaculated such applause as mothers emit on these occasions.

'I will say, Ada, you couldn't have picked a nicer young fellow. A real nice fellow, Percy is. I'll say you're both lucky, and I'll bet he knows he is. Well, fancy.'

It was, in fact, definitely established that Ada had done well, had taken a star part, and the spot-light played on her throughout the evening. It was not only amusing, it was creditable, to become affianced.

The corollary was that it was a little discreditable *not* to have become affianced. Ada's look at Daisy in answer to her congratulations, a nice look, half grateful, half apologetic, conveyed, I know you're thirty and I'm only twenty-four, and that I'm engaged and you're not. It's nice of you to overlook it, and I don't want to rub it in a bit. It's not your fault that some girls get off with men and some don't.

And Mrs. Arthur's glance at her conveyed, Never you mind, my lamb. Mother knows you could be engaged, too, if you had a mind. Anyhow, you're mother's clever girl.

But Amy looked at Daisy inquisitively, like a canary, to see how she took it.

Daisy felt, under these amiable regards, a pang of discontent, that she, Daphne Simpson, should be thrown even partially into a society which looked at engagement as one regards a new feather in a hat, or a medal for noble conduct. What did Thekla know or care about her various little friendships and affections? She had not, they thought, brought one of them to the only conclusion which is of importance; she had not, as Ed put it, roped anyone in. In the society in which Daphne moved, spinsterhood was merely the feminine counterpart of bachelordom, and no more discreditable, but in Daisy's simple and homely circle it savoured of disgrace, of having tried and failed. Daisy objected to this; it made her feel like those travellers, smiled on by gratified porters, who have failed to catch trains.

Mr. Arthur, with male tactlessness, made matters worse by saying presently: 'Well, Miss Printer's Ink, and when's that wonderful book of yours coming out?' kindly thus pointing out that she, too, could achieve something, even if not matrimony.

In about a fortnight, Daisy told him.

'Is it nice, Daisy?' Amy asked. 'Shall we like it?'

Daisy sadly feared that they would.

'People have been asking for it already,' Ada said. 'They've seen several reviews of it.'

'Advertisements of it,' Daisy mechanically corrected.

'They say it sounds ever so nice,' said Ada. 'Is it as nice as *Youth at the Prow?*'

'I expect so.' I fear so, was what Daisy meant, but they thought it the utterance of conceit. The faint melancholy of her tone was for the folly of Marjorie Wynne and of *Summer's Over,* Miss Wynne's forthcoming novel, but the family read in it a depressed admission that novels, even ever so nice novels, were but poor, dim achievements compared with engagements.

'Don't you lose hope, Daise, old fruit,' Ed admonished her, believing chaff to brighten situations. 'It'll be your turn next. You'll rope in an editor one of these days, and leave Adar at the post.'

It was a pity that Daphne, nonchalant, self-controlled, and heedless of the opinions of others, was not there. Without her, Daisy, vain, sensitive, impetuous, a lover of applause, lost her head, and shattered her own carefully laid plans to pieces with a sentence.

'Thanks, Ed, but the editor'll be too late in the day. I've roped in someone already.'

Sensation.

'Daisy! D'you mean you're *engaged?* Actually engaged, girl, or only working up to it?'

'Engaged, of course, mother.'

'But bless me, child, why didn't you tell me at once, the

moment you came in? I *said* you looked happy – now didn't I say you looked happy and bright? An' you never answered me "Mother, I'm engaged." Well, I never did, two girls engaged at one supper! Amy, are you sure you're not engaged? Now, Daise, you tell us all about him. Why, we don't even know his name yet!'

Daisy hesitated. It was apparent that her indiscretion had created a situation so delicate as to require the most careful handling.

'You see,' she began, 'It's all very private, so far. Very secret. We're not telling any one at all.'

'Why ever not, child? Who is he?'

Daisy paused, on the brink of replying 'I can't tell you his name yet,' for something in the curious, dubious regard of her half-sisters suddenly caused her to feel like one of those maidens of Hellas, such as Psyche or Semele, who, being wooed secretly by gods, could not reveal their lovers' identity, and whose tales were doubtless, in consequence, not well received.

'She's inventing it,' Amy's eyes, meeting Ada's, seemed to say.

'It's Raymond Folyot,' said Daisy. 'The son of Aunt Monica's friends that I was abroad with.'

The words, the statement of a fact so felicitously tremendous, seemed, like a golden aeroplane or a bottle of wine, to translate her above the clouds, so that she looked down on the world through rosy mists. What were those trifling fears and embarrassments that croaked like frogs beyond the mists? She was engaged to Raymond Folyot. . . .

They all knew about the Folyots, the west-end friends of Daisy's late west-end aunt, with whom she had spent the spring abroad. None of them had ever seen a Folyot, but now, of course, they would do so.

Ada's Percy seemed to recede a few steps, losing thereby an inch or two of stature.

'You can't surprise *me*,' Mrs. Arthur remarked. 'Oh no, not at all. I said to myself long ago, when first you got back from abroad, Daise, I said to myself, there's something up between Daisy and that young Folyot fellow. I'm always right, aren't I, Dad?'

And, indeed, she had said it. Observing her daughter's passionate lamentations in that she had been obliged to leave the Folyots owing to some trifling affair with a boar, she had known that there was more than a boar in the business. Boar's nothing! To account for such grief young men were required.

'Well,' said jovial Mr. Arthur, 'so our Miss Clever's found her Mr. Right. That's fine. Two of your girls got off in one day, Mother – how's that for brisk business?'

'I'm ever so glad, Daisy,' Ada repaid courtesy.

'Shall you be married soon?' Amy inquired. 'I wonder if you or Ada'll get married first.'

Married soon! The words of action dragged Daisy sharply down from above the clouds; her aeroplane grounded with a rush, and she sat, abruptly sobered, among the wreckage. What had she done? What should she now do, to avert catastrophe?

'No, not soon. He has to . . . to be earning more money first.'

'What does he do, Daise?'

'He lectures on science – biology.'

'Shouldn't think he'd get much for that. Who does he lecture to?'

'Empire University students.'

'He works in London, then. That's good. You must bring him down to supper one day soon, girl.'

'You see, mother, I can't yet, because no one's supposed to know about our engagement. I oughtn't to have told you, really. It's quite secret.'

'Well, bless me, child, he wouldn't mind *us* knowing. I suppose.'

'He might, because his own people don't know yet, and so it's best no one should. So please none of you say a word, will you.'

'A funny kind of engagement,' Amy commented. Amy, who admired normality, found a disproportionate number of things funny. 'Will his relations be annoyed when they know?'

'Annoyed, indeed!' Mrs. Arthur bridled. 'I should hope not.'

'No, not exactly annoyed. But they might think he oughtn't to marry anyone till he's got on more.'

'If his mother's got sense – and you always told me what a nice woman she was, Daisy – *she* won't think anything silly of that kind. She'll be pleased he should settle down with a nice girl he's fond of. It settles a young fellow so, marriage does. You'd much better go together and tell her all about it, girl. You take my advice, for I know.'

'Some time we shall tell her. Not just yet.'

Nightmare fears began to assault Daisy. Her mother, after a glass of wine or two, might take matters into her own hands, and, as one mother to another . . .

'Anyhow,' she hurried on, 'she's away just now. They're all away. They spend a lot of time away. They don't live in London much. Raymond's away a lot too.'

'Why, where do they all go to?'

'Oh . . . the Hebrides. Uist or somewhere.'

'Wherever's that? Sounds a queer place to spend time in. Does your young fellow give lectures there too?'

'No, he just looks for birds and things there. It's part of his work.'

'Shall you live in London when you're married, Daise?' Ada asked.

'I don't think so. Abroad, perhaps. . . . South America, perhaps.'

'*Daisy!*' Mrs. Arthur cried out, a smitten mother. 'Not South America. Not *South* America, girl! Why?'

Daisy retracted South America. Anything to get away from this subject in which she was entwining herself as with coil on coil of entangling rope.

'Well, perhaps it won't be. It will all depend on where his job takes him, you see.'

'One of these unsettled kind of jobs,' her stepfather inferred. 'He'd better leave it, and go into business. I might be able to get him a job in our firm, if he'd care for the work.'

'No, thanks, Dad. He likes his job.'

'Pity if he gets sent to the other end of the world, though, just as he's getting married.'

'Well, perhaps he won't. I didn't say he would; I said he *might*.' Daisy had definitely had too much of this subject. You can leave nothing vague with relations; they must always get to the bottom of things; they are like dogs worrying bones.

'But please do all promise to say nothing about my engagement,' she added.

'It's just the moment to publish it, with your new book coming out.' Edward knew the value of publicity. 'A little par about it would sell the book. It always does.'

'Ed, you mustn't. *Really* not. . . .'

Her voice shrilled with a note of anxiety that caused her relatives to look at her in surprise. There was something queer about this engagement, they thought.

'Another thing, Ed. I don't want it published anywhere that Marjorie Wynne is me. I know a lot of people know it, but I don't want it published.'

'Well, it seems to me silly, but it's your funeral. You'll lose a lot of good publicity.'

'Daise doesn't like publicity, she likes things private,' Amy remarked, and Daisy felt again the ignominy of Psyche or Semele, whose lovers could not be produced. She's not really quite pulled it off yet, she saw Ada and Amy thinking.

She changed the subject.

'When are *you* thinking of getting married, Ada?'

Ada and Percy, it seemed, had thought of Easter. There was nothing, in their case, to wait for. Percy was getting a good salary and had a settled job. No danger of Percy getting sent over the world, to South America or Uist. Yes, they thought of Easter.

Percy, during the conversation of the last few minutes, had advanced again to the centre of the stage, regaining stature. It was prouder to possess a public Percy than a so oddly private Folyot, a Folyot who could not be brought to supper, could not be mentioned to friends.

But Mrs. Arthur, as they talked of the Easter wedding of

Adar and Percy, said to herself: 'Daisy and me'll have a nice talk after supper. She shall tell me all about it. She's shy now, before every one.'

3

They did have a nice talk, up in Mrs. Arthur's bedroom, by the nice gas fire.

'Now, my pet, you tell mother all about this young man of yours. Do you love him a lot, Daise?'

'Yes, a lot.'

'And is he a handsome fellow – nice-looking? Have you a photo you can show me?'

'Handsome . . . I don't know. No, probably not. Nice-looking, yes. Dark eyes; tall; slouches rather. He looks . . . intelligent. No, I've no photo with me. I've got a snapshot in London, though. I'll bring it some time.'

'Do, girl. I want to know all about him. Now, Ada's Percy, he's been here a lot, I know him quite well. He and I have a rare time chaffing. A nice fellow, he is. I wish you'd bring your Raymond.'

'I'm sorry, darling, but I can't. I told you, it's still secret. He's not to know I've told you.'

'Seems to me silly. How long are you going on that way?'

'I'm not sure. I'll tell you later.'

Stabbed by fear, impatience, and remorse, Daisy, sitting on the floor by her mother's arm-chair, leaned her head against that capacious knee, and drew one of the kind and idle hands about her neck.

'Don't worry me about it, darling, will you? There are things to arrange . . .'

'Arrange! Well, I suppose so. Always are, with engagements. . . . Well, so long as you love each other, it's all right. An' he loves you a lot, doesn't he?'

'Yes. We love each other a lot.'

'That's good.'

The little thrill of satisfied emotion in her daughter's voice – that refined, literary, west-end voice that was quite different from any other voice in Thekla, but vaguely like,

in its accents and inflections, a voice that Mrs. Arthur
remembered thirty years back – pierced the mother with
keen memory. We love each other a lot. That was what *he*
had said – and it had been true, too, for a while – perhaps six
months or so. She hadn't married him; it wouldn't have
been fit, she'd have been a fish out of water, and she had
known, even at nineteen, that he would tire of her. But he'd
always been good to her and to the child, until he had died
of his lungs when Daisy was three. Oh yes, for a time they
had loved each other a lot – and what had that led to? It had
been worth while, but she didn't want Daisy to go that way
too. In the child's blood, it was. And this odd secrecy. . . .

'Daisy, my lamb. He *is* going to marry you, isn't he?'

'Oh yes. Presently.' Daisy dreamily gazed at the golden
fire. Nothing more beautiful than a gas fire, red-gold, hot,
and radiant like the naked sun. But it dazed and hypnotised.

'Well, Daisy girl, you won't let anything happen first;
now, will you? You've not done that, have you, mother's
own?'

'What? . . . Oh, I see. No, no, mother of course not.'

'Well, don't do it, girl. Believe me, I know what I'm
talking about.'

Daisy drew away. She was resentful, less at the idea than
the question. People, she held, should not interrogate other
people, not even daughters, on such things. Besides, where
was the use? If she could not have denied it with truth, still
she would have denied it. Her mother should have known
that.

She sat up stiffly, scarlet from the fire.

'Raymond and I mean to be married as soon as we can
manage it. We don't mean to live together first. Why should
you think so?'

Mrs. Arthur sighed, seeing that she had offended her
darling.

'That's all right, girlie. Course I don't think so. It only
just flashed into my mind, as it were, due to it's being kept
so secret, and to my thinking suddenly of me and your
father years back. But of course there's no such reason, you
and he being the same class. . . . Now don't you be vexed

with your silly old mother, Daise, always saying the wrong thing. Same way I was for ever vexing your aunt, saying things she didn't like. . . . Kiss me, child.'

So Daisy kissed her mother with affection, and caught the last train back to town.

4

On the way home she meditated cynically on vanity, the destructions, the wreckages of discreet and careful designs, that this most irrepressible of the deadly sins will cause. She reflected how vanity had wrecked continents, ruined empires, lit the fuses which had started wars, destroyed armies, sunk fleets, drenched worlds in blood; how it had caused, and would cause, great volumes to be written, and little volumes, and infinite columns in newspapers; how it goaded men and women to torrents of eloquence, to autobiographies, memoirs, and letters to the press; how it had drowned Narcissus, intoxicated Napoleon, Mussolini, and Lord Northcliffe, caused gods to ruin mortals, mortals to infuriate gods, ensnared women and entrapped men, built palaces, castles, abbeys, drunk up fortunes, emptied purses, all but ruined Psyche at the last, and now had imperilled the very life of Daphne. Yet what matter? Daphne's days, in any case, seemed numbered; the sword hung over her head, its cord fraying thin; one day the cord would part, the sword would fall, and so would Raymond lose his Daphne. Into the darkness beyond that loss, Daisy dared not look. Raymond might continue to love Daisy, but it was Daphne whom Daisy desired that he should love, not Daisy, the liar and the snob. Oh, she was trapped, she was trapped. . . .

Meanwhile, the sword swinging on its frayed cord, one could but dance in desperate felicity.

Raymond, Raymond, Raymond, sang the clattering train, jolting into the city. How could I tell I should ever mind like this? Oh, my darling, I can't, I mustn't think. . . .

That she might not think, she took up the *Evening Wire* and looked at it. There was a story of Ed's; he had been telling them about it at supper. An inquest on a murdered girl; parents in court; women join in rush for places, following four hours' wait in queue; surprise witness produced; a pathetic feature was struck by collapse of father; on showing him the hat his daughter had worn, he identified it and burst into tears; quite feasible that inquest might have to be adjourned, due to fresh evidence; disappointed crowds turned away from doors; many women among them.

But he had forgotten to say whether they were shingled and well-dressed, Daisy vaguely thought.

She reached home and hurried into a bath, drowning thought with hot water, then sank into bed, stifling care with blankets, till roused next morning by the sharp ringing of the telephone bell and a brisk voice that said: 'That you, Miss Simpson? Merton, *Morning Wire* speaking. We want you to do a short piece for tomorrow's issue – say two hundred words on "Do Men Like a Girl to Fix her Face in the Street?" And I wish you'd ring up the following and get snappy symposiums from them on it. Sybil Thorndyke, Gladys Cooper, Dean Inge, Dr. Barnes, Edgar Wallace . . . and – oh, anyone you can get hold of who'll answer. You read what Cardinal Bourne's been saying about it, of course? *Not?* Oh, it's in this morning's paper; we've given it a big show. A sign of the corruption of the age, he says it is, and what Jezebel did. It seems God doesn't like it. Mustn't touch on that, though; too controversial. Our question is, do *men* like it? Look sharp, won't you, and spill it across while it's still hot.'

CHAPTER 14

Discretion

The Folyot family took the engagement of Raymond with that appearance of pleasure and that acceptance of life which such occasions evoke. Since Raymond felt that he would be happier with Daphne than without her, since he felt competent to meet the additional expense, and since the two young people loved, it was well. Mrs. Folyot, a mother affectionate but occupied and detached, blessed the affair and got Daphne to assist her and a young French widow whom she often employed in such duties (her permanent secretary being very busy at the moment with a campaign for improving the morals of the police) in the matter of the Anti-Dictators' League, which she and Mr. Struther were starting for the benefit of their foreign friends, and also for that of the dictators, for it was a very civilised, constitutional league, the motto of whose organisers was not 'Say it with bombs,' but rather, ardent epistolophiles, 'Write to the newspapers,' so that MM. Mussolini, Lenin, Pilsudski, Primo de Rivera, Carmona, Paschitch, Bratiano, and the other European potentates had really reason to be grateful to the League, for they did not, for the most part, at all mind the British newspapers being written to about them, and no other newspapers printed the letters.

Daphne, though by nature epistolophobe, and with no strong feeling about dictators, assisted, when called on, in this good work, for she was a sympathetic girl, and liked to help Mrs. Folyot and the poor foreigners. So she spent a whole morning addressing envelopes that invited to a meeting such prominent foreigners as were visiting London owing to the dictatorial habits of their home governments, while Mrs. Folyot flitted between her permanent secretary and her casual helpers, bestowing attention alternately on dictated-to foreigners and doubtfully moral policemen.

Daisy preferred her job to the secretary's; she would not
have cared to be involved in casting aspersions on the virtue
of policemen, whom she had always found to be very good,
clever men, informing her of the way with the minimum of
effort and confusion, and never saying 'straight through.'
Who was good and policemen were not good? Must one,
then, seek out specks on the sun? Should one detect in these
good young men the flaws and frailties common to our
weak mortality and hold them up before a shocked public
for condemnation? Never would the English people stand
for this, for we love our good policemen.

But when, during a moment's pause in her own work,
Daphne ventured to express something of what she felt in
this matter of the police, Mrs. Folyot said 'Pish' (for she was
one of the few people who do really make use of these
ejaculations so frequent in literature), 'the police are only
human. They've got far too much power, and they often
abuse it. We can't have street dictators,' for she had,
naturally, dictators a little on her brain, and occasionally
mixed up the two works being carried on at the two tables,
speaking of the policemen as dictators and of the dictators as
if their private morals required at once a committee of
inquiry.

2

Mr. Folyot had come home from the British Museum to
lunch; he looked into the study, said good morning to
Daphne, with something less than his usual affability, and
indicated to his wife, by one of those movements of the
head by which husbands signal, that she was to come from
the room and speak to him. After a few further instructions
to her scribes she went out, but failed to close the door
adequately, so that they heard fragments of speech issuing
from the room opposite. It seemed to Daisy that Mr.
Folyot, her kindly, cheerful, and charming friend, had been
hurt by something which had occurred to him . . . or was it
something that had *not* occurred to him?

'I think I shan't go to the dinner at all,' he said. 'If they prefer that I should speak fourth, not first, well and good, it's their affair. But on the whole I prefer not to go, to be passed over like that in favour of Stenson.'

Mrs. Folyot made the soothing, indignant sounds that wives make when husbands have been passed over.

'It's not as if,' Mr. Folyot went on; but here, in order that Daisy, the secretary, and the French widow might hear no more, Daphne shut the door.

Odd, Daisy reflected, as she copied out the strange names borne by those who have dictators in their home countries, odd how you never know people, only on the outside. She would not have guessed that Mr. Folyot, so delightful, self-controlled, and humorous, so gifted a scholar, so gentle and kind a man, had these little feelings, ambitions, and resentments about the order of speaking at dinners. What else had he that she had never divined? Had everyone, then, some different self, that only a few people, that sometimes only they themselves, knew? How know anyone? She had put the same question to herself the other day, when reading the published diary of a man of letters, who revealed in his daily records a self strangely hidden from his friends. They had known him as one kind of person, and he was, between himself and his diary, quite another. Which was the more real? Both were real, but which the more? Not necessarily the secret, hidden self . . . Daphne was real as well as Daisy; the humorous, detached scholar who derided the world's small plaudits, as well as the disappointed man who had hurried home to complain to his wife that he was passed over and would not attend the dinner. What secret person lurked behind Mrs. Folyot's generous and bustling activities . . . behind Raymond's darling absorption? Further, if they all had these queer hidden selves, need they so much mind showing them to one another, need they be afraid?

Well, it all depended. . . .

Daisy was roused from these speculations by a loud sigh from the French widow, who was regarding with derisive distaste the neat white piles which covered the table and represented the morning's work she had done for humanity.

'Mon Dieu, quelles paperasses!'

The secretary lifted disapproving eyes from the Policemen's Morals. Daphne, suppressing a giggle, resumed the work of addressing an envelope to a Lithuanian doctor called Czarinatschiowski, which occupation took her until the lunch-bell rang.

3

Yes, the Folyot family were sufficiently pleased with Raymond's affair and with Daphne. But Daisy guessed that, under a polite childish exterior, which nevertheless concealed reserves, Cary was not sufficiently pleased. Cary, a child of pronounced affections, loved Raymond. A child, too, of curious divinations and clarities of vision, she had always looked through Daphne as if she had been a figure of gossamer and seen Daisy behind and within her. And what was her view of Daisy, who should say? She might mention it to Charles, but Charles, a child truly male, and no ethnologist, was not much interested in the characters of people, or in their views on one another. Charles took people for granted, without speculation, and went on his way. And it was certain that Cary would give her views on Daphne and Daisy to no one but Charles, her unexcited and unbetraying confidant.

Daphne would, when the mood and the occasion arrived to her together, woo Cary with the loan of books, with tales of adventure, with rational talk about the exciting and absorbing world, and with interest in Cary's own literary efforts. At times the child was a little won over. Daphne would answer her questions about those grown-up habits some knowledge of which is so essential to the best fiction. When she inquired: 'How can people stop being married when I'm tired of their being married?' Daphne told her, 'You can get them a divorce.'

'Oh, is that quite easy?'

'Quite easy for you to mention. The trouble would be all theirs, and you needn't go into it. Just say "They got divorced," and let them part.'

'Then which would have the children?'

'Oh, are there children? Better divide them.'

'There are thirteen. They won't go into halves.'

'Well, it would be six apiece, and the odd one could spend half its time with each of them.'

'So she could. And would they have a choosing of the others, turn by turn, should you think?'

'Probably.'

'You see, some of the children are bad and some are good, so it would be very important to the parents which ones they got. And some are clever and some are stupid. However, they're all good-looking.'

'I'm sure they are. How old are they?'

'One's thirteen, and four are twelve, and three are eleven, and after that they go down in ones – ten, nine, eight, seven, and six. And the mother's twenty-one now. She married the father when she was eighteen, because she met him in the Andamans where he was a convict and helped him to escape, and she liked him, and she wanted to have children.'

'Well, she seems to have got them all right.'

'Yes. But now I want her to go exploring in Patagonia, with her share of the children and with a faithful Indian, but without the father, so I shall divorce them.'

'What's she going to explore for in Patagonia?'

'Just treasure. She's found a document with a chart of where it's hidden. Spaniards hid it, years ago.'

The reticence suitable to hidden treasure descended abruptly on the novelist, who had been kindled by the narration of her plot to eloquence. She withdrew into courteous reserve; the eager author became the polite and aloof little girl.

'Thank you very much for telling me about divorce.'

'Don't mention it.'

At other times Daisy would find the impish child staring at her inscrutably out of clear green eyes, thinking what? Of wild boars? One got the impression that Cary was the only Folyot who remembered the boar, and that she not only remembered it but would not be at all surprised by precisely similar conduct on Daphne's part any day. It would not, one inferred, be Daphne whom Cary would ever invite to accompany her on exploring expeditions to Patagonia or the Andamans, though Daphne did well enough for giving information about the ways of the world. On the whole, Cary might appear to be thinking, Raymond had made a questionable choice. Was Daphne quite the companion to choose to take travelling round looking for animals? Now, if he desired a companion, there was Cary herself . . . or, if he would care for two companions, Cary and Charles. . . . However, Raymond seemed to like to go about with Daphne. I expect her talk amuses him, thought Cary. She does talk a lot. He won't let me talk much, but he lets her.

Sometimes, when Daisy was not making up to her future sister-in-law, or amused by her, she reacted towards her unspoken attitude with impatient annoyance. Why shouldn't the child like her? How dared she look at her with that queer comprehension, ignoring Daphne, refusing tacitly to accept Daphne's existence, penetrating, supreme impertinence, to the secret springs of Daisy's soul? Heavens, how much did she know? Was it possible that she discerned not merely Daisy, but – final insolence – Marjorie Wynne of *Youth at the Prow, Summer's Over,* and the *Sunday Wire*? Or rather (for she had surely never seen these novels or this newspaper, her parents only reading the so-called best contemporary fiction, and not, indeed, thinking very much even of that, and taking in only two Sunday papers, neither of which was the *Sunday Wire*) did she, perhaps, divine a potential Marjorie Wynne, one who might be expected to write like that if she wrote at all?

Well, why bother oneself about a tiresome child? What did Cary matter, anyhow?

4

Indeed, Daisy had not just now time or inclination to concern herself with Cary, for she had on her hands the task, sufficiently delicate and embarrassing, of segregating Marjorie Wynne, her new book, and all the activities and interests arising therefrom, from Raymond: *Summer's Over*

had just appeared, described by its publisher on the inside
flap of the wrapper as 'Youth's cry of perplexity and pain,
typical of this our post-War age of unrest, when, the old
values being submerged, youth, in hot revolt against Victorian standards, questions life as never before. No one who
takes up *Summer's Over* will put it down unmoved. It is pre-
eminently a poignant cry of youth to youth, but age, too,
will give heed.'

Pish, as Daisy imagined Mrs. Folyot saying. It should be
mentioned on Miss Wynne's behalf, that this blurb was not
her fault. Her publishers had done it without consulting
her.

When Daisy turned the pages of her advance copies, it
seemed to her that they were, these pages, no worse than
those that occurred in most novels. But then, of course, this
was not to say much. They were not ill-written; they had
even a certain poignancy, and, surely a kind of grace, less of
style than of sentiment and characterisation. And here and
there, so Daisy thought, there was humour. This Marjorie
Wynne – she was not, surely, on the lowest levels? There
were, thought Daisy, many novelists below her.

But, since to highbrows these slight differentiations
between one lowbrow and another are not obvious, all
appearing to be submerged in a common lack of intellectual
distinction and commonplace sentiment, style, and
thought, Daisy erected between Miss Wynne and the
Folyots a high wall of partition. It was not hard to keep any
of them from reading *Summer's Over,* for to none of them
(except Cary, whose appetite for fiction was at this time
catholic and omnivorous) would it have occurred to do so.
Mrs. Folyot sometimes read novels, but mainly those
which would, she believed, suggest to her some idea, state
some practical problem the solution of which seemed to her
to be of importance. Apart from these she occasionally
read, with little either of hope or of gratification, some
novel which she heard well spoken of, and, for the rest, Mr.
Wells, Mr. Bennett, and Mr. Galsworthy, as she had from
her youth up, for she found that these three distinguished
authors had often something to say to her, or, on the

occasions when they said nothing that she cared to hear, she liked at least to be sure that she had missed nothing.

Mr. Folyot read many more novels. He read the novels that he thought would amuse him, and detective stories. Raymond practically did not read novels at all; he did not care for this form of expression, and was not interested in the things with which most novels concern themselves.

No, there was little difficulty in keeping Marjorie Wynne's book out of the Folyots' home. On the other hand, mentions of it and reviews of it freely entered the house. It was fairly well reviewed, by reviewers who liked the kind of thing, and began that mysterious process known as 'getting about'. No one knows what starts this desirable activity in books, whether it is caused by publishers, booksellers, reviewers, the taste of readers, or those circular post-cards which say, brightly: 'I've been having flu lately, but have been quite cheered up by ——'s new novel, which made me laugh so much (and cry a bit, too) that I quite recovered.' It is, however induced, an activity, such as (among human creatures) roller-skating, ski-ing, and bicycling, which not all books ever learn to perform. *Summer's Over* showed, soon after its birth, signs of becoming one of these (mildly) active books. Ada told Daisy so.

'It's being asked for a lot,' she said. 'We've sold all the copies we had. They all say it's ever so nice.'

Thus Ada, kind girl, consoled her half-sister for not having a producible young man.

After some weeks *Summer's Over* was mentioned by a celebrated author in his weekly book-chat in an evening paper.

'I have been asked several times recently,' he said, 'if I have read a novel called *Summer's Over,* by a young lady called Marjorie Wynne. My answer is that I have not, and do not intend to do so. No adequate reason has so far been offered me why I should read it, and I see no likelihood of discovering such a reason. The only reason so far presented to me is that many other people have read it. This reason does not seem to me a particularly good one. (Towers & Smith, 7s. 6d.).' He then proceeded to speak of a novel by a

Scandinavian, mentioning favourably also short stories by Russians.

The publishers of *Summer's Over* were quite pleased with this attention, and with the statement that the book had many readers. Publishers always feel gratified if this is said of a book, not regarding it as at all derogatory, but sharing the view of many of those who try to sell goods that to hear of large numbers of others who have purchased them is a powerful incentive. 'We are selling a great many of these,' those employed to sell in shops persuasively say, predicating in their customers a touching faith in the good judgment of the majority. The only salesmen and saleswomen who appear to cater for a more exclusive taste are those who sell their wares not in shops but in streets, and who will seek to do business by informing potential customers that they have not, during the current day, so far, sold any matchboxes, violets, white heather, bootlaces, or what not. These street vendors seem to be the highbrows of the commercial world, making their appeal to an exclusive and esoteric pride; they are more flattering than their rivals behind counters, or than the proprietors of newspapers, with their announcements of extensive circulation.

Anyhow, the publishers of *Summer's Over* believed that the comments on it quoted above assisted in teaching it activity.

It proved to be the kind of book which pleases the editors of such newspapers as like to have little human articles blossoming like nosegays in their pages, and Marjorie Wynne suddenly found herself in demand. It seemed that she was to Speak for Youth, at rates higher than any she had been offered before. She was asked to write on 'Should Flappers vote?' Emboldened by success, and thinking that for once she would tell the truth about this affair of the flappers, she sent in seven hundred words, beginning: 'Flappers (when not meaning young wild ducks or partridges) are and have always been, since the first application of the word to human creatures, girls from about fourteen to eighteen. The name as thus applied derives either from the analogy of young birds, or from the fact that at this age the hair, not being yet what used to be called "up," used to flap on the shoulders, either loose or in a pigtail. I do not think it has yet been suggested that these young girls should have parliamentary votes. But I dare say they would do no more harm with them than other people do, and the expression of their opinions when educational questions turned up might be helpful.'

But the article was returned, with a letter from the literary editor which said, firmly: 'By flappers we mean young women from twenty to thirty years of age. We should be obliged if you would write the article on these lines. Our public is not interested in possible votes for schoolgirls.'

The remuneration was good, so Daisy, still cautious about the sales of *Summer's Over,* wrote the article on these lines. She did indeed alter the title from 'flappers' to 'young women,' but this was amended in the office, so no harm was done. If the press had decided, and it was apparent that it had decided, to apply a word formerly denoting ungrown girls to grown-up young women, no feeble protests from purists and pedants would curb it, any more than these had checked the same word's transference from young birds to young girls. If the press should elect to announce that flappers were women from forty to fifty, or men from sixty to seventy, nothing would check that either. Newspapers were like Humpty Dumpty; when they used a word the word meant what they chose that it should mean; they were the masters, never the slaves, of language.

As to that, Daisy reflected, they were but one with the rest of mankind. What, after all, is language, that it should dominate and hamper man who made it? And what right have any of us to demand that the meanings of words should be, what in point of fact they seldom are, static? Words move, turning over like tumbling clowns; like certain books and like fleas, they possess activity. All men equally have the right to say: 'This word shall bear this meaning,' and see if they can get it across. It is a sporting game, which all can play, only all cannot win. 'He altered the meaning of a word': is this a noble epitaph or the reverse? 'He refused to acknowledge a new meaning to a word': is this to be a hero or merely a linguistic backwoodsman? Still, why be coerced by Fleet Street? If words are changing their meanings, as assuredly they are, let each user of language make such changes as please himself, put up his own suggestion, and let the best win. It is unfair that, just because they have a staff of printers and a large supply of paper, newspapers should have it all their own way. The only people at present who have any adequate weapons with which to rival them are those potentates who command and sway the ether, and whose power to dominate the mind of man is alarming. If every day, in announcing the news, these should elect to say (for instance) weether for weather, how soon would it become common speech among that large class which accepts what it hears? Or if they should yield to the impassioned pleadings of certain Ulstermen and take to saying garrden, farrtherr, and dinnerr, how soon would they corrupt the speech of southern Englishmen, setting it rolling like a Scottish burn? Possibly never, for the English, in matters of pronunciation, are not lightly to be moved. But if, with calm assurance of correctitude, they should always say hindcast for forecast, would not this speedily become the accepted word? For the majority of the English, immovable enough as to the pronunciation of their words, are infinitely hazy as to their meanings and magnificently indifferent as to their etymologies.

Yes, these kings of print and air take unfair advantages, thought Daisy, as she tapped out her little thoughts on the voting of flappers. Such little thoughts as these and the others which were required of her by the press translated her into a world so alien from the world of Raymond that when she occupied it she felt lonely, as if she were on a visit to a star uninhabited by her lover, or to a lunatic asylum, where values and meanings were all quite transformed, where reason did not function, nor thought nor facts prevail, but, instead, a foolish coffle of words and phrases trotted round and round like jaded hacks in a circus, bearing on their weary backs marionette figures of wax, with dead simpering faces, and no life in their limbs. Lonely she felt among these, like an uncertified visitor to the asylum, and a little afraid, as if she might never see Raymond any more, so far away he was; but she found, nevertheless, a kind of foolish amusement in this odd world, to which those who knew Marjorie Wynne seemed so determined that she belonged. To her it was strange and frightening to open an evening paper and see 'By Marjorie Wynne, author of *Summer's Over*,' at the head of some little fragment of womanly chat, to see Raymond look through the paper, hold it perhaps open at that page, reading something else, pass 'Crinolines or Cocktails' without a glance, and turn to the contests of horses. It seemed impossible that he should miss that foolish black headline, with its lunatic alternatives, only linked by their initial letter. Did one wear the cocktails or drink the crinolines? One might proceed indefinitely on those lines, as Bustles or Bovril, Coats or Coffee, Jumpers or Gin, Lingerie or Lemonade, Waistcoats or Water, Mantles or Milk. But not even this much of comment did Raymond make; it was as if his eyes were holden so that he could not see such words as these in papers; or perhaps he saw them as some other readers see 'City Notes,' and 'Company Meetings,' and others, again, 'News of Books,' without comprehension, thought, or desire, so that they made no dint upon his consciousness.

From whatever cause, it seemed that Marjorie Wynne was inviolably lonely and secure behind her cage of print. And, if *Summer's Over* continued to be so active, the Marjorie Wynne of the newspapers might presently expire, thus removing herself from danger for ever.

But what of Marjorie Wynne the novelist? She must not expire; she was a breadwinner. She must continue to earn money, that Raymond and Daphne might be enabled to exist the more happily. It was Marjorie Wynne who would send Daphne dowered to her nuptials, who would furnish Daphne with economic independence. It was apparent to Daisy that, sooner or later, Raymond would have to become aware of Marjorie Wynne the novelist, and her degraded activities. And, after all, if these paid, they had justification enough. To pay – or rather, to be paid – was one of the few unimpeachable justifications for anything. Even Raymond, absorbed in his aquarium, his birds and his beasts, would scarcely deny that. If *Summer's Over* and its successors should afford them journeys abroad, feed and clothe their little ones, pay their income-tax, their gambling debts, their car and wireless licences, and Daphne's dressmaker, these words would not have been written in vain. After all, Raymond need not go so far as to read them. In fact, it was practically certain that he would not. It was as likely that Daisy would one day find herself perusing works on the Integral Calculus, or the Dean of St. Paul's 'Jesus Loves Me, by a Priest.'

So Daisy, though finding herself temporarily embarrassed by the entanglements twined about her by the secret children of herself and her typewriter, could look beyond them without excessive foreboding. Had Marjorie Wynne been her only embarrassment, the future, which now appeared so complicated and so uneasy, would have stretched before her even as a paved high-road.

CHAPTER 15

Cares of a Sister-in-law

Christmas drew near; or rather the inhabitants of the earth drew near to Christmas. The Folyots would have a happy Yuletide, for Mrs. Folyot, whose keeping of Christmas, as well as of other occasions, was an annual example of that competent eutaxy in which her life was ordered, not only shopped early but posted early, so that she had sent all her greetings (except those to her immediate family and household) by the fifteenth of October, thus leaving herself free to enjoy the happy season without further annoyance to herself. As to Mr. Folyot, he did not disturb himself much, leaving his wife to buy his children's presents for him and contenting himself, for his part, with being amusing and genial at home. Raymond's habit, contrary to Mrs. Folyot's, was to shop late. He devoted the first day on which the shops reopened after Christmas (usually the Feast of the Holy Innocents) to buying belated presents for his family in return for those received, then, having bestowed them, thought no more about this etesian worry until next Christmas. Cary and Charles behaved with the customary Yuletide abandonment of the young, and their excitement was not disagreeable to their parents. So this troublesome season was, on the whole, well managed by the Folyots, and passed over them without too much disintegrating them.

Raymond wanted Daphne to spend Christmas with them, but she said that she must spend it at her mother's.

'In Uist?'

'No, East Sheen. They'll be there for Christmas.'

'Better give me the address.'

'Darling, what's the use? I shall only be there two days; you'd have to write to me a week before I went there to reach me before I left. Let's spend Christmas Eve together, and meet again on the twenty-seventh. Mother'd be disappointed if we didn't all gather for Christmas.'

'I suppose you must gather, then. Will your mother stay long in East Sheen?'

'No, quite a short time. . . . I wonder what Cary and Charles would like for Christmas.'

'Oh, anything they get. Don't bother about them. Wait to buy presents till after Christmas; I always do. The shops seem less full then. No one with anything else to do can be expected to shop between the first and the twenty-fifth of December. The way people do it is another example of their meekness in bearing unnecessary torture. Like men's clothes on hot days, and women's on cold evenings. A form of asceticism, I suppose. Or else merely stupidity, not being able to think of a way out.'

'A few people really enjoy it. My mother does. Being in a big shop in Christmas week makes her feel like a child who's got to heaven, while every one round her feels as if they'd got lost in one of the Inferno circles.'

'I should like to meet your mother. She must be original. Is she like you?'

'Not a bit. I take after my father, I believe. Mother's a darling. Great fun.'

'Shall I come down to East Sheen and see her? I ought to, I think. I'm sure one meets one's mother-in-law before marriage.'

Unexpected things Raymond would say, suddenly recalling that people had mothers, families, and so on, when one supposed him absorbed in other affairs, and scarcely seeming to realise the world of conventions. The unconventional do have these disconcerting little attacks. Daphne soothed him out of it.

'Oh, you'll meet some time. It's no use trying to catch mother in Christmas week, she's never at home for an hour. She's one of the people Christmas was made for. She makes an orgy of it. I'll bring you together later, when life is calmer. But you probably won't care for her much. And I'm sure she and your mother wouldn't get on. I don't particularly want them to meet yet.'

'Why shouldn't they get on?'

'Oh, they're so quite different. Mother doesn't care twopence for any public causes; she's very frivolous. She'd give money if she was asked, but she'd never give attention. And she chatters away and talks an awful lot of nonsense. . . . No, they'd better not meet.'

My mother is not a lady; she doesn't come of educated people. What if one had said that and had done? It would have been like leaping into a gulf. At least it would have been over. And Raymond would have said, carelessly indifferent, 'What does it matter? What *are* educated people, anyhow? No one's educated much.'

How easy it would all be. But when they parted she would be leaving behind her the image of a Daphne slightly tarnished, vaguely marred, not precisely the same Daphne with whom Raymond had fallen in love.

She changed the subject, talking with that nervous gaiety and hilarity which seized her when she had looked into danger's face and passed it by. You'll get me some time, I suppose, she addressed it, but you shan't get me yet.

2

Three days before Christmas, Daisy, reduced by the frightful streets, the nightmare shops, to a state of tired nervous strain that made her flee from life as from a terrifying juggernaut, turned into a church to find peace. The misty and incensed air crept about her, as she knelt with her chin on her arms, staring through weary tears at the red sanctuary light. Here was comfort and security, something to hold to in chaos. If not objective truth – and who was to know that? – here to her was one kind of truth, shining like a lamp through the falsehoods and entanglements of her uneasy and frightened life.

Clergymen were hearing confessions, seated along the walls. Unobserving, Daisy saw people go up to them, come down. Unobserving, until a small, familiar figure, walking towards her, recalled her mind from its journeyings, for her eyes met those of Cary Folyot. The child had been making a confession; she had a paper crushed in her hand; her small face was pale in the foggy air, and half exalted, half conscious. Meeting Daisy's eyes, she reddened; never had Daisy seen such a tide of colour in that white, intelligent little face. She half stopped, then went on, and entered a seat behind.

Queer! Daisy suspected that she had intruded on some strictly private adventure. She could not imagine that Cary's parents had sanctioned, firm agnostics, this religious enterprise on the part of their young daughter.

Not wishing to intrude further on her future sister-in-law's devotional life, Daisy rose to leave the church. At the door Cary joined her, and they went out together.

'Hullo.' Cary spoke with a hint of nervous defiance, thrusting her hands into the pockets of her reefer coat and swaggering a little.

'Hullo,' Daphne returned. 'Going home?'

'Yes. . . . I say, there's a fog coming on.'

'Looks like it. How are you going? The tube? I'll walk to Oxford Circus with you.'

They walked down Margaret Street into Regent Street, and the Christmas crowds surged at them through the dark and fog like an army.

'I say, Daphne.'

'What?'

Cary's voice had a little quiver of nerves; it was hoarse, too, for fogs gave her colds.

'You're a silly child to be out this weather,' Daphne told her.

She ignored that.

'I suppose, of course, you'll be telling them that you saw me in that church.'

The tremulous assumption of negligence pleased Daphne. How little can children simulate, and with what courage they try.

'I shouldn't think so,' she returned, equally casual. 'Why should I? It wasn't specially interesting.'

Cary thought that over.

'Well,' she said, after a moment, with candour, 'I think it

was rather interesting for you, seeing me like that, going to confession, when you didn't guess I went, did you? I'd have thought it interesting, if I'd been you. Even I think it's rather interesting that I go, and it's nothing new to me, of course, because I've been several times now. Only,' she added, 'no one knows.'

'Is it a secret, then?'

'Yes, kind of. You see, I'm not sure they'd like me doing it.'

'I should think you were quite sure they wouldn't, aren't you?'

'Well, yes, quite, really. But still, now I suppose you'll be mentioning it to Raymond?'

'No reason why I should. Raymond wouldn't be interested.'

'You don't tell Raymond everything, do you?' Was it a question or an assertion? The queer green eyes were raised suddenly to Daisy's, and Daisy felt startled, accused. What did this strange child mean? What did she know?

'No one ever tells anyone everything, I should think,' she answered shortly.

'Well,' Cary's eyes dropped again, and she trotted on through the encumbered forest of Regent Street in silence for a minute, before saying, 'Then you won't be mentioning me to anyone?'

'If you don't want me to, I won't.'

Daisy for a moment had an absurd feeling that they had made a mutual compact.

'But,' she felt obliged quickly to add, 'it seems a pity to hide it, don't you think? I mean, if you really feel you want to go to confession, and tell them so, they'd let you, I expect.'

'I don't think they would,' Cary was doubtful. 'In any case, they wouldn't be pleased about it. I'd rather not mention it, at present.'

'Well, why do you go?' An impertinent question, Daisy admitted, even to a person of twelve. But persons of twelve are well broken in to impertinence, and expect it. Cary replied, simply, 'It's interesting. And I expect it's good for me. You see, there are lots of things you can't *tell* anyone, not ord'rily. But in confession you can. You can talk. . . .'

Daisy understood. This child desired an outlet.

'You can argue about religion and things,' Cary went on, warming to her theme. 'Only there wasn't enough time to-day, he was in a hurry. He doesn't usually let me talk a great deal,' she added, with a sigh. 'But he listens to me saying what I've done, and the thoughts I've had.'

'What put it into your head first?'

'I read about it in a book. And I saw people doing it in the church at Solio. They were Italians, of course, but then I read about how English people go, too, so I went. . . . I wanted a lot of things explained, and I didn't like to ask Daddy and Mummy, so I thought I'd better see a clergy-man, so I did. He makes me feel a lot better always. . . . I think perhaps when I grow up I may be a nun, and write my books in a convent, and not have any name on them, but just "By a Nun".'

'Why should you be a nun? I don't suppose you'd be at all a good one. I don't believe you're a bit religious, really.'

'No.' Cary considered it honestly. 'I'm not really very religious. Only interested in religion. But I think I shall be a nun. Then I needn't marry.'

'You needn't marry in any case. Lots of people don't. But I thought you wanted thirteen or fourteen children.'

'I don't now.' The child seemed suddenly, standing in the tube entrance, to shrink and become frightened and babyish. Her eyes were on her muddy little shoes.

'I don't like the way they come,' she muttered, so that Daisy barely heard, and added something about 'Beastly.'

Dear me, thought Daisy. This child knows too much. One must look into it. She asked, 'Has your mother been telling you about that – babies, I mean, and things?'

'No. Not Mummy.'

'Who then?'

'No one.'

'Then you've been reading something, haven't you?'

Cary was silent and flushed, kicking one foot against the ticket-machine.

'What *have* you been reading, Cary?'

'Well – a book about dreams.'

'Dreams? Who by?'

'A man called Frood.'

'Frood? . . . Oh, I see. But it's a pretty nasty book, Freud on dreams. I don't wonder you didn't like what you read. How did you get hold of it?'

'It came from the library once, and I looked at it. Then I got it out again, and no one knew.'

'A pity you did, because he's so nasty. There's nothing horrid really about how babies come, or about marriage or anything; only he'd make anything sound filthy. He's got that kind of mind. . . . Did you tell that in confession, that you'd been reading books like that secretly?'

'Yes. He said I wasn't to. He said to think nicely, and not about that. So I try to. But sometimes in the night . . .'

The self-contained child was on the edge of tears.

'Oh yes,' said Daisy, 'I know about the night. Nights are like that. You know what you'd much better do – tell your mother what you've been reading, and get her to talk to you. Those things are all right really, and nothing to bother about. They simply don't matter twopence. Will you tell her?'

Cary rubbed her eyes dry with her woollen-gloved fist, and thought.

'I don't expect so,' she said, after a moment. 'I may think I shall now I've been talking to you and just been to confession, but I don't expect I shall when I think it over.'

She seemed to pull herself together, and reserve descended on her.

'I shall be late for tea if I don't hurry. Are you coming to tea with us?'

'No, not to-day. You'll get back all right alone, shall you? . . . Well, that's what *I'd* do, Cary, and I wish you would. Think it over, will you.'

'Yes, thanks very much,' said Cary politely. 'Goodbye.'

She was cursing herself, Daisy saw, for having given herself away. She got a ticket to Holland Park out of the slot and was swallowed up by the hurrying throng, a small,

frail, spindle-legged little girl in a red tam-o'-shanter and
reefer coat. So small and frail and spindly and young that
she melted the heart, like lambs or colts that are new to this
difficult world, and yet one cannot help them through it.
Daisy felt absurd inclinations to pursue her, to offer her
warm milk and good advice, to wrap her in blankets and
carry her safe home through the fog, feeling her less a sister-
in-law than a child who had scared itself in the dark.

3

So this was Cary's secret life. The clever, self-contained
little creature, who looked at her sometimes with such
alarming elfish comprehension, and at other times romped
about and talked normal childish nonsense – in her other,
her hidden life, that no one guessed at, she alternately
sickened herself with reading hints at a life so disgusting
that it kept her awake with nightmares, and sought emotional and spiritual outlet in secret religious practices.

Daisy felt suddenly like a parent, helpless before the
disconcerting plight of childhood, desiring to shield and
guard, yet knowing no way. She wished that Cary liked
her, that she might be of some use. She almost wished that
she had not made that promise of silence, but, after all, what
is the use of telling parents what goes on in their children's
lives? The children have to work it out in the end for
themselves. Cary had brains, and Daisy believed, probably
erroneously, that brains are apt to pull people through. So
long as she did not have a nervous collapse. . . . Was that
priest suitable? Was he looking after the child, not merely
furnishing her with an outlet for her intellectual and
spiritual vanity, pandering unknowingly to her interest in
discussing herself? Cary had said he didn't always let her
talk much, so perhaps he was sensible enough. But had he
told her to tell her parents she came to him, or didn't he
know she came secretly like Nicodemus? Priests, like other
people, differed; some had more sense of honour, some
less. One could but hope, concerning Cary's father in God,
for the best.

Daisy wished that Cary would give her opportunities of talking to her casually, cheerfully, about marriage, as if it was quite all right, and not at all beastly really. To pass from childhood into adolescence with that sinister shadow brooding over life – for a nervous child, that was a misfortune. Daisy resolved at least to give Mrs. Folyot a hint as to that, though it seemed too late to begin now those cheerful little discourses on the propagation of the vegetable kingdom with which first bird life, then the life of beasts, and finally the embarrassing life of man, is gently broken to the young. Mrs. Folyot had, in fact, probably taken her children through these first courses in life years ago, only they had not made such an impression but that the Viennese professor could trample it out and foul it with his dirty boots.

And Daisy fell to musing on the oddness of life, how it is such that most of its beginners, first learning of its mysteries, are disgusted. Is it, then, really so disgusting, or is it we who are too readily disgusted? What a perverse anomaly, that we should revolt in displeasure from the methods of our own origin. Do the other and less intelligent animals show this strange lack of intelligence? One believes not, and that they, being great acceptors, take it quite for granted, scarcely even speculating on it until the time arrives when they desire to put it into practice, if then. How fortunate are the animals, arriving into this world without the sense of fastidiousness that so deranges and dualises the mind of man. Or so we imagine; but who are we to judge? We are not present to observe the squirrels when first they are informed of the Facts of Life; we do not see the young rabbits scuttling abashed into their burrows after their mother's revelations, nothing left but the twinkle of white scuts. Too easily and too lightly we make pronouncements on these our reticent and unfathomed fellow-creatures.

Too readily, also, we fall into the snares spread before us by children, attributing to them as tragic obsessions what are but fleeting and occasional thoughts, brooding in anxiety over what to them are little passing revulsions, impermanent shadows that fall into place and are quickly forgotten in the swift procession of their thronged and moving lives. Parents fall into this snare, and by the time they have made up their minds what procedure to adopt with regard to a child's trouble, the trouble has been forgotten by the child, till forced on it again by anxious elders. Why, thought Daisy, be a parent before one's time? She put Cary from her mind, and turned again into the nightmare streets.

The things she had to buy for people had become, in her fancy, a legion of monsters, like the distorted objects in a fever dream. Giddily they slipped in and out of one another, making her head ache. Shopping, or trying to shop, against that phalanx of shoppers, was like trying to row a frail boat against a river bore; one was driven back, submerged, drowned. What was the use? For what did it serve, this tormenting folly? Since one had not been rational, like Mrs. Folyot, and shopped in early October, why, in the name of peace, not be rational like Raymond, and shop in the Feast of the Holy Innocents, or rational like Mr. Folyot, and not shop at all? Daisy, thus questioning, knowing herself one of those unfortunates to whom rationality in the practices of life has been for ever denied, continued, choked, blinded, drowned, to drive her frail barque against that surging mass. We are as we are, and each Christmas finds us as we were last year, leaves us as we shall next year and through all the years be. All Daisy could do about it was to desire, but how vainly, to be as vanessa or a polar bear, that she might sleep the winter through.

4

What, she suddenly wondered, as Christmas swirled violently and blindly about her like a stampeding herd of cattle, was the hidden life of Charles? Would hints of that, too, be irrelevantly, surprisingly, tossed at her out of darkness, out of the abyss where souls lie hid?

Boxing-Day

Christmas Day, when at last, after all the turbulent fret and disorder of its preparation, it arrives, is like a house, blinded and barred, in which groups of relations are confined together. Friends are shut out, lovers are sundered; it is the apotheosis of family life. The Folyots' house on Campden Hill was temporarily closed to revolutionaries, refugees, committees, Armenians, and those who desired to hold bazaars. It became, for two days, merely the home of two parents and three children, shut in Yuletide confinement together. They gave one another little presents (except Raymond, who had not yet shopped, but would shop on the twenty-eighth) and ate too much. Mrs. Folyot and the children heard carols at the Abbey in the afternoon, Cary went to children's Mass in the morning, the children stayed up to dinner and they had games afterwards, and from the outside world poured in, in the middle of the morning, an avalanche of greetings from those whom they had, during the first half of October, either remembered or forgotten.

A strange, gay, isolated day, more like a dream than a day, emptied of responsibilities, cut loose from those little understandings with time and with humanity which moor most days to the world at large. Christmas Day resembles an island such as Delos, that rocks unattached in an open sea, unanchored to that floor which holds most islands so firmly in their places. On the Feast of St. Stephen, however, lines begin to be thrown out once more to the mainland. Families cease to be so self-sufficient; they go to parties at the houses of other families, and present rewards to those who have served them the year round with milk, letters, groceries, and meat, delivered them from that overflow of unwanted possessions which they summarise tersely, inclusively, and often euphemistically, as 'dust,' and paid them the other little attentions without which their lives would have been even more troubled than they have been.

Yes, Boxing-Day opens the doors; Boxing-Day is a more normal, responsible, grown-up kind of day, even though lacking newspapers, shops, places of business, and posts. But one cannot deny that this descent on to the flats of Boxing-Day induces in many subjects a fretfulness, a lassitude, even an inclination to annoy the relations with whom they have been marooned, which does them small credit.

Cary and Charles Folyot, for instance, fought in the morning over the division of their presents, some of which had been sent by ignorant and tactless relatives vaguely to the two of them together. Having quarrelled over that, they proceeded to quarrel over a game of ping-pong. Raymond, who was reading in the room, said, with impatience, 'Oh, shut up, Cary.'

Cary said, aggrieved, 'It's not me to shut up, it's Charles. He served a fault and won't count it against him.'

Charles said, ''Twasn't a fault. It was right,' because it was Boxing-Day and he was cross, though he knew all the time it had been a fault.

Cary said, 'It wasn't. Liar,' and hit him on the head with her wooden racket. At that Raymond looked up and said sharply to Cary, 'If you lose your temper at games, you've no business to play games,' for he, too, was cross, since it was Boxing-Day, he missed Daphne, and what the B.B.C. weather announcers call 'conditions' were cold, damp, and dismal.

'I can't,' he said, 'read a word in this infernal row you make. Chuck it, both of you. Cary, you've no business to hit him with that thing; you might hurt. You want spanking, that's the fact.'

He returned to his book. Cary scowled at him. He had taken Charles's side, and she was hurt and angry, for it *had* been a fault, and she knew that Charles knew it, and Raymond hadn't even bothered to inquire.

Charles climbed down suddenly. He was an honest child, and wanted to go on playing.

'All right, then. It was a fault. Your game. Now it's you to serve.'

He handed her her racket. But she threw it down on the table.

'I shan't play any more. You cheated. I'm going to read a book.'

'I didn't cheat. It's not cheating unless you go on saying it is.'

'Yes, it is.'

Cary, gloomily offended, but less with her younger than with her elder brother, left the room. Charles took to his soldiers, until better might be.

Presently Cary returned with a magazine. She sat down in the arm-chair by the fire, opposite Raymond, and read it.

'Fancy,' she presently remarked.

No one answered. Neither of her brothers was given to fancying, and one may assume that they ignored the command.

'This is awfully funny,' Cary tried next, and gave a mirthless laugh.

'What?' Charles, hoping for a joke to be read him, looked up. He was a sweet-tempered and forgiving boy.

'It's a bit about Daphne,' said Cary, looking sideways at Raymond. She gained her object; her elder brother looked up from his book at the name.

'What are you talking about? What's that you've got?'

'*Monthly Bits*. It says: "The other night I was at a literary party at Mrs. Roland Lancaster's (Mrs. Lancaster is one of the only women in London who may truly be said still to hold salons)" – What's a salon?' Cary broke off to inquire, aware of the dramatic value of suspense.

'Don't know. A party, I suppose, it means.'

'Well, but don't lots of people give parties? It must be some funny kind of party, that hardly anyone has.'

'Dare say. It probably means a party at which the people think they're important. It doesn't matter, anyhow. What about Daphne?'

Cary resumed: '"There, appropriately enough, since I had lately been reading her clever novel, *Summer's Over,* I met

Marjorie Wynne, who is, needless to say, in private life, Miss Daphne Simpson. She told me that she is not yet at work on another book; to judge from the frequency with which her name figures above newspaper articles just now, she cannot have much time for novel-writing."'

'Isn't that funny,' Cary commented. 'Daphne writing novels. Did you know, Raymond?'

'Rot. That's not Daphne. Must be some one else. Daphne hasn't published a novel.'

'Yes, she has. *And* articles. I've seen them in papers. They're signed Marjorie Wynne. There's one in this. And I've seen *Summer's Over* in the library, when Mummy's sent Charles and me to change the books. I looked inside it.'

'Very likely. But Daphne didn't write it. She'd have said so.'

'She did write it. I know she did.'

'As if you knew anything about it.'

'I do know. Because I read a bit at the beginning, and it was a bit I read before, at Solio, when Daphne had just typed it. I remembered it. So I know it was by her.'

Raymond looked at her with disapproval. He believed her, for she was one of those accurate children who are seldom mistaken on points of fact.

'A bit of a Paul Pry, aren't you. Anyhow, it doesn't seem particularly important. People needn't run round telling every one when they write novels, I suppose. What made *you* keep it so dark, by the way, all this time?'

'Well,' Cary blushed a little, 'I didn't know. I thought, as Daphne hadn't told us, perhaps it was a secret. So I didn't say anything to her or anyone.'

'Not till now.'

'No.' Cary grew redder, and fiddled with the button of her shoe. She felt suddenly embarrassed and ashamed; uneasily she feared that Raymond perceived the motives of her revelation, divined that she had read aloud that paragraph to annoy him, out of revenge, to show him that here was something about Daphne that she had kept hidden from him. Partly that, and partly to enliven the flatness of Boxing-Day by a little drama, a surprise sensation mystery.

Now that she had exploded her little bomb, she felt ashamed. The schoolgirl code of honour, of not telling tales, that had kept her silent, respecting Daphne's silence, for all these weeks, returned to sting her. After all, Daphne hadn't told of her. . . .

'Perhaps,' she stammered, 'it was a secret. . . . I didn't mean . . . I expect Daphne'll tell us when she wants us to know. . . .'

'I've no doubt she will,' Raymond drily returned. 'A little late to think of that, though, isn't it. However, it doesn't matter twopence, anyhow. Pass me that thing.'

He read through the paragraph again. It was one of a column of such items. Raymond looked through them. It was his first acquaintance with the style, and its felicities bewildered him; it was so different from anything else he ever read. *Salons. Appropriately enough.* Why was it appropriate to meet people whose books one had read? *Needless to say.* Doubtless everything this writer said was needless, if you came to that.

The next paragraph was about a friend of Raymond's: 'Mr. John Desmond, who lives and writes, of course, in Bloomsbury, the very temple of the intellectuals.' . . . What was all this nonsense about Bloomsbury? There was more of it farther on. People who lived in Bloomsbury were just like anyone else; just like the people on Campden Hill, in Hampstead, Kensington, Chelsea, Bayswater, Piccadilly, and Sloane Square. Raymond knew any number of them, and they were quite usual. *Temple of the intellectuals.* What were intellectuals? One was always seeing that word about now. Presumably it meant intelligent people. But one didn't say intelligents, or clevers, and only stupids in nursery parlance. Why then intellectuals?

This writer seemed a very discursive, romantic chatterbox. Reading his (or her) statements as to those he had met, and of what they had informed him, Raymond (always, like the men of Emmaus, slow of heart to believe) felt, as he had unjustly felt while reading a recent book on desert adventure, that there appeared to be no particular evidence that the writer was not making it all up. Raymond wondered for whose benefit these items were written, and who (besides himself and Cary) read them.

He turned the pages till he found the article signed 'Marjorie Wynne.' It was called 'After Love's Rapture – What?' and was captioned by the editorial staff as 'The fourth of our series of little talks on Modern Married Life. The authoress of *Summer's Over* and *Youth at the Prow* emphasises the necessity of having a basis of Comradeship in marriage, which shall survive the inevitable dying down of the first love rapture.'

Raymond looked at the little talk. One cannot, perhaps, assert that he precisely read it, since certain words are incapable of establishing enough *rapport* with certain minds to penetrate within them. He was like a little boy confronted with a theological treatise by a Father of the Church, or an old lady with an essay on dynamics; he saw the words written, but they scarcely impinged on his brain. What was all this? Love . . . comradeship . . . the basis that endures. . . . How in the world did Marjorie Wynne think of it all? The fourth little talk in our series – had three other people also conceived and emitted thoughts on this odd topic? Did many writers do so? Was this kind of thing the stuff of which all these magazines one saw about were full? And did it interest anyone to read? How much, he wondered, were they paid, the writers who wrote this?

'I suppose it's all right,' Raymond, on the whole a tolerant young man, conceded, 'for those who like the kind of thing.'

But could this Marjorie Wynne really be Daphne? He had never heard Daphne talk at all in this vein, but, of course, given the pay was adequate, people might, he supposed, turn their hands to anything, break out anywhere. After all, why not? Raymond suppressed, fair-minded scientist, a faint feeling of disgust, and admitted that it wasn't necessary only to write on subjects which demanded information and a modicum of intelligence; probably quite a number of people liked to read discussions of things about which they themselves knew as much as the writer; it would make them feel pleased and set up. Most novels, were, possibly,

like that – about people, what was called human stuff. Why
not, Raymond asked himself again. It wasn't what he
personally cared about or could read, but then plenty of
people wouldn't care to read about his subjects. It might
even be rather clever to be able to write about love and
comradeship, men and women.

Also, for these, too, seemed to be quite a topic, children.
On the next page to 'After Love's Rapture – What?' there
was a column headed: 'Points from Letters received from
correspondents with reference to our series of Talks on
Marriage.' The first point was:

'SIR, I think homes without children are like rooms
without windows.

E. E. PIGOTT.'

That was all. Mr. Pigott (or was it Mrs?) did not explain
his analogy. He merely, with a fine simplicity, made his
'point' and left it there. Or had there been, possibly, more
of the letter as he wrote it, in which he had enlarged a little
on the similarity of children to windows? Both, he had
possibly explained, frequently have sashes, and pa(i)n(e)s.
. . . But his remark, as it stood, was bald. It would have
been better in riddle form. 'Why are homes without children like rooms without windows?' with a prize for the best
answer.

All down this column, other correspondents had made
points a little similar to this, and very strange reading it was
to Raymond. In the new light thrown on Daphne's habits
and powers, he ran his eyes down the column to see if her
pen-name was there. Vaguely relieved, he found that Miss
Wynne had communicated to the journal no points with
reference to marriage beyond those to be found in her Little
Talk.

Cary, making as if she read *Sard Harker,* watched her
brother over it, saw how he held *Monthly Bits* a little way
from his eyes, brought it nearer, held it slightly sideways,
like someone trying to decipher a difficult handwriting,
pored over it with a puzzled frown, knocked out his pipe in

the grate, turned the pages, gazed in surprise at what he found, lit and sucked at his pipe, placid yet puzzled, like a schoolboy who is no good at mathematics doing his algebra, became reflective, laying the paper down and staring at the fire.

What had she done? She had betrayed a secret, betrayed Daphne, possibly made a breach between her and Raymond, who would be annoyed because she had written things all this time and never said. Daphne had not betrayed her, but she had betrayed Daphne. And now it would only be just and natural if Daphne, who had been decent to her that afternoon in the fog, should betray her, should, when Raymond said to her: 'Cary tells me you write novels, and are called Marjorie Wynne,' reply, 'As for Cary, she goes secretly to confession.' Cary, who had her pride, would never ask Daphne not to do that. In fact, she felt it would be a fitting punishment for her own treachery. A Paul Pry, Raymond had called her in contempt, and she had had to admit the name to be apt. It was the worst of things to be. A Nero, a Medea, a Mussolini – there was something grand and large-size about these infamous persons, but a Paul Pry! Cary could not endure that Raymond should thus think of her.

Boxing-Day was a desert, a day of ashes and dust. And just after her Christmas confession (before she had seen Daphne) she had felt uplifted, essorant, as if she would be for ever good, quite removed above the plane where one hit Charles on the head and sulked, and told secrets out of revenge.

She furtively sniffed, and fumbled in a pocket of miscellaneous objects for her handkerchief. It was not there.

2

Mrs. Folyot entered, bringing into the stale crossness of the family Boxing-Day a breath as of fresh windy air and energetic good-humour.

'Children, are you going to take Jimbo for a run in Kensington Gardens before lunch?'

'Yes.' Charles scrambled to his feet, and reached for his new boat.

'No, dear, don't take that; there won't be time. You must leave it till after lunch. Just a quick run down there and up again, that's all. Cary, put your book away and get your things on quickly. Your thick shoes, mind; the roads are all wet.'

Cary, struggling with tears behind *Sard Harker*, muttered: 'All right,' in a voice which her mother recognised.

'Why, what's the matter, child? Not crying, on Boxing-Day? Oh, that *is* silly. What's happened?'

'N-nothing.' Cary, attention focused on her, crossly drew her hand across her eyes. 'I'm not crying.'

'Well, hurry up and get out; it'll be good for you. And get a handkerchief. I suppose you and Charles have been fighting; I'm ashamed of you,' said Mrs. Folyot, a breezy mother.

It perhaps occurred to Charles that, if there was crying to be done, it was he who had received a whack on the head. However, he was aware that not for anything so usual as a fight with him was his sister in tears. She probably had a tummy-ache, and didn't want to say so for fear of not being allowed to go to the party this evening.

The children went off together to take out Jimbo.

Left alone with Raymond, Mrs. Folyot asked casually, 'What was wrong with the child, do you know?'

'No. Just Boxing-Day, I imagine. She's been tiresome all the morning.'

Raymond thoughtfully folded up the magazine he had been reading and put it in his coat pocket.

'Well, she seems all right now.' Mrs. Folyot heard her younger children leaping noisily downstairs, shouting to a yapping dog, and rushing out at the front door, which banged behind them.

'Noisy little creatures,' she observed. 'Good for them to work some of it off out of doors.'

Raymond said, 'I think homes with children are like rooms without windows,' trying it on his mother to see if it made sense to her, but having slightly forgotten how it went.

Mrs. Folyot was going rapidly through a packet of Christmas greetings. Although those which she had herself despatched in early October had been long since forgotten, still her friends remembered her. She glanced up at her son in momentary surprise, pleased that he should be taking an interest in the housing question.

'What, dear? Rooms without windows, did you say? *Of course* they ought all to have windows. It's perfectly scandalous. Tiny little slots that will scarcely open. They ought to be pulled down. The House Investigation Committee . . .'

'I said, mother, that homes without children are like rooms without windows.' Raymond, a determined person, was bent on getting his remark across. He had forgotten that certain remarks from certain people cannot get across; they lack the necessary verisimilitude.

'And, as you say, when there are children windows are far more important still. Growing children *must* have air.'

Mrs. Folyot, her mind on her packet of cards and notes – how anything in paper form appealed to her, her son thought – was, in her efficient and rapid way, glancing at each and tossing it on to its appropriate pile. She did not seem to have taken his point at all. Raymond wondered what line E. E. Pigott's mother took with him when he made his little epigram to her. But families, of course, seldom take one's best points; perhaps this partly accounts for letters to the press, which, however, does not always take them either.

CHAPTER 17

Meet Miss Wynne

Daisy, on December the twenty-eighth, returned to Maynard Buildings, full of family life, lavish Christmas foods, and the happiness attendant on returning to one's home after three days' absence. Her flat appeared to her very beautiful, seductive, and gay, and in the best of taste. It actually was scarcely these, but so it seemed after three days at Thekla. Staying at Thekla always made Daisy feel quite highbrow by comparison, after she had left it. As has been well said, every one is somebody's highbrow, and she was that of her family. It is probable also that every one is somebody's lowbrow. At times Daisy met people who looked at her (or did not look at her) as if she were not only somebody's lowbrow but probably nearly everybody's. That was, of course, due to the popular young author, Marjorie Wynne. It was Daisy's distaste at the prospect of being so looked at by members of the Folyot family which had hitherto inhibited her from avowing her connection with this young lady.

But when Raymond, having tea with her at Stewart's after they had together performed his Innocents' Day shopping, said, 'Oh, by the way. What's this story about your writing novels and signing them Marjorie Wynne? *Do* you?' she fobbed it off gaily enough.

'I do then. I wondered when you were going to find that out. I wouldn't tell you, just to see how long it took you. Someone mentioned it, I suppose?'

'Yes, Cary did.'

'*Cary?* How in the world did she know? That's an amazing infant, Raymond. Knows a lot too much, if you ask me.'

'Very probably. Anyhow, she had some magazine with a paragraph about someone meeting you at a salon. What's a salon, by the way? Cary asked how it differed from ordinary parties, but I felt vague about it myself.'

'So was I, till I looked it up in the dictionary once. It said, a periodic gathering of notable persons in the house of some social queen.'

'Oh. Well, anyhow, that's where this chap said he met you. The social queen was Mrs. Roland Lancaster. One would have to look up queen, to grasp that. The fact is, you need a dictionary the whole time, reading that magazine.'

'Dictionaries wouldn't help you much with it, because so few of the people who write that special style seem to have used one. I think they find they get on better without. More untrammelled. . . . I saw that paragraph; it annoyed me rather.'

'He said you'd "told him" something or other. I didn't suppose you had. In fact, I didn't think it was you at all, only Cary came out with some story of how she'd seen part of your novel in type once, and knew it again when she saw it in print.'

'Curse that child. I always knew she knew too much about me. Serve her right if . . . Well, no matter. You had to know some time. Skeletons will out. Meet Miss Wynne, Mr. Folyot. She's an awful little fool, but she earns my living for me. Someone has to do that, you'll admit.'

'Why, yes. It's very clever of you to be able to do it in that way. . . . I read your Little Talk on marriage.'

'Darling, I'm sure you didn't. You may have tried. It's not the sort of thing you *could* read.'

'It's not the sort I could write, anyhow. I certainly couldn't have thought of all those things to say about it.'

'You couldn't have thought of anything at all to say about it, my blessing. Not a single word. Nor could I, off my own bat; it's being a woman journalist; one gets into the atmosphere and picks it up. It's quite easy, really; I could reel off pages and pages of that kind of stuff to you now this minute, over tea.'

Raymond's momentary look of nervousness stung her, revealing how she, who had already exhibited to him such unguessed-at talents and habits, had become to him an enigma, a dark horse, a person who was not safe not to do anything.

'All right, I'm not going to. But I assure you it's quite easy, once you know the trick; anyone could do it.'

What was the use of that? She knew that he knew that plenty of people couldn't and wouldn't.

He shook his head. 'They certainly couldn't. I couldn't, for one. I'm sure mother couldn't. I don't believe scarcely anyone I know could. I bet you Geranium couldn't, if she tried for a year.'

Geranium? Daisy was amazed and frightened at the sharpness of the stab that pierced her at Geranium's name on his lips in that context, at his classing of Geranium and himself together in a group contrasted with herself.

'Geranium. . . . Why not? I dare say she could. For all I know, she does. . . .'

He smiled at that. 'Not she. Theo might; not Geranium. She'd be as hopeless as me about it.'

He didn't care for Theo much; Daisy knew that.

'Well.' She lit a cigarette, striving after blandness. 'I don't see what Geranium has to do with it, anyhow. We neither of us know her well enough to say for certain what she does or doesn't do in private. People lead the oddest secret lives, Raymond. Not only me; lots of people. Mine's no queerer than yours, I dare say. You probably preach in Hyde Park on Sunday afternoons sometimes, or dance as a lounge lizard in the evenings, or are a secret cocaine doper, or write verses for Christmas cards, or live on blackmail. Heaven only knows *what* you do. No, don't tell me; I'd rather guess. We'll tell each other nothing more of our secret lives; it's much more exciting hiding them.'

With such prattling badinage as this did she seek to charm out of mind recent revelations, to smooth over the new situation, to exorcise Marjorie Wynne from between them with Daphne's gay derision, and to forestall future catastrophes, arranging that even these might be seen, if and when they should arrive, in the harmless light cast on them by her present jests.

'I once saw an aunt of mine,' said Raymond, 'eating

cream cakes at Buszard's all by herself in the middle of the morning. She was simply pitching into them, one after another. She looked awfully shaken when she saw me looking at her. That must have been her secret life.'

'Yours, too, it seems. If not, I don't know what you were doing at Buszard's in the morning yourself.'

'Ordering a silver wedding-cake for my parents,' Raymond replied, with dignity.

Was Daphne tarnished? Was she dimmed and cheapened; had she lost the least edge of fineness, the frailest gossamer of glamour? They talked so much that Daisy could not sound the inarticulate, delicate, uncharted deeps (or shallows) of her lover's regard for her, could not tell how his love fared, or in what relation to her and to himself he placed the cheap and babbling authoress, or know what her secretiveness in the matter had wrought in their friendship. Vaguely, there seemed a shadow.

2

It was not till they were back in the flat that she could say: 'Darling, you don't *mind* about that horrid Wynne girl, do you? Or about my not having told you? You see, I knew you'd hate her, and I didn't like to mention her. . . .'

'Why should you mention her? She was no one's business but yours. And how could I mind? Of course not. It's your show. In my view, no one ought to mind what other people do. You don't mind my going lizard-hunting, even if you don't care to keep one yourself as a pet——'

'But I did, Raymond! Only it ran away, the poor little thing – I told you.'

'You *are* a prize liar, aren't you. As it happens I know it didn't run away, for I saw it this morning in that animal shop in Southampton Row, and the man there told me a lady had asked him weeks ago to take it from her, as she found it tiresome in the house. So I bought it off him. I always wanted that creature myself, only I thought you'd like it, so I gave it to you.'

'Oh dear. So that's out. Ran away was a euphemism, my

love; I thought you'd prefer it. One doesn't like to tell people that one has disposed of the rare animals they've given one to shops. No one likes to, do they?'

'The only thing about it was,' Raymond said, and his voice was plaintive and proud, 'that you might have known I'd like it if you didn't want it yourself, and have told me. Not that it matters now, because I've got the animal, but it was by the merest chance, you'll admit.'

'Oh dear,' Daphne again ruefully lamented. 'What an afternoon of revelations! Fragments of my under life pushing up all over the place. You'll have to forgive me, darling, about Pedro *and* Marjorie. Do you think you can?'

It seemed that he did think so. But the vague shadow that had hovered was now defined; it had been less Miss Wynne than that disagreeable little saurian half-breed who had come between them. Naturally, since to Raymond saurians were of so much greater significance among God's creatures than novelists and human journalists. These could not matter to him; they pursued their curious ways through fantastic worlds by him not realised, impinging nowhere on his consciousness. Perhaps, if they must function at all, it was better that they should not mention it.

'But I'm afraid your parents won't like Marjorie at all,' Daphne said, and sighed.

'Oh, they won't bother about her,' Raymond comfortably assured her. 'They haven't time for much reading.'

Vaguely impatient of the subject of Miss Wynne, a tiresome but unimportant girl, he changed it.

3

Daphne was right as to the reactions of her prospective parents-in-law towards Miss Wynne's literary activities. They thought them most odd. Mrs. Folyot sent for a copy of *Summer's Over* from Bumpus and looked at it kindly, though she perceived at once that it was not the kind of novel she read. She perused the comments on the paper cover with distaste.

'Did *you* make up that, my dear?'

'Oh no, indeed. Indeed not. The publisher did. They do, you know. Isn't it silly!' Daphne explained, uneasily emphatic.

'Well, I must say it is.' Mrs. Folyot read it through.

' " . . . this post-War age of unrest, when, the old values being submerged, youth, in hot revolt against Victorian standards, questions life as never before. . . ." Is that what it's really about, dear?'

'Oh no,' Daphne protested. 'Not really much; no indeed. But publishers always think that goes down, you know — the revolt of youth against Victorian standards, and all that. They see it everywhere, like the people who write to the papers. It's a kind of disease, like seeing snakes when you've got D.T.'

'Poor things. What an odd thing to think they see. Why do they think people living in the present day would be revolting against *Victorian* standards? They must mean Georgian, surely. We don't revolt, in the reign of King George, against Victorian, Jacobean, or Elizabethan standards. He's forgotten who's on the throne. And "questions life as never before!" As if people hadn't always questioned life the whole time. He'd better read the Book of Job, your publisher. Well, dear, what about the book? Is it what I can leave about safely? Cary gets hold of anything she sees, you know, the monkey.'

Daisy suppressed an inclination to say: 'Considering she's read Freud, *Summer's Over* won't teach her much, I should think.' Instead, she said, 'Well, I don't know quite what she's supposed to read, really. Perhaps you'd better look at it first and see. It has love in it, and . . . and all that, you know.'

Mrs. Folyot rightly interpreted 'all that.'

'All you young writers are so fond of loose living. It's so dull, really. What's the matter with the people you all write about is, they've not enough to do. If they'd do a little work for their neighbours, or take up some cause, they wouldn't have so much time on their hands for philandering. If *I* had my way with all these young women in novels who go off for jaunts with men, I'd give 'em all babies. Twins. *That* would keep them out of mischief in future and give 'em a job of work. But it never seems to happen in these books. . . . Well, then, I *can't* leave it about for Cary, that's clear. I'm not prudish with her, but I don't see why she should clutter up her mind yet with these ideas about the way people live. It's one-sided, and I'd rather she was interested in other things.'

Besides, Mrs. Folyot thought but did not say, *Summer's Over* was obviously one of a third-rate class of novels, not written in an intellectual style. It would not assist Cary's education. She believed that she kept trash out of her daughter's way, by no means aware of her omnivorous literary activities.

4

Alone with Cary, in spite of some considerable manoeuvring on the part of her sister-by-troth to evade this situation, Daphne accused her tartly of prying.

'I never said you could read my papers, you little sneak. You must have pried round my room and found them. And if you did, you'd no business to bring it up later and tell something which you must have guessed was a secret. It wasn't a particular secret, but I was going to tell myself, in my own way.'

'I read it in *Monthly Bits*,' Cary sulkily returned.

'All right, but when Raymond didn't believe it you proved it by telling about something you'd no business to have seen. You were a little sneak, and you know it quite well. It would serve you right if I told them things about *you*.'

Cary looked at her darkly, refusing to plead.

'I may quite likely,' she said, 'tell Mummy myself soon about that.'

'Well, I should think you'd better. However, it's your show. I shan't really tell, of course; I don't.'

It was no use. Daphne might assume what fine and graceful pose she liked; Cary, sceptical and unimpressed, consistently looked clean through her at Daisy beyond.

'I'm sorry I looked at your papers,' she said shortly, thus dissociating herself from dishonour by apology. 'I went in to get a pencil. They lay on the table, and they were typed, so I read a bit. I didn't know they were private. 'Twasn't a letter. And I told Raymond because I was cross with him, because he'd been beastly to me. So I read him *Monthly Bits*, and told him, to show I knew something he didn't. But,' she added, 'I don't believe he minded.'

'Why should he, you little ass? People don't tell each other everything, even if they are engaged.'

'No,' said Cary, indifferently, and as if that question did not concern her, since, for her part, she would be a nun.

CHAPTER 18

Little Exposures

Mrs. Folyot, during one of those little reveries which make the last days of a year so melancholy a period, decided that during the past twelve months she had been an idler, a sluggard, a spendthrift of time, a cumberer of the earth, and that during the twelve months to come she must display more energy in good works. Good European, ardent citizen of the two hemispheres, she had a poignant vision of the world's revolutionaries unaided, its dictators undeposed, its policemen living in corruption, its white slaves being deported, its black citizens despised. Committees she might have formed, meetings she might have held, letters to the press she might have written, foreign languages she might have learned, cabinet ministers she might have interested, started up before her with reproachful faces. Here was life speeding on – she would be fifty-six this year – and what was she doing in comparison with the vast undone?

A thousand eager little desires assailed her; she would liberate Russian prisoners, separate Catalans from Spain, Armenians from Turks, raid those Italian islands where anti-Fascists lived deported, restore the Dodecanese to Turkey, the Trentino to Austria, Corsica and Nice to Italy, Alsace to Germany, Vilna to Lithuania, India to itself; she would console American negroes, give the Scots and the Basques Home Rule, hunt down the traffickers in women and children, brighten Moscow, free South America from the Monroe Doctrine, learn Russian, Chinese, Czech, and modern Greek.

Full of such resolves as these, and of the high courage that derives from the punch-bowl, she went to bed on the last day of the year. On the first day of the next she wrote a letter to *The Times* about destitute and patriotic Cantonese and the remodelling of the Kuomintang, sent for a large Russian at eleven and a small Greek at twelve, and learnt for an hour the tongue of each, which, however, proved a mistake, leading to some confusion in the mind by lunchtime.

This business of the Cantonese Kuomintang – she would have a drawing-room meeting about it, and Li-Hung-Fwat should speak, in his disintegrated but courtly English. All sorts of people should come. . . . Raymond must come, and bring a train of young men. Mrs. Folyot wished that Raymond and his friends would feel more interest in the world's affairs. They all seemed busy with their own jobs. Mrs. Folyot liked to have interested young men about her; she valued the co-operation of male creatures, young and old. They were so clever, and so male. She had always preferred them to girls and women. Women were the idealists, and more interested in causes, but men, as a rule, knew more; more women were stupid, or silly, or both. Plenty of men, too, of course, but more women, and stupider. Men went about more, were better informed. Like so many women, Mrs. Folyot had always preferred their company and conversation. As a young woman she had been handsome, and had liked also their admiration. She was still handsome, but now, fifty-five and thick-set, and with scarcely any neck, could only win admiration by vivacity, capability, and mental energies. Anyhow, who wanted admiration? She dismissed it. What she wanted, she admitted, and what she got, was fellowship, intellectual companionship, co-operation with intelligent men in her activities. She loved to have a group of them in her drawing-room, important men, lawyers, politicians, writers, all talking with her about something that mattered. Women, too; sensible, clever, vivacious, active committee-women; but these could never be quite so stimulating and encouraging to her as men. How acceptable is (as has always been found) the company of a sex other than one's own!

For this reason, among others, Mrs. Folyot regretted a little Raymond's engagement at twenty-seven to Daphne. She would have preferred that her son should remain longer a bachelor, bringing his men friends about the place.

Women friends, too, he had always brought, for he liked both; but his atmosphere had been that of bachelor maleness. Now he would become a married man, perhaps soon a parent, and be interested in a flat, or even a small house, in geysers, central heating, the painting of the doors scarlet (for young wives like to paint doors scarlet), servants, cooking, and such domesticities. His work would, of course, continue to be his main preoccupation, but the background to this would become littered with the toys of matrimony. His book on the minor bivalves would suffer, and he would take less interest than ever in the Freedom of Foreigners.

For Mrs. Folyot was less inclined than before to believe that her daughter-in-law would be a link between this freedom and her husband. She had begun to suspect that Daphne, always interested and helpful, was merely obliging, and that neither her heart nor her head was involved in schemes for world-liberation and relief. To judge from the two novels of hers which Mrs. Folyot had conscientiously read and then put on a high shelf out of Cary's way, it was the personal aspects of life which interested the girl. 'Trash, I'm afraid,' she had told her husband. 'Oh, well, they're like a hundred other novels which seem to come out every year – not exactly stupid, and not quite tosh, and with a kind of bright naturalness in the dialogue and characters. But no intellectual background, and nothing to it but the personal note, and that shocking sentimentality novelists have. They're written in more or less literate English, but they're not *educated* books. I'm rather surprised that Monica Ashley's niece shouldn't produce something better. She should have been sent to a university.' For Mrs. Folyot, herself a university woman, quite thought that those three years of education made people much more intelligent.

When, however, she was shown by her husband, who had chanced on it in an evening paper, one of Marjorie Wynne's little articles, she was really shocked. It seemed that a number of persons had been asked to write a few brief thoughts on Home Life, for a bishop had said that this form of life was, in Great Britain, extinct. So the Causerie was entitled: 'Is Home Life Dead?' From Mrs. Folyot's point of view, the only possible reply to this inquiry was: 'Obviously not, since people do not all live in the streets and fields, and since thousands of new houses are being built annually.' But Marjorie Wynne, sliding easily over this truth tackled the question manfully, discussing how many meals each day the people who lived in homes must eat in their homes to qualify their life as Home Life, and how many inhabitants of the home must be present (*a*) at each meal, (*b*) at bed-time, (*c*) at getting-up time; and for how many weeks in each year the home might be shut up while the occupants were away, and whether, if servants and a cat were left in it, it would still remain a home, and whether flats and houses hired furnished from others were homes, and if so whose homes, and, if home life were really dead, what the houses wherein people lived must in future be called, and other such complexities of the question.

'You really shouldn't discuss such nonsense at all, my dear,' Mrs. Folyot said to Daphne next day, for the public remarks of the clergy on our national life and habits it seemed to her only decent and kindly to ignore. 'You'll be joining next in discussions on the Modern Girl.'

'Oh, dear, I do hope not,' sighed Daphne, and blushed. The blush was for the past, the sigh for the future, for it was apparent to her that Miss Wynne's literary income was going to suffer.

It was these little exposures that were making Mrs. Folyot more doubtful than before about Daphne as a daughter-in-law, more regretful that Raymond should be about to renounce bachelordom. If he must marry, why not have selected a girl of intellect and fastidious taste, who would not even be aware of what foolish people had said about home life?

2

But Daisy, feeling common and inferior, was elevated a little nearer, in her own estimation, to Mrs. Folyot's level – or rather, Mrs. Folyot was a little depressed towards hers –

one afternoon, early in the year, when they were shopping
for garments woven by peasantry (for Mrs. Folyot was of
those who consider that peasants make garments well, and
she liked to encourage them, not deterred by the extra price
which is caused when people do jobs out of their own line,
and which affects, similarly, potatoes hoed by tailors).
Anyhow, buying these garments, Mrs. Folyot suddenly
caught sight of her figure, full length, in a long mirror, and
suffered the experience of shock normally attendant on this
incident.

'Heavens,' she cried, 'I have no neck! None whatever!'
And, indeed, she had not much.

'I must leave you,' she added to Daphne, and hurried out
of the shop. Daisy supposed that she had somewhere an
appointment with a committee, a Cantonese politician, a
large Russian, or a small Greek; but no, she was seen to
hurry down the street and dash into a beauty parlour,
where, presumably, she would have her neck elongated
forthwith by one of those processes known to plastic
surgeons, Procrustes, and those who slay fowls.

This little incident cheered Daphne, seeming to draw her
and this public-spirited woman closer together. Never had
she thought of Mrs. Folyot as spending any portion of her
busy days on those premises where the personal appearance
is improved. Perhaps, however, she often did so; possibly
she had massage, and reducing processes other than the
dieting which she openly practised. She showed, indeed, no
results, but Daisy, though she had, when she could afford
it, an occasional face massage herself, was not so simple as
to believe that any such processes made any actual difference in the human appearance, which remains as it is and
will be.

To have happened thus on a glimpse of activities so
unexpected in a life lived on so high a plane enabled Daisy to
put a better face on her own dark secrets. Even the great and
good have their weaknesses; that is apparent. Daisy was
further encouraged by the fact that Mrs. Folyot, recounting
at dinner that night her day's activities, made no mention of
that which she had done immediately after shopping for

peasant clothes. Obviously, then, a secret. Mr. Folyot
would, to his wife, reveal his complaints, grievances,
egotisms, and small ambitions, but not even to him would
she reveal, self-respecting wife, her attempts to arrest time's
work on her pleasant face and form.

Her secret, anyhow, was safe with Daisy.

CHAPTER 19

Birds and Bivalves

The days lengthened, becoming the cold, pale days of early spring, when blackbirds whistle from naked orchards and dig in hard soil like sextons, and larks spring up from bleak and windy ploughlands pricked with frost and patched with snow, and thrushes flute once or twice, then, forgetting song in meals, hack the cold earth for snails, and birds in general fall eagerly, passionately, into love, and the brooks chatter full with rain, and, in the purple-brown woods and pale dun fields, summer seems a hundred years away, unimaginable, a fantastic dream of beneficence faintly remembered, scarcely expected again to occur in these our days.

How Daisy hated cold! It assailed her heart and soul, body, blood, nerves, and brain, stabbing, paralysing, strangling. Her feet and hands had no feeling, her blood seemed to have no motion, her brain no power to formulate a thought, even of the most mediocre description. Her face was stiff, her mouth frozen so that it could scarcely be moved, her nose cold and pink, her eyes red. If she had ever any charm of appearance, of manner, or of spirit, it left her when she was out in cold weather. Nothing shielded her from the bitter winds that blew in February; fur and wool, leather and tweed, were as so much paper wrapped about her wincing body.

The old biological puzzle obsessed her, as she followed Raymond on his explorations after life in the home counties, striding over naked windswept fields in a hard black frost, lurking ambushed with glasses in shivering coppices – why have not man and beast adapted themselves to the climatic conditions of the world in which for so long they have lived? How did creatures so imperfectly adjusted to the world's weather ever come to take life and develop on its surface? What becomes of any theory of natural adaptation, in view of the so terrifying mutual misunderstandings between the creature and its environment? Above all, how does earth come to have thrown up a being like man, who passes his life in perpetual and painful discord with himself?

They discussed it a little, but Raymond, though a biologist, could not throw much light. He was more interested, for the moment, in watching the wheeling of a flight of fieldfares over the sloping ploughland on whose brow they stopped to watch. They formed a spiral pattern against the sky, like a dark current running over a pale sea; they wheeled, they turned, they changed, as if they performed patterns in a country dance.

In fact, thought Daisy, they behave like a flight of fieldfares. Why do we trouble ourselves to observe them? Have we, then, not seen fieldfares going through their antics before? Is it worth this anguish to see them once more?

For, indeed, it was anguish that she felt, drowned in that bitter, whispering wind as cold as death, standing stark and rigid on the bleak hill's crest, in the pale and frozen country, whose bounds were shrouded in pale mist. There they stood, frail human creatures, vulnerable targets for the cruel assaults of earth and heaven, defying the gods to do their worst, while the gods, as always, took them at their word.

'Is it worth it?' cried Daisy, suddenly and shrilly breaking the silence.

'Is what worth what?' Raymond was peering through his bird-glasses, deciphering the wheeling pattern, absent and intent.

'Watching birds. Standing here in this field, freezing to death. Yes, to death, darling. I shall probably die, quite soon. You won't notice; you'll be looking at birds, but I shall sink into that frozen sleep from which people never wake again. I shall be glad. This anguish is too great.'

'Feeling chilly?' Raymond thus, with tranquil meiosis, interpreted and summarised the eloquence of his betrothed.

'Yes,' Daisy returned, bitterly ironic. 'Feeling chilly. My

God, Raymond, how can you bear it?'

He looked round at her then, in mild surprise.

'You're so sudden. You seemed all right till just now. What's happened?'

'I wasn't all right. I've been all wrong ever since we got out of the train. I tell you, this is no pursuit for a day like this. It's rotten, and I'm dying. Who wants to see birds, anyhow? I'm always seeing birds. Can't we go home?'

'Home? Well, I suppose we can. But it's only two o'clock; we've only just begun. I wanted to go into the woods. But if you don't want to. . . . Look here, are you really frightfully cold and bored, and do you really hate birds?'

He was looking at her now in puzzled concern, seeing, as she seldom let him see, Daisy. Not Daphne, the interested, spirited companion, the bird-lover, the woodland elf, the adventurer who didn't mind hardship, but Daisy, the cowering, shivering creature, who didn't give a damn for any bird that flew, but suffered excruciatingly from physical cold and spiritual ennui, to whom his researches were a tiresome game, only pursued by her to please him. Yes, he looked straight at Daisy for the space of half a minute before she fled to cover, and pushed Daphne out in front of her to shield her.

'Cold,' said Daphne brightly, 'I certainly am. As I say, all but dead. But not bored; it's much too exciting for that. And of course I like watching birds. Come on into the wood and look at courtships, and then we'll go up to the Yew Tree and have tea and drinks. I shall feel better in the wood, I expect. You'll admit it's a trifle exposed here.'

Raymond was relieved. Daisy had disconcerted him; but Daisy had gone to earth, and the familiar Daphne was there again, cold indeed, but not bored. After all, it *was* cold. Perhaps, as Daphne had suggested, it might be warmer in the wood.

They entered Burnham Beeches, and possibly it was a little warmer; anyhow, the bitter wind blew muffled by great, bare beech boles and shivering birches. Daphne, when they stopped to look at birds, crept within hollow trees,.from which she peered forth as if, like her namesake, she was undergoing dendroid metamorphosis..

They busied themselves with watching the courtships of bullfinches, and great tits, and the passionate quarrels of thrushes who were rivals in love. What birds go through in February! What anguish of love and hate, jealousy, passion, and desire, these little creatures endure before they can settle to tranquil nidatory life. What excitement of pursuit and propitiation, vanity, and display, what coy advancings and retreatings, dancings and bowings, nods and becks and wreathèd smiles, between those who love! What flauntings of natural elegances; for birds, like human beings, and with far more reason, consider that beauty in their own species exists.

And yet what a small part sex and its attendant emotions and activities play actually in their lives, as in man's. From courtship they will be lightly and easily distracted, caught away into hunting for food, pecking at bark, swinging on twigs, flying up into the sky and down again, practising mass flights in elaborate and complicated patterns, opening their beaks and trying little tunes, playing hide-and-seek among branches, leaping, full of *joie de vivre,* from bough to bough. Their courtships, their little nuptial occupations and engrossments, seem to be to them exciting, but not absorbing.

'As to human beings and other creatures,' Daphne commented, when, waiting for tea at the inn at the edge of the Beeches, they discussed sex and its usually over-estimated importance in the life of man. They agreed that much imaginative literature had here struck a false note from all time.

'And now the pseudo-scientists,' Raymond said, 'like Freud, poor old man, who's hypnotised himself with observing diseased erotomaniacs and thinking them normal, till he can see nothing straight. . . . But, if you come to think of it, it's not really queer that anyone should be sex-obsessed; it's rather really queer that we're not all, considering that we all originated from an impulse of sex emotion. It shows how strong all the other things must be, that we're not all quite tied up in it. Now, if we reproduced like paramecia, merely splitting quietly into two with no emotion directly we were full-grown, we shouldn't have all this concentrated excitement and absorption.'

'Sex is depressing,' sighed Daphne, thawed out and fluent again, now that she was sitting by a fire and expecting soon to drink hot tea. 'Sometimes it all seems a great mistake. . . . I think it's depressing, for one thing, all this woman-baiting that goes on – the way, I mean, some men seem to hate women merely as women. They keep writing books and articles about them, saying how horrid they are, and how they have no moral sense and no intelligence or imagination, and no idealism or decent impulses, and no irony or humour, and no anything else worth having. I do call it depressing; I sometimes quite get to feel we must really *be* like that, even though I know we're not. Do they just make it up, or is it simply that they haven't met any decent, civilised woman?'

'Oh, I imagine they make it up. It's just a convention – a fashion of writing or something. I don't know why women don't do the same about men, just to show up its silliness.'

'Women don't want to. They don't dislike men. A few women pick up the woman-baiting fashion from men and do it themselves, like parrots, but most don't bother about sex generalisations at all, it doesn't interest them.'

'They're quite right. It's dull and not important.'

'Yes, but listen, Raymond, I get a horrid fear sometimes that it *is* important, that, if men go on and on saying these things about us, we shall *become* like that, hypnotised, you know, by labels. We shall become like the woman of man's theorising. Ghastly. She is such a gruesome creature.'

'Well,' said Raymond, thinking that Daphne was getting maudlin, 'I can't understand why you read all the toshy articles and things you see about. I don't. There's no need. Have some more tea. It's too strong, it wants filling up.'

'And the worst of it is,' said Daphne, filling it up, 'that even the men who think women are like that go on wanting them to live with. They despise them, yet pursue them. Why?'

'Oh, well, that's merely biological. That's natural enough.'

'It doesn't seem to me natural.' Daphne gloomily surveyed the dingy business of living. 'If I thought a man was a degraded, uncivilised being, unfit for me to talk to, I shouldn't want to live with him. It must be women who are the idealistic sex.'

'Possibly. I don't know. Temperamental differences between the sexes are much too boggy ground to tread on. I don't. Too many contradictions. You no sooner think you've got hold of something than it slips out of your hand. Because temperament and hereditary qualities cut clean across sex. It's easier with animals, rather.'

'Some things one can say,' Daphne mused. 'Men – taking the average, I mean – are enormously abler, for instance. Really enormously, both in body and mind. Stronger all round, in nerves and muscle and brain, more creative and inventive, and with more sense. They carry heavier guns. If the woman-baiters would stick to baiting us about our frail intelligences, they'd be right all the way. Oh, dear, women seem to be very nearly imbecile often.'

'They are pretty often imbecile. But so are men.'

'Oh, yes, often and often. But not *so* often. Men should stick to that. They do tell us about it a good deal, of course, and point out how much less well we've always done nearly everything than they have, but they spoil their case by going on to all the other things, that aren't true a bit. It's like kicking people when they're down, for things they've not done. Why can't they let us alone? Women on the whole are so nice, so generous and decent.'

'Not worth bothering about, that kind of unscientific punk. You do bother too much about punk, you know, darling.'

Raymond had got out his note-book, and was jotting down records of his day's observations. He was not much interested in discussing human creatures.

'Oh, well, I suppose it comes from writing it,' said Daphne.

She was happy now, and relaxed, warmed with fire and

drink and that talk about human beings that bored Raymond. How much more at ease was Daisy thus than when shivering frozen in the wood, watching the amours of birds, for whom she cared less than Raymond cared about men and women. There were sometimes moments when out with Raymond, such as the moment on the ploughed hill to-day, when Daisy felt that she must make a stand, tell Raymond that in winter she could not go out with him for whole days, that flesh and blood could not and would not endure it. Yet she never told him this, so eager was she to be the perfect playfellow, as well as the perfect lover and the perfect companion. One day, later on, perhaps she would say to him that, in cold weather, she must either stay within doors or keep moving, that she would not crouch in naked woods or stand on frozen fields swept and pierced by harsh winds, while he peered through glasses at those little feathered beings who so engrossed him. What would he say?

'Oh, I thought you liked it. You said you did. Geranium does. . . .'

Oh, no, she could not say it yet. Daisy might break out, in the anguish of a moment, but Daphne would always step forward and cover her words, efface her impression from Raymond's mind.

Life was getting all cumbered up and blocked by the things which she must say one day but could not say yet. She was like a housewife who puts off from day to day the clearing up of the litter that has accumulated in her dwelling, thinking that one day she must tackle it, but not yet; or like one who should have many teeth pulled out, and will one day call on the dentist, but oh, not yet, not yet.

Meanwhile, present, past, and future swam rosily together in the lamplit, firelit room, throwing a lovely haze over the table with its check cloth, the horsehair sofa with its woollen mats, the china dogs on the chimney-piece, and the pictures of King Edward VII, Lord Kitchener, pheasant, horse, and girl life, and their host and hostess in the wedding-costumes of thirty years ago, that adorned the flowery walls.

They would walk to Beaconsfield station, the wind at
their backs, harmless to pierce their new armour of
warmth; they would entrain for London, their rural ramble
over; suitably cleaned and changed, they would have supper at the Folyots' house, and attend afterwards an Arts
Theatre Club play, for Mrs. Folyot was a member of this
club, and liked to see what Sunday drama was up to. In
Raymond's opinion, neither Sunday nor week-day drama
was up to much, but he would now and then attend it, if
Daphne wanted to. As to Daisy, indiscriminate drama
devotee, her felicity at being at the play, any night of the
week, was not seriously marred by the undoubted fact that
most plays, on any night of the week, are bad.

So Daisy regarded with pleasure the evening stretching in
front of her, now that the cold February daylight and its
ornithoscopic activities were over.

2

But Raymond had his troubles. Instead of being happy in
the train, talking, or looking at Daphne or at the view, or
brooding over and amplifying his bird notes, he read a book
he had with him called *A Study of Lamellibranchs*, by
Humphrey Dysart, Cambridge University Press, 10s. 6d.,
which had been sent him for review by the *New Statesman*.
This book annoyed him, since he was late with his own
lamellibranchs, and had now been forestalled. Humphrey
Dysart, whom he knew and rather disliked, wrote well, and
made several new and good observations concerning the
little creatures, observations which Raymond had also
made in his forthcoming treatise. The affair was saddening.
Raymond, reading the book, perceiving that it was good,
even important (in so far as lamellibranchs can be considered of importance), gave way to depression. He wished
that he had been less dilatory with his own treatise. What
was the use of bringing it out now? It would look silly. No
one demands a continuous flow of books on lamellibranchs,
more especially when they make some of the same points. If
Dysart's book should be praised, and achieve a position in

mollusc literature, he might as well scrap his altogether. Raymond was no purely disinterested and single-minded investigator. As to that, who is? He inherited from his father – if indeed it is required that one should inherit this quality from any source other than universal humanity – a liking to see the rewards of his labours. He did not feel disposed to make much of this book; it was possible to find in it a few faults, disagreements with himself, even mistakes, and to make it seem of small importance, in a short notice obviously only written to be set up in minion, or even in nonpareil type. He saw no reason why he should puff the book.

Gloomily he marked a passage or two as questionable, and made a few notes. Daisy, sitting opposite him, watched his absorbed attention. She loved it, that absorption of his. She loved the scientific mind, its disinterested zest for knowledge, its clear, close, impersonal thinking, so remote from her own darting impressionism. She saw that what Raymond perused was a book on lamellibranchs, his own subject. Naturally, then, he was interested. And interested in the subject in itself, the little shelled creatures, to most people gastronomically but not otherwise important. The dictionary described oysters as 'inactive creatures, usually eaten alive,' and so, indeed, to all but the Hebrews, who may not establish even this relation with them, they are. But Raymond saw them more as God must see them, objectively, sitting encased in their little homes, pursuing their little avocations (however inactively), making their little clicking songs, courting, loving, marrying, bringing forth, exasperated into making pearls – to be eaten alive, perhaps, in the end, if unfortunate, but meanwhile what a life was theirs to lead! Not the bustling, loquacious, advertising life of birds, nor the peripatetic, adventurous, busy life of man and beast, but a life thoughtful, philosophic, dignified, bedridden yet quietly gregarious, wrapped in tranquillity and dreams, bounded by green swaying seas, infinitely prolific, so that their progeny was as the sand of the sea in number, yet never permitting their serenity to be ruffled by family life.

It was thus, when one thought of them apart from vinegar and brown bread and butter, that one thought of oysters. It was thus, Daisy reflected, that Raymond must see them and read literature concerning them – objectively, without any personal rivalry, jealousy, or afterthought of any kind. Such, thought Daisy, was her darling Raymond's approach to life.

She wanted to reach out her hand and touch his leg, stretched out beneath her seat, to stroke it, as one strokes a dog one loves. He was so adorable, dear, and fine.

Raymond wished that his little review could be set up in pearl type, or – last ignominy – in diamond, scarcely legible by the naked eye.

So, by the end of that February Sunday, Raymond had encountered his Daphne's hidden self for a minute, but Daisy had not apprehended her Raymond's even for so much as that.

CHAPTER 20

Burglars

Cary (it was often the poor child's fate) was awakened from sleep in the small hours by burglars in the house. Usually on these occasions, after a period of lying tremulous, listening to jemmies in action, stealthy footsteps creeping upstairs and down, furtive hands trying at doors, swag being dropped on floors with muffled thuds, fearful imprecations being quite smothered, and the other little sounds incidental to burglar life, she would, against her will, fall asleep again, lulled by the thought of her parents and Raymond, who would surely, when it should become necessary, take notice of these noises and send for the police.

But to-night she was not so lulled. Mr. Folyot was away, and Mrs. Folyot lay ill with influenza. Raymond, indeed, was in the house, but Raymond, a sound sleeper, did not appear to be taking any notice of the intruders. Daphne was also in the house, spending the week-end. But Daphne, in Cary's view, would not be much use with burglars. As to the cook, the housemaid, and the parlour-maid, these with burglars are no use at all, but as inexpert and unwilling as old ladies with bulls. To be useful with burglars; it is an art by itself, like being handy with a broom, efficient with a typewriter, good with children, discreet with Alsatian dogs, clever with house-agents or needles, or intelligent at bridge. Cary felt sure that her mother had more gift at burglars than anyone else of the household, but her mother had, besides this gift, influenza, and must not be disturbed.

But really the burglars to-night were disturbing. Cary, lying tense and trembling in her bed, had never heard them so bad before. Burglars, like weather, varied from night to night. On this Friday night of late February, both the fog and the burglars were bad. 'Burglars bad to-night, miss' – did the people in shops and streets who told you what the

weather was like also ever comment on the burglars?
Anyhow, they *were* bad to-night, terribly bad. Along the
passage they crept, and up and down the stairs, creaking,
stopping to listen, creaking again, whispering, dropping
jemmies, revolvers, and silver with muffled thuds, dragging sacks of swag about the floor.

Oh dear, oh dear, oh dear. Cary sat up in bed, shivering
and sweating, pricklings of terror lifting her hair. It was too
much. Never before, even in her rich experience, had
burglars made such noise, behaved with such freedom.
Cary was sure that this time they would even steal something, an error in taste which, to do them justice, they had
never before committed in the Folyot's house, where,
apparently, they called as a rule merely for a little harmless
jemmy-practice. But to-night seemed to be the night to
which all their years of rehearsal had been leading up, for
surely they were really and truly now performing. If it was
their *première,* Cary felt that they should be supplied with an
audience to watch them, not merely an audience that heard
them, trembling, from behind bedroom doors. What was
the matter with Raymond, that he did not wake, besieged
by so unquiet an army?

Cary desperately crossed herself and sprang out of bed.
Be the danger what it might, she must run along the passage
to Raymond's room and wake him.

Gently she opened her door and peered into the dark
passage, praying that here, for the moment, no enemy
lurked ambushed. Then her heart lifted, for, at the end of
the passage, down the three little stairs, Raymond's door
stood open, and the room beyond it was lit. He was awake,
then. Cary dashed along the passage, down the little flight,
into the lit room.

It was empty. The bedclothes were flung back as if
Raymond had sprung from bed in haste. He must have
gone, then, to beard the foe downstairs. Cary, shivering on
the landing in her pyjamas, listened. The muffled sounds
went on downstairs, but no voices. One did not hear
Raymond's voice raised in displeasure, saying, What are
you doing in our house? How dare you? Go out immedi-

ately, or I shall call a policeman. Had he, perhaps, said this already, and had they fled? No, for they were still there, making their frightful burglar-sounds. Then what of Raymond? Oh, God, what had happened to Raymond?

Cary pressed her two fists against her mouth, a childish gesture she had used of old to restrain screams of terror, excitement, or rage. What was she to do? Call her mother? No, not that. Her mother must not be made worse. Not all her gift with burglars would carry her through an assault on them without damage to her health. Call Daphne? Daphne at least was grown up, and Daphne would want to save Raymond. Cary ran back along the landing to Daphne's room, and burst in at the door.

Daphne's light, too, was on; Daphne was sitting up in bed, rather pale, with startled, blinking eyes.

'Cary!' she whispered, at the little pyjamaed figure that stood shivering by the door. 'Are you frightened? Did you hear noises? Do you want to come in with me? Come along, then.'

But 'Raymond's gone down,' Cary hoarsely whispered. 'It's burglars. I know it's burglars, and Raymond's gone to them, his room's empty, and they may have killed him! Oh, Daphne, come down and see!'

'Come down. . . .' Daphne looked at her, but did not move. 'Nonsense, Cary. It's not real burglars, you know: it never is. Only noises. If Raymond's gone downstairs, it was probably him making them.'

'No, no, no!' Cary's voice rose, still whispering, but shrill. 'It *is* burglars, I know it is, and I heard Raymond go down after they'd been there for ages, and now he's quite quiet, and we must go and help him and call the police. *Come down, Daphne!*' She had caught hold of Daphne's hand, and was tugging it.

'Cary.' Daphne, with her free hand, caught the child's sharp shoulder. 'You're being silly. You're working yourself up about nothing. Come into my bed and go to sleep quietly, and everything will be all right in the morning, you'll see. You *know* it always is. Raymond probably went down to fetch something, and made a noise looking about for it.'

Cary, knowing better, pulled herself free. For one second she paused; her queer green eyes, searching the other pale face, saw that it was Daisy who sat there in bed, uncertain, frightened, unable to conquer her fear, refusing to believe, no use with burglars, even when Raymond was down among them.

'Oh, you're no good,' muttered Cary, and fled from the room, pursued by Daisy's whispered cry, 'Cary, Cary, go back to bed!'

Cary knew then that she must descend alone among the burglars and rescue Raymond by herself. The maids, even were it possible to imagine them willing to assist in this enterprise, were at the top of the house. Charles . . . well, Charles might get hurt; he'd better not come. But, as Cary passed Charles's door, next her own, habit made her look in, to see if by any chance her constant companion in adventure were awake. He was not awake. Switching on the light, Cary saw him lying in bed, his head hanging outside it, his face smeared with jam. On the table at his side was a small empty pot which had recently held, it would appear, strawberry jam. Charles must have pilfered it from the larder; if he had been given it he would have told Cary and offered her a share. Charles had been a thief and a glutton, and had foolishly and prematurely fallen asleep, bearing on his countenance the traces of his sin. Here, Daisy would have perhaps noted with interest, was a glimpse into the hidden life of Charles. But Cary, who doubtless already was familiar with Charles's hidden life, since between brothers and sisters little is hidden, noted it merely with annoyance. Charles was dead asleep after his orgy; it would have taken ages to wake him and make him understand the situation. Cary, remarking in a loud whisper, 'Little hog,' picked up a cricket-bat from the floor and entered on her dark and frightful adventure alone.

2

No sound now rose from the black pit of downstairs, as

Cary paused to listen, leaning over the banister. All was silence. Had they killed one another, the wicked gang, and killed Raymond, too? Or did they merely lurk in silence, waiting? Even as she listened, she seemed to hear gentle footsteps, and the creak of a door or window being quietly opened or closed. Oh God! Grasping tightly Charles's bat, she ran downstairs, and, with a deep gasp, switched on the light in the hall, determined to see the worst. The hall was empty, but, surely, queerly dishevelled, with a kind of turbulent, ransacked look, the oak chest open, the Indian cloths in it flung on the floor. The dining-room door stood open, and in the cavernous blackness beyond it something moved, thumped, grunted like a beast.

'*Who's there?*' Cary cried, in a faint, thin, dying voice. 'Go away *at once*. A policeman is here. Oh, policeman, there's burglars in there, do go in and arrest them. . . .'

Again something grunted. Cary, the bat raised for defence, crept forward until she could feel the switch inside the dining-room door; click, and the fearful room was disclosed; it was confused, disturbed, and empty, but for a figure that lay on the floor by the window, trussed with cords and gagged. The blood seemed to rush from Cary's head; sick and giddy, she bent over Raymond and pulled the gag from his mouth. He gasped and swore hoarsely. Then, 'That's better,' he said. 'Now undo my arms, can you.' Cary fumbled at a knot with shaking fingers, and at last pulled it loose. He dragged his arms free, and unwound the rope from his legs.

'Oh, Raymond . . . are they gone?'

'Yes, worse luck. With a lot of silver, too. Not all, because I surprised them at it, and they got the wind up lest the house should be roused, so they downed me and tied me up and made off. I must get on to the police-station at once. Lord, though, I feel giddy. They fetched me one on the head. . . . I say, how did *you* come into it?'

'I heard them. So I came down.'

'Good for you. Complete with bat for attack. Why didn't you fetch someone, though? Weren't you scared?'

'Oh, no,' said Cary, loftily. 'I just supposed it was

burglars, as usual, so I came down to send them away. I
went to fetch you, but you weren't there. And I went to
fetch Daphne, but she didn't think it was real burglars, so
she didn't come. And Charles was asleep, and Mummy's
ill, so I came by myself.'

'Helpful child. You deserve a medal.'

He proceeded to have a telephonic interview with the
constabulary.

'They'll be round here in a few minutes. I shall sit in here
and drink whisky till they come. That gag made me thirsty.
I say . . .'

Cary lay back in a chair, pale, with closed eyes. She
opened them heavily.

'I feel sick.'

'I don't blame you. It's reaction, after all this rescue
work, and not feeling at all frightened and everything. I feel
rather that way myself; it's a nasty jar, finding burglars all
over the dining-room and kitchen. Worse than black-
beetles. Come on; I'll carry you up to bed.'

'No. I want to stay down here with you and see the police
come.'

'Nonsense; you'll be cold. You've nothing on. Come
along.'

He lifted her up and carried her upstairs and deposited her
in her bed.

'Better now? Like anything to eat or drink?'

'No thank you. Raymond.'

'Yes?'

'Noises *are* burglars. I always told you they were, and
you said they weren't, and, you see, they *are*.'

'Not as a rule. Just once in a way, perhaps.'

'Every time, I expect.'

'Well, we won't make a habit of disturbing them, anyhow. I like a quiet night.'

'Still,' said Cary, 'a night like this is 'stremely exciting,
don't you think? Just like a night in a book. I expect you'll
have a lovely talk with the police. Couldn't I come down
for it?'

'No.'

'Oh, well.' Cary lay back, shivered a little, and yawned. After all, she had had her night.

Daphne came in in her dressing-gown, pale with ruffled head and bright eyes.

'What is it? Has anything happened?'

'Only a few burglars,' Raymond told her. 'They knocked me out and trussed me and made off with some silver and things. The police are coming. I suppose I should have been on the dining-room floor all night, only Cary came to the rescue.'

'Raymond!' Daphne blanched paler. 'Not really! Cary told me she thought she heard something, but I supposed it was nothing. I thought she'd gone back to bed. I wish I'd gone down with her. . . .'

'Oh, she was quite adequate by herself.' Still, Raymond thought that Daphne might, with advantage, have made sure what Cary was doing, not let the child go off by herself. Discomfortably there returned to him a half-forgotten scene on the island hillside, and he did not meet her eyes.

'If only I'd guessed what it was. I thought it was just night noises; one's always hearing them.'

Daphne, sounding flustered and on edge, was displaying less interest in the adventure itself than in her own non-participation in it.

'They're always burglars,' Cary asserted with conviction. 'I knew it was burglars. I told you it was. An' I thought *you* thought it was burglars too. Because you were frightened.'

'Rot, I wasn't. Of course, I didn't think it was burglars.'

'Oh.' Cary gave Daisy an impish glance, and curled herself up in bed like a little hedgehog.

'Charles will be jolly sick he missed it all,' she said, and giggled a little into her pillow, remembering Charles and his jam-pot.

'That's the police,' said Raymond, and went downstairs.

'Do go to sleep quickly,' said Daphne to Cary. 'You're much too excited. You're very nearly hysterical.'

But Cary only giggled again, either at Charles and the

jam-pot, or at Daisy, or perhaps she was nearly hysterical. Daisy went back to bed.

3

Mrs. Folyot, waking ever and anon from feverish slumbers, thought: How noisy they all are by night! They should really try and be quieter. In and out of each other's rooms, talking, and bumping things about. People should be quieter by night. Particularly when other people are ill.

CHAPTER 21

Food for the Press

How do newspapers know? Is it the police who recount to them as they occur those little nocturnal events that adorn their pages in the mornings? Or do they rely on their delicate apprehensions and intuitions, which whisper in their ears like little birds the tales of mystery and sensation wherewith they like to please us? It matters not. The fact remains that they do know. Nothing of moment occurs by night but the news' staffs of daily journals are aware of it before morning, and send out their spies hot-foot in battalions to gather in decorative detail.

The *Evening Wire,* hearing by the customary means of the burglary on Campden Hill, sent forth, the first thing in the morning, a smart and alert young man to look into it. He arrived at the house soon after nine o'clock, and encountered in the strip of front garden two children who crouched in a laurestinus bed and dug like dogs.

'Good morning,' said the pleasant young man, who had learnt the value of tactical rather than direct approach to houses where news had occurred.

'Good morning,' the children returned, indifferent yet polite, and proceeding with their occupation, which appeared to be the interment of an empty but sticky jampot.

'Had a little affair here last night, didn't you,' the young man brightly and educatively continued. 'Quite a little burglary, I understand.'

The small girl stood upright and looked at him, wiping earthy hands on a holland overall.

'It was a *big* burglary,' she corrected him.

Edward Arthur gave her the pleasant smile that made his task as a collector of information easier than that of some of his colleagues.

'Why, yes, of course it was. Now, do you think anyone

in there would care to give me a little story about it, for my newspaper?'

'Oh. Do you write a newspaper?'

'Well, some of a newspaper; not quite all, you know. But I want to write up this burglary of yours, and make a good story of it. Think I could see anyone?'

Cary was silent. Into her face came that light which transfigures the countenances of ladies who rise to great situations. Then she spoke, casually, indifferently, in what her relations called her society voice.

'*I* can tell you all about it. I was there myself throughout.'

'You were? That's great. I wish you'd spill it out right now, will you?'

Edward saw the headlines: 'West-End Burglary. Child's Amazing Story.' Here was a scoop. But they mustn't stand by the front door like this, to be caught by all the other fellows who came.

'Where can we go to talk?'

'Come inside,' said Miss Folyot hospitably. 'Into the schoolroom.'

She opened the door and they went in together. Charles would have followed, but his sister said distantly, 'It's no use your coming, Charles. You were asleep. You'd better finish burying your jam-pot. Anybody could see there'd been something buried, the way you've left it. Jimbo will think it's a bone and dig it up. . . . Will you come this way, please?' she said to her guest, in the best manner of the parlourmaid.

She led him to a small room which had the customary features of those rooms where the lessons and amusements of children are carried on. It was here that the younger Folyots did their school preparation in the evenings and on Saturday mornings, and here that they normally pursued those less tedious occupations which are, however, even more unsuitable for drawing-rooms and dining-rooms.

'Well, now.' Mr. Arthur seated himself at the scratched table and produced his note-book and pencil. 'Do you think you can tell me all about what transpired last night?'

Cary collected her forces. A dreamy expression came

into her face; she felt like a great but hitherto little known actress, who has been suddenly cast for a star part, and is facing for the first time her tremendous and invisible audience.

'Yes, I'll tell you,' she said. 'I had gone to bed at bed-time as usual, but was woken up after some hours by the most 'strordinary noises. Obviously it was burglars.'

'You knew that at once?'

'Oh, yes. You see, we often have them here. I hear them slightly most nights.'

'Is that so? My word! Do they take much?'

'Oh no, they don't take anything as a rule.'

'I see. They just pay a little visit, for luck.'

'Well, they're rather apt to take knives. Mine and my brother's, I mean. Several times we've missed our knives.'

'You think they collect them? That's sinister.'

'Well, we think they must. You see, we get a lot of Russians here, even by day.'

'Russians?' The reporter became alert. To say 'Russians' to a newspaper man is like mentioning rats to a dog. 'Bolshevists, I presume. What do they come for?'

'No, not Bolshevists. I think they ran away from Russia because of the Bolshevists.' Cary had picked up in her home a little news of the affairs of foreigners.

The *Wire* looked disappointed. 'Oh, Whites. But *they're* all right. *They* wouldn't steal knives.'

'Yes, they would. I expect they have a great criminal organisation. International crooks.' Cary had not read her Edgar Wallace in vain, and to her the word 'international' stood less for those gallant sportsmen who represent their nations in contests of skill than for those sinister figures who bandy crime about between land and land. 'Oh, we've any number of them coming here.'

'What for, may I ask?' The journalist's eyes glistened. This seemed like news.

'Well, you see, my mother likes them. She really collects foreigners. They have meetings here, and often meals. They hatch conspiracies against their governments.'

'That's very interesting. Your mother's a bit of a

politician, I take it?'

'Oh, yes.' Cary was not sure what 'politician' meant, outside people who sat in parliament, but she was sure that her mother was everything of that kind.

'She works for women's rights, doesn't she?'

'Yes. And men's.'

'And you think it was these international chaps who broke in last night?'

'Well, they sounded like that. They often come, but I don't believe they usually get right inside the house, only try round it, making noises. But last night, of course, I knew they had got in, and were doing their nefarus deeds downstairs.'

'You must have been frightened, weren't you?'

'Oh, no, not to speak of.' Cary met the intent and expressionless stare of her younger brother, who, having completed the interment of the jam-pot, now firmly entered the schoolroom and sat down in a corner. A swift struggle against embarrassment seemed to betray itself for a moment in the manner of the *raconteuse*. She emerged victorious, refusing to allow her style to be cramped by the presence of relatives, and proceeded firmly.

'Not at all frightened. I'm quite used to it, you see. So I thought I'd just go down and look, and send them away. So I crept quietly out of my room, and went to my brother's.'
. . . For a moment she paused, and glanced at the listener in the corner, just to remind him, as it were, that she might, if she cared, here blast his reputation, make public a tale of gluttonous orgy next door, for the world to read that afternoon. Charles returned her regard with wide and innocent blue eyes. She continued, with an air of chivalrously refraining, 'My elder brother, I mean. But he wasn't there. So I knew he must have gone downstairs to attack the gang. So I went downstairs, armed with a bat.
. . .'

'I wonder you didn't wake someone else,' the reporter commented.

'Well, my father's away, and my mother has influenza, and the servants were on the top floor, and my younger

brother was asleep. . . .' Again an ominous pause; this time
Charles stirred uneasily.

'So,' the narrator continued, losing herself now in her
subject, submerged and swept along in the flow of the
fiction-writer's entrancement, 'I crept quietly downstairs,
grasping the bat firmly in my hand. Everything was pitch
dark, but I heard the suppressed noises of the gang struggling in the dining-room with my brother, who they were
trying to overpower.'

'Did you hear them speak? *Were* they foreigners?' the
interested journalist inquired.

'Well, not exactly *speak*, but they made noises.'

'Foreign kind of noises, I take it?'

'Yes. Like international crooks make. So I went down
quietly and looked into the dining-room. Quick as thought
I switched on the light, but the room was empty. The
robbers had scattered and fled when they heard me coming,
and all was quiet but for my brother choking on the floor.'

'*Choking?* You don't say!'

'Yes. He had a gag in his mouth, and he was tied up
tightly and left on the floor for dead.'

'For *dead*. . . .!'

'Oh, he *wasn't* dead. He came to presently, and had a
drink of whisky and rang up the police. It was a very near
thing, though. You see, there was a whole gang of them.
He could have coped with one or two, or even three, but he
was quite overpowered.'

'Gee, yes, he must have been. Well, now, that's a capital
story, and it'll all go in. Now, do you think your brother
could give me any account of the men?'

Cary seemed to drop back to earth. The exalted I-have-
laid-my-dreams-under-your-feet expression she had worn
at the end of her narration changed to a dubious hesitation.

'Well, I don't know. I think it was dark during the
struggle.'

'Think I could have a little chat with him? Is he at home?'

'Yes, I think he's in, but he's rather busy, I expect,
working.'

'Well, I wish you'd take me in to him just for a minute. I'd like to have his story as well as yours.'

Cary looked as if this was superfluous, even a mistake. But the journalist, a firm young man, snapped his notebook together and rose with brisk determination.

'Lead me to him, please.'

'I'll go and ask him first,' Cary doubtfully suggested, but this was swept aside.

'Nix on asking him first. If you don't mind taking me right in, I'll do the rest.'

'All right.'

Overborne by this strong personality, Cary led the way to the dining-room, where Raymond, she believed, was. But, looking in, she saw only Daphne.

'He's not there,' she told her guest. 'If you'll go in and wait I'll see if he's upstairs.'

Edward went into the dining-room.

'Why, Daise!' he exclaimed.

2

Daisy, startled, sprang from her chair, her book tumbling to the floor. It was a surprise sensation, a west-end house mystery moment, even an amazing scene. To Daisy a scene of fear and anger, to Edward of startled recognition. *Folyot* . . . why, of course . . . what a mug he had been. He had not identified these Folyots of the Campden Hill burglary with Daisy's Folyots. Then this young chap he was about to interview would be Daisy's chap. . . .

'Lord,' he chuckled, 'that's funny.'

But Daisy, staring at him with open mouth and startled eyes, did not appear to be amused, though, after a moment, she put on nonchalance, as a lady surprised in déshabille hastily assumes a garment.

'What in the world are you here for?' she inquired, low-voiced.

'On my job, of course. The how–de–do last night. That kid gave me a first-class story – she can spill it out all right – and she's gone to fetch her brother to give me his. Any objection?'

He was a little nettled by her first expression of alarm.

She struggled for ease. 'No, of course not. Only you mustn't mention *me,* or seem to know me. You see, I've not told them yet.'

'Told them what?'

'About the family. . . . I mean, that I've told the family about our engagement. You see, it's supposed to be a secret. . . .'

'Right-o. Mum's the word. I'm here to talk crime, not engagements. But I don't get that idea about seeming not to know you. What's the big idea there?'

'Oh, just for a joke. I want to tell them myself about the family, later on, do you see.'

He looked at her queerly, satirically, his head cocked like a bird's, his bright, quick eyes seeing quite enough to go on with.

'Right,' he agreed, in a new, dry voice. 'It's your show. But in that case hadn't you better go while the going's good? I mean, it'd look a bit funny afterwards, you and me being in the same room and acting strangers. It may be a joke, but I can't see it's going to be such a damned good one. However, it's your show. *I* shan't butt in.'

Ed was angry. He had his pride, and he and Daisy had always, he thought, been pretty good friends. And now, because she'd written a successful novel and got engaged – or said she had – to a west-end johnnie with a 'varsity education and a good job, she was turning up her nose at her relations, including her mother and an *Evening Wire* star reporter who was making good hand-over-hand. In Ed's opinion, Daisy had swelled head, and was a damned little snob.

'You needn't worry,' he told her. 'I don't want to claim acquaintance with anyone; I'm here on business. As a matter of fact, I've put in quite enough time on this job already, and if your young man keeps me waiting much longer, I shall go off without his story.'

But here Raymond came in. Ed saw, critically, a tall, pale young man, with a swollen bruise over his right eye and his left arm in a sling. He looked sleepy and bored. Miss

Simpson left the room as he entered it. Like a mask she wore the debonair calm of Daphne over any perturbation which Daisy might be experiencing.

3

Edward said, briskly, 'Good morning, Mr. Folyot. Been a bit in the wars, I see. Handled you pretty roughly, I dare say, those fellows?'

'Good morning,' the sleepy young man replied. 'My sister told me you represent a newspaper. Would you mind getting any information you want from the police? They know all about it.'

'Oh, that's all right, Mr. Folyot. It's only one or two little details we want – all publicity helps the police in these affairs, you know. Now, for instance, did you get a close look at any of the thieves so that we could publish anything about them that might help to identify them?'

'No, it was dark. I'm afraid I really can't help you at all. I've told all I know to the police, and it's not much.'

'Foreigners, I hear they were?'

'Foreigners? Very unlikely, I should think. Who said they were foreigners?'

'Your sister had that impression.'

'My sister? She didn't see them. They were gone some time before she came on the scene. I'm afraid she knows nothing about it. I hope she hasn't been spinning you yarns; if so, you'd better forget them.'

'Oh, well, we don't attach undue importance to anything we're told, you know, but we like to get a little picturesque detail. For instance, Mr. Folyot, I wish you'd give me a line on your sensations when you came down and found the burglars, previous to their attack on you. What you felt, you know,' he lucidly explained, as Mr. Folyot stared at him stupidly.

'How do you mean, felt? What anyone else would feel, I suppose – that there were burglars in the house. There wasn't much time to feel anything before they scragged me and trussed me up.'

'No doubt you were very anxious to spare Mrs. Folyot alarm. I hear she is ill.'

'You seem to have heard all I can tell you, and probably a good deal more. I'm afraid I'm rather busy this morning, so perhaps you would excuse me.'

Ed, who recognised a blank wall when he was up against it, put away his note-book. Daisy's young man, he perceived, wasn't a patch on his kid sister as a story-spiller. He seemed only half awake, as well as stand-offish.

'Well, many thanks, Mr. Folyot. We'll get the rest from the police station. You'll recognise, I'm sure, that the greater the press publicity the greater the chance of running the thieves to earth. All in a good cause, you know.'

'Oh, quite.' Raymond was politely opening the door.

'I am very interested,' said Edward, going through it, 'to hear of Mrs. Folyot's political activities.'

'What? . . . Oh yes . . .' How this tiresome person went on chirping about this and that.

'Quite a little international centre you have here, I believe.'

'International what? . . . Oh, centre. Well, I don't know about international. I expect you mean that my mother knows a good many foreigners. . . . Good morning.'

'Good morning, Mr. Folyot. Thanks very much. Forgive me bothering you; it's my job, you know. The public nowadays must have new details. They lap up a good burglary and assault story like kittens lap up milk.'

'I suppose so,' Raymond vaguely agreed, and shut the front-door after the loquacious young man.

Daphne came through the hall.

'That was a very conversational reporter,' Raymond said. 'He wouldn't go. I must tell them not to let any more of them in. I suppose he was rather amusing, really, only I haven't any sense of humour this morning after my rugger night. Marvellous people they are. You ought to have stopped and listened. Cary seems to have been feeding him up with melodrama, by the way. Where *is* the little liar? Cary!'

Cary appeared at the schoolroom door, with a touch of

defensive swagger.

'What?'

'What in the name of nonsense have you been telling that reporter?'

'Oh . . . nothing in particular. I just told him a little about last night.'

'What business was it of yours, you little ass? Who said *you* were to talk to the press?'

'He asked me himself,' Cary said loftily. 'So nach'ly, I told him things.'

'Apparently you did. What nonsense did you spin him about foreigners? Those men weren't foreigners; why should they be?'

'Well, I thought most likely they were. It's so often foreigners here by day that I thought it would be them in the night, too. International crooks.'

'Lord, did you tell him that? If that gets into his paper you'd better keep it away from mother, my poor demented infant. Her pet menagerie figuring as crooks in the *Evening Wire*; she won't be pleased.'

'Well, they *look* like crooks.' There was a faint, defensive quiver now in Cary's voice. She was suffering the normal reaction after the stimulating experience of holding the stage. In cool blood, in sober family life, she neither enjoyed making a fool of herself nor displeasing her mother.

'What else did you tell him?' Daphne asked.

Cary looked at her, seeing through Daphne's casual indifference to Daisy's apprehension.

'Nothing about you. I didn't even say you were here. I just told him about the gang, and Raymond's struggle with them, and me finding him tied up. It was all true,' she added, with pride.

'She said she wasn't frightened,' Charles put in.

'I wasn't,' his sister retorted. 'Anyhow, not much. And I said Charles was lying asleep like a hog, with . . .'

'You didn't.'

'Well, I shall. I shall telephone it.'

'No, you won't. If you did, I should tell how you . . .'

'Shut up, you ass.'

Children have too many holds over one another. They lead lives of reciprocal blackmail, like the members of criminal organisations.

'Well,' said Raymond. 'I suppose we'd better get that paper this evening. I wonder if father will see it on his way home, by the way. If so he'll be rather surprised. That reporter has a pretty telling style, I shouldn't wonder; he seemed all out for sensation. . . . I might try and modify it by ringing up the paper, but I don't imagine they'd take the slightest notice.'

'Not the slightest, I'm sure,' Daphne agreed, knowing the paper.

'You look pretty cheap, old thing,' her lover said, hearing in her voice a depressed cadence, and observing that she wore a drooping mien.

'Oh, we all look cheap this morning.' Daphne moved away, nervous and on edge. 'I dare say the international crooks do too.'

Brinks of chasms seemed to Daisy to be crumbling away beneath her feet, leaving her poised precariously above cold, engulfing seas, struggling for foothold and slipping ever down. Every step she took was a false step, every rock she clutched for support broke away beneath her hand. Why was she thus blindly heading, demented fool, for destruction, when, at each point, the simple truth, casually and lightly uttered, would lay a safe and unbreaking pathway for her feet? What was this fear of a momentary ignominy, a little fall from pride, that was goading her down the crumbling slopes into the abyss of shame that waited to receive her soon or late?

4

Mr. Folyot walked into his wife's room at five o'clock in the afternoon with an evening paper which he had purchased at King's Cross. Mrs. Folyot was sitting up in bed having tea and feeling what is called, in patients, brighter, as is usual at tea-time.

'Well dear,' she said, 'have you heard our news? We had
the most tiresome night of burglars; they blacked poor
Raymond's eye and gagged and bound him and went off
with a bag of silver. Most annoying. But they say it always
happens at last to every one. Did you enjoy your
conference?'

'No. Very poor.' But the little cloud which the memory
of a conference not enjoyed had summoned to Mr. Folyot's
brow was dispersed by the contents of his newspaper.

'You certainly seem to have had an odd night. Or,
anyhow, it comes out well in the *Evening Wire*. Where did
they get all this stuff from?'

'I'm sure I don't know. Newspapers do, don't they.
What do they say of it?'

Mr. Folyot read it aloud, in those scholarly, cultivated
accents that make the press sound so surprising.

'WEST-END BURGLARY SENSATION
INTERNATIONAL CROOKS SURPRISE ATTACK
FOILED BY CHILD
WELL-KNOWN BIOLOGIST BOUND

How the courage and devotion of a child of twelve saved
her brother and foiled the surprise raid of a gang of foreign
criminals at 180 Campden Hill, the residence of Mr. and
Mrs. Hugh Folyot and their family, was related this morning to an *Evening Wire* representative. Mr. Raymond
Folyot, the well-known young biologist and clubman, was
disturbed in the night due to noises downstairs. On going
down to investigate, the gang surrounded and overpowered him, and left him gagged, bound, and seriously
injured on the floor of one of the rooms. Following this
incident, Mr. Folyot's young sister, who is aged twelve or
thirteen, disturbed from sleep by the burglars, adventured
downstairs to her brother's help, armed with a cricket-bat.
On hearing her coming, the gang fled, taking with them
some silver and other objects, and she released her brother.
By hearing some words spoken by the gang, it seemed to
Miss Folyot that they were foreigners, and she suspects
them of being identical with some Russian Bolshevists who

have been frequently at the house. Mrs. Folyot, well known
in social and political circles, and a prominent committee
worker for women's and men's rights, had taken a great
interest in foreign politics, and frequently invites alien
malcontents and revolutionaries to the house. It would
appear that some of these aliens are members of international criminal organisations, and may have taken advantage of their knowledge of the house to effect a night entry.
Certainly the gang's cowardly assault on Mr. Folyot sug-
gests the Bolshevist mentality. Mr. Folyot himself was too
surprised by the sudden attack to be able to identify the
nationality of any of the gang. The comparative smallness
of the haul was owing, of course, to the interruption by
members of the family. Mr. Folyot, who was seen this
morning by an *Evening Wire* representative, said that he
experienced no sensation of surprise or alarm on finding
burglars in the house. His sister also said that she was not
alarmed, due to being quite used to hearing them, as they
often attempt to break into the house by night, though
usually the family take no notice. Both brother and sister
had been chiefly intent on keeping the alarm from their
mother, who was lying ill. 'I felt,' said Miss Folyot, 'that on
no account must my mother be disturbed.' The police are in
possession of important clues, and sensational developments are expected shortly.'

5

After all, one cannot learn too young not to talk to the press.
In adult life Cary Folyot, remembering this episode in her
youthful career, will perhaps thank her kind parents and
brother for all they taught her this Saturday evening concerning discretion, reticence, and accuracy. But one small
point she stuck to, between sobs.

'I never said *Bolshevists*; I never did. I said they weren't.'
And so this minor lesson, too, her trouble taught her – that
to the minds of many of those who write in papers and
elsewhere, and even of those who write nowhere, all
Russian revolutionaries are Bolshevists, even though

Bolshevism is what they are in revolution against. The profound conservatism that is always at least ten years behind the times dawned before her shocked eyes.

For the rest, she took a deep and undying dislike for the agreeable young journalist who had made such trouble for her. So disgraced was she made to feel by this indecent figuring in the press that, instead of the pride with which she had anticipated narrating the night's exciting adventure to school-friends on Monday morning, she experienced merely shame and disgust when they besieged her with interested inquiries.

'The newspaper made it all up,' she sulkily replied; for this, she had learnt from her relatives, was the correct tone to adopt with regard to the major portion of the Fourth Estate. You told it nothing, and you disbelieved very nearly all it told you. In fact, you offered it no kind of encouragement, except that, rather illogically as it might seem, you regularly bought it, or some specimens of it; you encouraged it thus far, which was perhaps odd.

CHAPTER 22

Lily, Milly, and William

Mrs. Arthur's elder sister, Milly Barker, came to tea at Thekla. Milly was unlike Lily, who had always been the big, merry, wild one of the family. Milly was smaller, primmer, more conventional, of a respectability intense and never spotted, except vicariously and long ago by that youthful escapade of Lily's which had resulted in Daisy. Milly was married to an accountant in the city, and had a very respectable grown family of four. She was fond of Lily, but had never approved of her policy with regard to Daisy, nor, greatly, of Daisy herself, though she found her writings very readable. Daisy got her writing talents, she supposed, from her father, the peccant youth who had seduced Lily and expired. Both sisters would have experienced surprise had it been possible for them to know, or for the deceased father to express, his views on his daughter's literary productions.

'There she was, you see,' Lily was saying, finishing a story as she poured out the tea, 'there she was, staying in the house – Ed was struck all of a heap finding her there, for he hadn't guessed it was those Folyots at all, Daisy having always made out they were up in the north somewhere and never in town – but there Daisy was, popping up in one of the reception rooms when he was shown in, and scared dumb to see him, he says. . . . Drop o' something in it, dear? Do you good. I always do. Settles one's tea, I always say, especially when there's crumpets.'

'No, thank you, dear. I'm not troubled that way. And I don't think you require it either, Lil, if you ask me. These little nips you're for ever taking – they don't do you any good, dear.'

'They do, though. That's why I take them. They warm up me heart.'

'Your heart! You are a one. Your heart's warm enough
already, my dear, and always has been. Well, never mind,
you get on with your tale.'

'Well, as I was saying, the girl seemed all upset seeing
him, though she tried to pass it off. And she begins begging
him not to say a word to the family about who he was, or
about her or anything. For a joke, she said, because she
wanted to tell them herself later. But, as Ed says, that's just
nonsense, because there's no joke *to* it. No, she was just
downright scared about something. Ed says it was all
vanity, and that she's ashamed of having her west-end
friends and her young man know she comes of plain people,
and maybe that's what it is.'

Milly clicked her tongue.

'It doesn't seem sensible for *her* to be proud, does it?' she
suggested. 'Considering everything, it seems a bit funny.'

'Oh, well.' Lily drank her tea in two generous mouthfuls
and felt better. 'Daisy's got good blood in her, one side, and
she was brought up by her aunt in the west end and attended
a good school and made classy friends, and it's only natural
the girl should feel she's a bit above the rest of us and be half-
ashamed. Any girl would,' she added, defending her eldest
with spirit. 'And more than ever now she's picked up with
this young fellow. A regular clubman, Ed says he is. Yes,
Ed saw him afterwards. In he walks into the room, and out
goes Daisy, with never a look at Ed, nor a sign she knows
him. He was a poor fish at telling a story, Ed says. Ed
couldn't get a word out of him. All that piece he had in the
Wire, that was from his little sister, whom he saw
previously. A real cute little thing, Ed says she was. But
Daisy's young fellow, he was a dumb fish. There, I dare say
he was feeling poorly, he'd been all knocked about by those
foreign gang chaps. Well, anyhow, he was no use to Ed,
and Ed didn't take to him much – thought he was stand-
offish and proud. Of course Ed said not a word to him
about Daisy, and he never guessed who Ed was. So Ed
came away, and got his story in the paper – and a very
interesting piece it made, didn't it? – but he came home
in the evening real cross with Daise.'

'I don't say I blame him. That's no way to treat relatives.
It's not right. I'm afraid Daisy's got spoilt, Lil. You've been
too soft with her always. And this is her gratitude. I always
say it doesn't pay to spoil them; they give you no thanks for
it later.'

Lily finished her second cup of heart-warming tea.

'That's right. But do you know what's worrying me
mind, Milly? I don't believe for a minute it's all just pride in
Daisy. She's taken such a queer line all along, hiding things
up and scarcely telling us a word, and pretending this and
that. . . .'

'Now, that's not right, is it. I always do like people to be
above-board. I suppose it's being naturally of an open
disposition myself. That's what that fortune-telling woman
told me long ago – you've an open disposition, she said, and
you find it very hard, she said, to understand or to pardon
false dealing. And you're so sensitive, she said, that you
suffer very deeply when people hurt or deceive you; she'd
never seen such a sensitive hand, she said, and proud, too; I
could be led, she said, but never driven.'

'Now, I'm just the other way,' her sister said. 'No use
trying to lead me, but, good gracious, every one's for ever
driving me! Daisy's like me. She can't be led either, only
driven. And not always that. She's proud and sensitive, like
you.'

'Well,' Milly was rather annoyed, 'I don't suppose any
fortune-teller ever told Daisy she was open, anyhow.'

'She's an open nature, Daise has, she was always open as a
little thing, but it's a funny thing, she's been ever so sly
lately. And when a girl gets sly, one begins thinking
things.'

'That's right.' Milly's mouth took the primmer lines
suitable to the things one begins thinking when a girl gets
sly.

'And I don't mind telling you, Milly it's worrying me.
Suppose this young fellow isn't playing straight with her,
and that's why he makes her hush it up so. When I get
thinking of it, I get all heated up, and I nearly rush up to
town to see the girl and warn her. But what's the use? I did

speak to her about it, at the very beginning, when first she told us, but of course she said it was quite all right, girls always do. Dear me, I remember saying the same to mother myself.'

Milly shook her head. 'You had your lesson, Lily, and perhaps Daisy's got to have hers.'

'Well, I was happy enough.' Lily gazed into the past as into a dead dream. 'I had my troubles, but I was happy with Ron, and then I had Daisy, and then William came along. I didn't do badly. The worst that happened to me was Ron dying. So long as he was alive, even though he wasn't with me and I scarcely ever saw him, I was happy enough, but when he died like that, and me not able even to go and see him, well, I thought the world was over . . . But there, it wasn't.' She sighed, and took another cup of tea.

'But,' she added, 'I don't want Daisy to go that way.'

'I should think not, indeed! Such a disgrace for a girl, not to mention her relatives.'

'Disgrace, yes. . . .' Lily appeared to muse over this aspect of it. 'Anyhow,' she went on, 'a girl and a fellow, they'd better be tied up safe, or else not come together at all. That's what I think.'

'That's right. I mean, laws are laws, and God made them, and they're righteous laws. You can't get round that, can you, however you look at it.'

'What I say is,' Lily evaded the legal question and concentrated on the practical point, 'what I say is, if this young fellow is playing fast and loose with Daise, he's got to know Daise has a mother to look after her.'

'That's right, dear. It's your duty to Speak, that's what it is.'

A little helplessly Mrs. Arthur contemplated this duty. Speak, yes. But to whom, and what should she say? No use speaking again to Daisy.

'Well,' she temporised, 'you never know. We must look on the bright side, mustn't we. Perhaps we're quite wrong, and it's something else than what we think.'

'It's feasible,' said Mrs. Barker, 'but it's not probable. Now, dear, if you ask me I'd say you'd had quite enough of that tea of yours, if not too much. That sipping habit is easier to commence than to stop, as many have found.'

'That's why I've commenced it and not stopped it,' Mrs. Arthur intelligently replied. 'Commence with the easy thing, and go on to the harder thing later, as we say to the children. Train yourself up gradual; that's me. Never try to move mountains before you can move molehills; I remember writing that out in Sunday school.'

'Now you're getting silly, dear.' Milly became the reproving elder sister. 'Once get a slave to anything out of a glass——'

'A cup,' Lily interpolated.

'Out of a bottle,' Milly compromised, 'and you don't know where it'll cease, or where it'll lead you.'

'Can't be led,' Lily explained. 'Fortune-telling woman said not. Only driven.'

'*Or* where it'll drive you. And that's the very word. Drink drives many into very peculiar situations.'

'Oh come, Milly it's not *drink*; a little drop to brace up one's tea.'

'And I say it *is* drink. It's the small beginnings that count. Little drops of water, little grains of sand, make a mighty ocean, build a mighty land. It *is* drink, Lily. For it's not food, dear, is it?'

'Nor are tea and milk food, come to that. But you'd never call them drink. You drink them, and they're drinks, but not drink.' Lily's mind, after a little bracing, functioned with a lucidity unusual in her family and unknown to her sister, who never split hairs over niceties of speech, but knew what she meant.

'It does you no good, Lily, and you'd be better not touching it. It's no kind of example for your children, is it, now?'

'Well, one kind of example, but not a good one perhaps.' Lily was increasing in logic and precision as her tea worked in her brain. She was quibbling now rather as Daisy quibbled, and in a way that always annoyed her sister, who now sighed, pursed her mouth, and gathered herself together to depart.

'Well, dear, you know what I think, for I've never
shirked saying it. I'm always open, and I never keep things
back, and I'm sure I've always talked to you quite straight.
Drink is drink, however you take it, bottles or glasses or
cups, and you take too much of it. And God's laws are
God's laws, as I said before, and we must all keep them, and
it's your duty to see Daisy does. I say you should speak,
before it gets too late. Of course it well may be it's too late
already, much too late, but better late than never. Now,
don't you go letting things drift. You don't want that girl
on your hands with a baby. It might be twins, you never
know, for Daisy's getting on, and nature often makes up for
lost time that way.'

'Daisy isn't getting on all that,' the mother protested.

'Thirty-one, dear, next month. I remember when she
came as if it was last week, and how upset we all were.
Daisy's no child, Lil, but you must see after her just the
same. Now, you call on me if you want me. I've helped you
before, and I'll help you again. Now I must be off. . . . Did I
tell you I've joined our chapel mothers' meeting, that meets
on Mondays at seven?'

'No. Why'd you do that?'

'Well, what a question. Why shouldn't I?'

'You should, Milly. I never said you shouldn't. People
always think when you want to know why they do something you mean they shouldn't do it. What I say is, reasons
don't only belong to the things we shouldn't do. There's
reasons for doing even the things we *should* do. Like
brushing our teeth.'

'How you do ramble on, to be sure. Here's William.
Good evening, William; and it's good-bye, too, for I'm just
off. Good night, Lil, dear. You'll think of what I've said,
won't you.'

William came to the front-door with his sister-in-law,
and helped her on with her coat. She turned on him a grave
and warning face, whispering, 'Keep her off it, William. It's
not right, all this sipping she does. You look after her.'

'Oh, that's all right, Milly,' he cheerfully but uneasily
replied. 'Don't you worry. She knows what she's about,

Lil does.'

'Not she,' the elder sister returned, putting up her umbrella against the March rain. 'And never did.'

2

Returned to the sitting-room, Mr. Arthur found his wife in tears beside the tea and whisky. He put his arm round her ample form.

'Why, what's the trouble, old lady?'

She sobbed that it was Daisy, who was, it seemed only too likely, being let down by a fellow. He patted her shoulder and consoled her for this possible catastrophe.

'Don't you go looking on the dark side, meeting troubles before they come,' he recommended.

She added, mopping her eyes and blowing her nose, that Milly thought she ought to Speak.

'Who to? Better be careful. Lot of harm done by speaking, that's what I've found. Too much speaking brought the Great War about, and too much speaking ever since has stopped us getting ahead with the peace. Women are for ever wanting to speak. They think it settles everything. You're just like all these statesmen, you women are; always think you're going to set the world right talking round a table. If we all kept our mouths for eating and drinking there'd be less harm done. And talking of drinking, old lady . . .'

'Now, don't you get talking of drinking, too, William. I've had enough of that from Milly. Drinking's not a thing to talk about; it's a thing to do, when you feel you need it, and if you can carry it. What do you want me to drink? Glaxo? Well, you're wrong, because that runs to fat. Gladys' new baby, he's Glaxo-fed, and I always think he's going to melt when they put him near the fire. I don't need Glaxo, thank you; what I need is bracing and stimulating. Tea by itself spoils the nerves and wears the system, they say, but a drop in it bucks you up. So there, old gloomy-face, and don't you go looking on the dark side. Now, I'm going to run round and see Mrs. Dean's new baby before the children come home, and give myself a good laugh. They're so comical at that age, they'd make a cat laugh. When I'm feeling down and can't go and see a funny picture or anything, and my book's not a bright one, I always wish I had a baby under six months to laugh at. Gracious, when they first showed me Daisy I nearly killed myself – couldn't stop laughing. The doctor thought it was hysterics, but it wasn't, it was just that comical little creature looking at me. Well, we must laugh at them while we can; they get past a joke later on all right, when all this male-and-female business begins, drat it. Male and Female created He them, of course, but, thank goodness, at six months they don't know it.' (For Mrs. Arthur's cheap books had not included the works of Dr. Freud.)

Mr. Arthur settled himself in his arm-chair and lit his pipe.

'Now, don't you go gadding about after funny shows when I'm just in, old woman. You sit down and have your good laugh at me. Ain't I comical enough for you? Turn on that wireless, then; might be something bright.'

'Might. You never know.' Hopefully Mrs. Arthur turned it on. Through the mouth of a black trumpet a tired, cultured voice remarked, 'A book has recently come out . . .'

'Oh Lord.' Mrs. Arthur switched it rapidly off. 'Of course it has. All these books! If they're not translated from the Russian then they're from the Scandinavian. Anyway, they're all dry, the books that chap likes. I'd almost sooner hear about the wet – the chap that always says rain fell in the Hebrides and Northern Ireland. Fancy troubling to mention it! If it was me I'd wait for a day when those places had been dry, and mention that. I'm all for something new. But, of course, if you think *you're* new enough to do for me this evening, you silly old man, s'pose I must stay with you and give that kid the go-by.'

'That's the stuff. That's my old girl. Looking so bonny, too, in spite of being a bit mottled with crying and gin.'

'Mottled with gin! Impudence!'

'Mottled with gin,' William firmly repeated. 'Nothing

like spirits for spoiling a nice skin. You take care of that
schoolgirl complexion, my girl. You'll miss it when it's
gone.'

CHAPTER 23

Raymond, Daphne and Daisy

After the day of the visit of the *Evening Wire*, Daisy increasingly experienced the sensations of one who treads on quicksands or over a light volcanic crust that may at any moment heave and explode. The hour was at hand, she perceived, in which she must make to the Folyot family her little narrations, opening her mouth and saying, I am, on the maternal side, of a very common family. Yes, that was my half-brother, that vulgar young reporter who called on you. No, I did not wish to recognise him just then; I had my reasons. My mother has even less education and chic; she married a very respectable house-decorator, and it was thought quite a good match, and they live not, as I told you, in the Hebrides, but in East Sheen. Oh, yes, she is very common, though I love her. I have, further, two aunts; they are respectable and prim and good chapel members, and talk in a way which would surprise you very much. Yes, it is true what they will tell you, that I am thirty-one next month. Why did I say I was not yet twenty-six and that my mother lived in the Hebrides? Well, I should think even you could imagine why; it is scarcely worth inquiring into.

This embarrassing hour certainly appeared to be drawing near. Far better would it come from her than from others, and that others could not for ever be kept from landing on the island of dreams on which – fool's paradise – she stood huddled above the threatening seas, she had been reminded afresh by Ed's inadvertent intrusion. Tell them, then, and be done, she admonished herself, but still from day to day could not, would not, did not tell them any such thing.

Instead, when Raymond said, 'What about getting married in early May?' she answered 'Yes, do let's,' and felt a storm-tossed mariner sighting harbour lights. Certainly let them get married in early May; at least then she would be, in a manner safe. She would make her narration, and try after it and before it to be so charming, so irresistible, that in Raymond's eyes she would be tarnished scarcely at all, but loved, esteemed and desired by him as much as ever. He should meet Daisy and love her, as he now loved Daphne.

2

But she at times vaguely, at other times sharply, felt that Raymond was already meeting Daisy, and not loving her quite as he loved Daphne. And, indeed, this was the case.

Raymond, not analytical, but trained to observe scientifically and with interest the temperaments, habits, and activities of the world's creatures, could not be blind to those of one linked to him by the thousand little intimacies of the betrothed. He did, on many occasions, perceive Daisy lurking behind Daphne, or encounter her slipping inadvertently into Daphne's place, a changeling. With a vague, resentful sense of loss, he would look for the charming, clever, amusing, companionable creature with whom he had fallen into love, and find in her place someone different, someone less intelligent, less charming, less entertaining, someone, even, who appeared (surely) to have just lied about some trivial matter, deceived him for no reason of importance, when all he wanted was straight, blunt frankness. Her duplicity in the matter of the little lizard, her secretiveness about that queer literary life of hers, were not solitary instances. More often than she knew, Raymond encountered Daisy the deceiver, and was, without analysis, instinctively vexed by her. Then Daphne would reappear, and he would, for a time, forget the puzzling image which, however, lingered still in the recesses of his mind. His desire for her, moreover, seemed to burn lower as the spring weeks went by; had it ever been truly, deeply, and directly passion, or was it merely an emotional story that his mind had invented and related to his senses, which had quickened in second-hand response? What was this love, of which so many and so diverse varieties are known to science and to humanity? It was, at least, very certain that Raymond did not love Daphne with the fiery abandon of body, soul, and spirit with which Daisy loved Raymond. Since, however, Raymond was not very deeply interested in human love, but prepared to accept it with a tolerance less critical and analytical than that with which he examined the emotions which engross crustaceans and bivalves, the passions which unite birds and shake the hearts of reptiles, the desires which animate frogs and overwhelm snails, he did not subject it to any such close scrutiny. His mind was too busy for him to spare it for the investigation of his emotions, which took their own way unquestioned and uncensored, like children whose tutor is engaged in pursuits higher than minding them, and who will only be recalled to their doings by some audible disturbance. His book, his lectures, his work, his amusing hobbies, engrossed his mind and his time, and Daphne, so he supposed, engrossed his heart, and they would be married in early May.

But, disturbingly, in and out of the absorbed unconsciousness of the scientist, ever and anon Daisy flitted, like an ambushed bird that peeps from cover, flutters a wing and is again concealed; or like one of those felons who hide themselves behind statues in houses, occasionally emerging by inadvertence and hurriedly retreating again, so that the impression they make on those who chance to observe them is disturbing but not lasting.

CHAPTER 24

The Undoing of Daphne

On Palm Sunday, which fell on a fine day in mid-April, Mr. Struther lunched with the Folyots, and after lunch Mrs. Folyot and he sat in the drawing-room and spoke of Lithuanian freedom.

'Freedom from what?' Cary inquired from the window-seat, where she had curled herself up with her pencil and manuscript book to write her novel unhindered by the interruptions of Charles.

'From Russians and Poles, darling,' her mother told her, and then they both forgot her and plunged into business, for they expected a Lithuanian, a Ruthenian, a Livonian, two Esthonians, and a Lett to tea, and had to settle a number of small Eastern-European points before these Baltic visitors should arrive.

Hearing that they spoke of Vilna, of Kovno, of minority schools, of plebiscites, of Zelikowski, of Pilsudski, and of Radziwilischki, Cary perceived that Lithuanian freedom was dull, and absorbed herself in the composition of 'The Sinister Footsteps, or the Mystery of the Mansion.'

Through the open window the April sun shone, the April wind blew, carrying smells of spring, of budding London gardens, of blossoming country lanes. Cary, sucking her pencil, sniffed the spring and heard the cuckoo, and for a moment the Sinister Footsteps became as irrelevant in that sweet air as were Vilna, Kovno, and plebiscites.

But Mrs. Folyot and Mr. Struther, being older, and having had, therefore, more springs and heard more cuckoos (as to that, Mrs. Folyot, with her usual efficiency, always made a point of hearing the cuckoo on the tenth of April, and then thought no more about him), had attained to more balance, and were not to be turned by an April breeze or a vagrant bird from the business of delivering Baltic-dwellers from

Russians and from Poles. Still, while the birds sang sweetly
and gaily in the garden trees, they spoke of minority
schools, of plebiscites, of Ruthenians, of Latvians, and of
the League of Nations.

2

The bells of St. Mary Abbott's church rang three times,
and, synchronistically, the bell of the Folyot's front-door
rang once.

'Good gracious,' said Mrs. Folyot, 'I hope it's not the
Lett. Letts never have the right time,' she generalised, and
with that sweeping injustice characteristic of the Nordic
attitude towards the Slav races. 'My little tailor in Church
Street is never by any chance ready for me at the time we've
arranged. They're quite hopeless on committees.' Almost
better (it seemed from her tone) that Letts should not have
freedom, but be dominated by Russians and by Poles, who,
however, only too probably never have the right time
either. The right time is, in the main, the property of
Anglo-Saxons, who present it, by request, to the young in
streets and parks. Celts and Latins frequently have the
wrong time; Slavs too often no time at all.

However, those who were now heard in colloquy with
the maid in the hall were Anglo-Saxons.

The maid appeared at the drawing-room door, unin-
terested and well-bred.

'Mrs. Barker and Mrs. Arthur to see you, ma'am.'

So accustomed was she to announcing to her mistress
callers of an almost feverish strangeness that Mrs. Barker
and Mrs. Arthur seemed to her of quite unusual normality.
Not ladies, but, no doubt, arrived to assist in some good
work, or to call Mrs. Folyot's attention to some hitherto
unnoticed little grief endured in some part of the globe by
those unfortunate people, the foreigners.

'Who in the world are they?' Mrs. Folyot murmured,
trying to remember. 'Oh, probably aliens,' she surmised,
for she was busy about the wrongs endured by British aliens
and had invited any who would like advice to call on

Sunday afternoons.

'Show them in,' she said, and in they were shown.

But they did not seem like aliens, unless they might perhaps be aliens by marriage. Two middle-aged female Britons, who appeared to be of what is commonly, in our curious geometrical parlance, called the lower-middle class. One was small and neat and dressed in brown, with a boa of feathers, a toque of velvet, a hair-net, and one of those prim faces and tight mouths whose owners, in the pits and upper circles of theatres, click their tongues and say 'Fancy' when there occurs on the stage a joke, a surprising remark, or a kiss. The other was large and dressed in purple, and had bright yellow hair and plenty of colour and looked more like one of those who disturb audiences by laughing too loud.

'Do sit down, won't you?' said Mrs. Folyot, brisk and polite, and added, according to her practised and efficient habit, 'I have an engagement in a very short time, so I'm glad you came in now instead of a little later. You wanted to see me about something?'

'You're very kind,' said the smaller lady, speaking in the accents of Essex, refined by long residence in Middlesex. (Certainly, then, not an alien in her own right.)

'It's rather a private concern,' the prim little woman proceeded, looking towards Mr. Struther. But Mrs. Folyot, with a gesture, included this clergyman in all concerns likely to be raised between her and her visitors. 'That's quite all right. Mr. Struther helps me in everything.'

Since Mr. Struther seemed a clergyman, and since she did not observe Cary behind the window curtain, Mrs. Barker accepted her audience and said, 'My name is Mrs. Barker. This is my sister; her name is Mrs. Arthur. So we felt we ought to call.'

Mrs. Arthur, who sat on a sofa, her stout legs crossed, her purple hat askew, said, 'That's right.'

Certainly they were married to aliens. Mrs. Folyot assumed the encouraging look she wore for these.

'Yes? And you find things difficult and awkward, I

expect? As I'm sure you know, we're organising an agitation about it. There's to be a procession on May the first. . . .'

Mrs. Barker looked surprised and as if she did not see how a procession would help in this matter, but Mrs. Arthur smiled sweetly, for she was of those who believe processions to help in all matters. It was apparent to her that the Folyot family was taking Daisy's part in the affair Raymond, and would agitate and process until he was persuaded to make an honest girl of her.

'Procession?' Mrs. Barker, less imaginative and ritualistic, as beseemed a chapel member, commented.

'We believe that they help, you know,' Mr. Struther explained, answering the surprise in her tone by enunciating this widely held, if curious, creed.

Mrs. Arthur turned on him an approving eye. The clergyman, too, then, was on Daisy's side. Well, of course, so a clergyman should be. These seemed nice people, well-disposed and right-thinking. She was relieved and pleased.

Mrs. Barker, however, was finding them distinctly odd.

'Well, fancy,' she observed, a little baffled. 'I don't see how a *procession's* going to do Daisy any good, Mrs. Folyot.'

Daisy? Oh yes, her sister on the sofa, of course.

'But these processions, you know, really do make a great impression, both on the public and the government. We had one for the white slaves shipped to South American ports, and another for the black ones in Sierra Leone, and government took action quite soon afterwards about both. It's the sight, I suppose, of so many people walking in double file, so far and so slow. One wouldn't guess it, *a priori*, but it does seem to be a psychological fact that processions produce results. They start questions in the House quite often. In parliament, you know.'

'In parliament?' Mrs. Arthur gasped. Must, then, all the forces of the British constitution be set in motion before Daisy could have right done her?

Mrs. Barker looked still more surprised.

'Oh, but Mrs. Folyot, that wouldn't seem very nice,

would it? To have Daisy asked about in parliament, I
mean . . .'

'Not by name, of course – oh no. No individual cases will
be mentioned, only the whole question raised and discussed. You see, there are thousands of women in England
in just this difficult position. Something *must* be done to
help them, and quickly.'

'*And* quickly,' Mrs. Barker repeated, and nodded her
approval. 'That's just what I say. It mustn't be left till too
late, must it.' She had dropped her voice to the tone suited
to this kind of too-lateness.

'But,' she added, 'it seems a dreadful thing that it should
have to be brought before Parliament. Couldn't your son
do the right thing by Daisy without that?'

'My son? Well, I'm afraid *he* hasn't anything to do with it,
you know.' Mrs. Folyot wondered if this good lady
thought her the mother of the Home Secretary.

'Well.' They both stared at her.

'Considering,' said Mrs. Barker, 'that he's led her to
believe he wants to marry her – or so she told us,
anyhow——'

Mrs. Arthur sat up straight. 'Of *course* he led her. Daisy'd
never of said so if it hadn't of been true. Always truthful,
Daise is,' she added, defiantly, to her sister, rushing gal-
lantly into the eternal contest between parent and aunt.

Mrs. Folyot was looking dazed. Less aliens than lunatics,
she was beginning to fear that she was entertaining. Or
could they be Sunday afternoon blackmailers? The purple-
clad lady on the sofa was also, of course, slightly but
definitely the worse for liquor; or possibly the better, for
she did not speak with incoherence or articulate with
thickness, but with an exhilarated animation familiar to
Mrs. Folyot's experience.

'Well,' she said briskly, 'I'm afraid I don't quite understand, but perhaps it's all rather long to go into now, as I'm
expecting some callers on business.'

Firmly she stood up, making those little movements of
departure (the departure of others) which are the only way
to cause aliens, lunatics, drinkers, and Sunday afternoon

blackmailers to leave houses, and even this way is not always effective.

It was not effective now. For though Mrs. Barker stood up too, she made no movements of departure, but quite the contrary.

'Pardon me, Mrs. Folyot,' she said, and smoothed her brown kid gloves.

'Not at all,' said Mrs. Folyot, and signed to Mr. Struther to ring the bell.

'*Pardon* me,' Mrs. Barker repeated, with the firmness she evinced at chapel parish meetings.

Even as Mr. Struther pressed the bell, Raymond came in.

'I say, mother . . .'

He spied strangers, and stopped.

His presence seemed to inspire Mrs. Arthur with animation and energy. She rose from the sofa and advanced towards him, remarking, 'So you're the young fellow my Daisy loves. Well, you've a nice face.'

He looked at her in some surprise.

'Your Daisy . . .?'

His mother indicated to him that the bell had already been rung.

'Yes, Daisy. Why, you look as if you'd never heard of her before; upon my word you do, don't he, Milly?'

'I'm afraid I never have,' Raymond, polite but blank, replied.

'Oh, don't be silly, young chap. It's not a bit of use. We've just been talking it over with your ma, and she's going to have a procession about it, and questions in parliament, if you don't do the right thing by Daisy. Not that *I* want to go to such lengths. I always like young people to please themselves and not be forced, and I say if you don't want to marry Daisy, then she's best not marrying you. . . .'

The maid was visible in the background, waiting to conduct Mrs. Barker and Mrs. Arthur to the hall door. She was very much interested in this scene; it seemed as if Mr. Raymond had not been acting right by some girl, and he engaged and all.

Mr. Struther was firmly but unsuccessfully guiding the ladies towards the hall, when Daphne walked in.

3

Daisy stopped, and turned a curious yellow grey, as if she were about to faint, or to succumb to the ocean. Well, then, here it was: it had at last occurred, and here one stepped over into the waiting abyss. No use to fight any more for footholds on the crumbling banks; they had all given at once.

'Why, Daisy!' Mrs. Arthur's voice was not assured; it faltered, for she knew, even though supported by Milly and by port wine, that she had done wrong.

'Well . . .' Daisy closed the door behind her, shutting out the eager maid, and leaned limply against it. She really did feel very dizzy; it was so unexpected.

'Aunt Milly and I, we just thought we'd call,' said Mrs. Arthur, lamely excusing herself. 'Aunt Milly thought we'd better. . . . Don't mind, dear, do you?'

'Oh, yes,' Daisy faintly replied.

Mrs. Folyot pulled herself together. Her customary power of dealing with situations, however peculiar they might be, seemed to be failing her.

'My dear Daphne, what *is* all this about? I shall really be glad if someone will explain.'

'Oh, Daphne – of course that's what you'd call her.' Mrs. Arthur seated herself once more on the sofa. No point in not being comfortable while one chatted. 'Daphne. That's what her friends always seem to call her. Her aunt Monica did, too. We call her Daisy at home, you know; it's her second name.'

'You're Daphne's mother, then?'

Mrs. Folyot, so used to exercising courtesy to surprising people, was politely non-committal, but revealed faintly her surprise. Anyhow, Mrs. Barker bridled a little.

'I hope you've no objection, Mrs. Folyot.'

'Oh – oh, no, of course. I'm very glad to see you. Daphne should have told us you were coming . . .'

'Well, you see,' Mrs. Arthur apologetically explained, 'Daisy never meant us to come. She always said I wasn't to, on any account. That's why I thought there must be something funny about it, if you see what I mean.'

Daisy, standing limply against the door, muttered: 'Oh, mother, be quiet,' further embarrassing them all.

They all regarded one another for a moment in silence, and it seemed like one of those domestic catastrophes which used so frequently to overtake the Greeks, who made such serious errors regarding the identity of their near relations as to marry their mothers, slay their fathers, and shoot their children, all in ignorance, believing them to be strangers or creatures of the chase, and then were overwhelmed with horror and surprise when their relationships were disclosed.

'Do sit down again, Mrs. Barker,' Mrs. Folyot hurriedly rushed into the pause. 'I must really apologise for my stupidity, but, do you know, at first I didn't a bit know who you were. I'd forgotten what Daisy's mother's name was, and I confused you with some ladies I was expecting on business. We were quite at cross purposes, weren't we. It was really quite amusing. The fact is, I wasn't a bit expecting to see you, Mrs. Arthur, because I thought you were in the Hebrides.'

'In the Hebrides? Fancy that!'

'Yes. In Uist, where you live. Daphne never told us you had come on a visit south.'

'Me live in Uist? Why, I've never been near it. That's you, not me, Mrs. Folyot. I never even heard of it till Daisy mentioned what a lot of time you all spend up there.'

'Oh, no, we never go to Uist.'

It became apparent that no one present ever went to Uist. These two families were simultaneously cleared in one another's eyes of this curious and unnatural habit.

Mrs. Arthur was amused by this, though others present were embarrassed.

'Fancy, isn't that funny? Can't help laughing, can you? We live in East Sheen, and have done for years. Mr. Arthur's a builder and decorator, and has premises in Baker

Street. Now, isn't that amusing, Mrs. Folyot, you thinking we lived on a comical island like that, and us thinking you did. Whatever made you put us all on Uist, Daise, you funny girl?'

'Oh, just for a joke.'

Daphne, now casually seated on the arm of a chair, lighting a cigarette with unsteady fingers, was fighting for her life, with a foolish and spurious smile on her colourless lips. She was playing her part before Raymond; indeed, she felt herself to be alone with him, and as if the foolish explanations and inquiries going on around them were no more than the chatter of the starlings in the April garden. What did anything matter now, but that Raymond was for the first time truly face to face with Daisy, and was regarding her with questioning, puzzled, embarrassed eyes?

'Well, really!' her aunt Milly commented. 'Not a particularly good joke, that I can see.'

'Oh, well, it's all been just a silly misunderstanding.' Tactfully, Mrs. Folyot passed it off. 'Now, I wish I had more time this afternoon, but I have a deputation of foreign visitors coming, so I'm afriaid I can't be with you much longer. Daphne must be your hostess at tea instead of me, and we must get to know one another some other time, mustn't we?'

'Mothers should,' Mrs. Arthur agreed, nodding and smiling. 'I always say, the mothers should get well acquainted. Daisy wouldn't have it – I expect she thought you wouldn't think us smart enough, not being west-end people but living in a small way, but I always knew we should get on. And I feel I shall get on with you, too, young man. Mr. Arthur tells me I always take to the young fellows, and I like your face. You must pardon my sister and me thinking he'd led the girl astray, Mrs. Folyot.' She lowered her voice to a loud whisper, 'and didn't mean to act rightly by her, for I'm sure now we were quite wrong. It was her hushing it up so, and saying you weren't to be told of the engagement, made us think there was something funny about it, but I knew Daise better all the time really. And now I can see it's quite all right, and I'm ever so happy about it.'

'I certainly can't imagine why you should have thought anything of that kind, Mrs. Arthur.' Mrs. Folyot was more distant than with any aliens, any deputations, any Baltic dwellers; she had assumed the chilly tone in which one addresses oppressors, such as Fascists, Bolshevists, police-agents, and Turks.

Mrs. Barker resented this tone, which was, indeed, unjust. What minorities had they oppressed, what frontiers violated, what liberties threatened, that they should be treated like the perpetrators of these deeds? Had they not, on the contrary, come forward in defence of a girl's rights?

'It was Daisy's own doing, Mrs. Folyot. She should show more sense, a girl that's turning thirty-one next week.'

Thirty-one? It had been, surely, Daphne's twenty-sixth birthday that was to occur next week. What was this tissue of silliness, vulgarity, and duplicities that was being so tiresomely displayed before them, piece by piece, like shoddy fabric over a counter? Mrs. Folyot glanced impatiently at it, and at Daisy, the foolish, lying girl with relations whom she really ought to keep in their homes, though, to do Daisy justice, she did seem to have done her best about this.

Daisy, turned now from pale to scarlet, saw Raymond's face, empty of comment, turned from her. Embarrassed and made uncomfortable by the odd remarks of these women, he was endeavouring politely to escape from the room.

Into the little awkward pause broke a sharp sob from the window-seat, and Cary came out among them, her hands clenched over her face, shaken by tears.

'Cary! You here?' Her mother turned on her, venting her vexation. 'You know very well you oughtn't to have stayed there like that. . . . What's the matter? You're not hurt, are you?'

But Cary made no answer. Shaken by sobs, she fled from the room.

Mr. Struther, the only person present with soul undisturbed enough to make such observations, thought how the child's had been the only voice uplifted to bewail this tragedy, and how, like a Greek chorus, she had appeared, made her sad comment, and vanished.

As to Cary, she rushed up to her room and sobbed upon her bed. People had stood round the drawing-room and hurt one another; each speech and each silence had wielded a knife, and the knife had plunged into Daphne, and Daphne had stood before them all like Indians at a stake, trying not to scream. That was how Cary had felt, from the moment when Daphne had come in; she had felt it until at last she had herself broken into shamefaced tears and fled. Cary had not been surprised at Daphne's funny mother and aunt, or at anything that had transpired concerning Daphne; vaguely and unconsciously she had realised it all along, had known that Daphne told lies and hid things. She was not surprised, but she suffered; she did not love Daphne, but at Daphne's exposure she wept for shame and anguish, as if she had watched someone pelted in a pillory.

'Poor mite,' said Mrs. Arthur in the drawing-room. 'It's the earache, I shouldn't wonder. I remember Daisy taking on just like that with the earache when she was a kiddie. It's wonderful what children can suffer, to be sure. Warm wax I always dropped into their ears. . . . And is that the clever little kiddie that told Ed that beautiful story about your burglary? Ed's my son, you know; he called here from the *Evening Wire,* do you remember?' She addressed Raymond. 'But he didn't get near as much from you as he did from your little sister! She told it ever so cutely, he said. You remember Ed coming that morning, don't you?'

'Oh, yes, I remember,' Raymond politely assented. Still he did not look towards Daphne; so many things were being piled up, one by one, between them, that it seemed to Daisy that he would never look at Daphne again. What he was seeing instead was the young reporter standing in the dining-room that March morning, and her own unrecognising face as she left them together.

What Mrs. Folyot was seeing was the story in the *Evening Wire* about the burglary. The temperature of the room seemed to drop still a degree or two.

'Warm wax,' Mrs. Arthur repeated. 'Or, if it's tummy, a pill. . . .'

As if he hastened to administer these consolations to his young sister, Raymond, murmuring something about some unfortunate obligation he had contracted elsewhere, left the room.

At the same moment, the hall was heard to be full of Lithuanians, Ruthenians, Livonians, Esthonians, a Lett, and a Pole, all arrived for tea and Baltic chat.

'My deputation,' Mrs. Folyot superfluously remarked, and the next moment the maid appeared at the door, observing that the foreign gentlemen were arrived. She made no attempt to announce them by name; this enterprise she had long renounced with Mrs. Folyot's visitors.

'Show them,' said Mrs. Folyot, keeping her head as usual, 'into the dining-room. Daphne, perhaps you will give Mrs. Arthur and Mrs. Barker tea in here. . . . I am so sorry,' she explained to these ladies, 'but I must say good-bye now. One can't keep them waiting.'

She and Mr. Struther hurried away to join the Eastern Europeans in the dining-room, where all was heard to be animation, as if a great number of those little tailors with curly heads and broad noses who inhabit small London streets had got together. The animation was the greater because of the presence of the Pole, who had not, in point of fact, been invited, but, learning of the little gathering, had perceived that a representative of his country should adorn it, in order that the case for Poland might be clearly and accurately stated.

4

The East Sheen party – wholly East Sheen, since even Daphne was departed, leaving Daisy in the bosom of her family – were left in the drawing-room, in possession of the deserted field.

'Well,' Mrs. Arthur said, 'I'm sorry Mrs. Folyot had to go. Perhaps we shall see her again after tea. She's what I'd call a quite distinguée woman; shouldn't you say so, Milly? Seems busy, too. Why don't you take your hat off, Daisy, and sit down and be comfy? You look tired, child. Not cross with mother, are you? I bet you half think we shouldn't of come; don't you, girl? but look how well it's turned out – all of us as thick as thieves already.'

Mrs. Barker was gathering her feather boa, gloves, and bag about her.

'You never were one to come away at the right moment, Lily. But *I* was never one to stay anywhere a minute longer than I was wanted, and quite plain one can see that we're not wanted here, neither by Daisy nor her friends, so we're going right off, and if you want tea before you get back we'll get it at a Lyons'.'

'Why, Milly . . . Mrs. Folyot invited us herself to tea. You don't want us to go, do you, girl?'

'Yes, please.' Daisy's voice had become small, expressionless, pale, like her face. Wrestling, quite in vain, with an overpowering universe, she seemed to have dwindled, been emptied of personality and emotion, become a wan automaton. Neither Daphne nor Daisy she seemed, but some sad changeling, who, mislaying both selves, had mislaid the universe.

'Yes, please,' she dimly said. 'I'm going too.'

Through the pleasant glow that encompassed her, the mother felt her child's grief pierce. She stared at the small blank face.

'Daisy, girl. . . . What's the matter? You don't really *mind* us having come, do you, goosey? Why, it's all been as nice as it could be . . . hasn't it?' Dubiously the last two words fell. But . . . hadn't it? Mrs. Arthur felt like the producer of a play which has seemed to him to be going well until the curtain and then the first doubt strikes at his heart, for the applause is faint and there is, here and there, a hiss.

'Well, *I'm* all right here, but, if you both say so, we'll go.' She heaved herself from the sofa.

Raymond came into the room. He had fought with shyness and returned to act host to Daphne's mother,

whom he rather liked, in spite of the odd things she had said
to him. The other woman seemed tiresome, but this one, in
her frank and exuberant naturalness, rather pleased him.
Anyhow, someone, since his mother was now with Lithuanians, must see that they had tea. Daphne seemed so odd,
so little kind, to her mother; she might not even give them
tea.

'You're not going?' He hovered by the door, shy, yet
friendly and hospitable. 'But you must have tea. . . .'

'That's what *I* say,' Mrs. Arthur agreed. 'I'm always for
my tea. But Daisy's for bustling us off in a hurry.'

'Nonsense. Of course you'll have tea. It's just coming in.'

In it came as he spoke, and Daisy, pale automaton, strove
no more. She sat down, she poured out tea; they all ate and
drank. Mrs. Arthur talked to Raymond, merrily chaffing
him, telling him anecdotes of Daisy's childhood. She liked
young fellows. Raymond listened and talked; he got on
well enough with her, in his shy, polite, rather puzzled
way. What he said made her laugh, and her sense of humour
pleased him.

Daphne joined in the conversation, feverishly bright.
Daisy listened to her, to Raymond, to her mother and to her
aunt, and thought, he likes mother. If I'd told him from the
beginning it would have been all right after all – at least, it
might. Thinking this, and of her hateful, wasted lies, her
shame and bitterness and trouble welled in her anew.
Across a dark dividing gulf she reached to find her lover,
but found instead an aloof, puzzled spirit, that turned from
her in non-comprehension, bewilderment, and embarrassment. Contemptuous, no doubt, he was, resentful even,
and hurt; wondering who and what was this changeling
into which the gay and frank Daphne of his dreams had so
fatally been transformed.

Oh, she could no longer endure it, it was no more to be
endured.

Abruptly she rose.

'I must get back. I'll walk with you to the tube, mother.'

Mrs. Arthur, having had her tea, admitted that the
Sunday afternoon call might now be called over.

'Well, it's been a real nice afternoon, that it has. And I'm ever so pleased to have had such a nice chat with you, Raymond. I may call you that, mayn't I, and when you feel you can manage it you must call me Ma, the same as Ada's Percy does.'

Raymond, not committing himself on this point, helped the ladies into their coats, conducted them through the hall, found their umbrellas, said good-bye, shepherded them out through the front door.

'I shall see you to-morrow, shan't I,' he said to Daphne.

'Yes, to-morrow evening.'

Their voices were as usual; you would not have known that each groped blind, the one for a lost lover, the other for a vanished wraith.

'Good-bye, Raymond; pleased to have met you. Tell your Ma she and I must have a proper talk one day soon.'

'Good-bye, Mr. Folyot.'

'Good-bye, Mrs. Barker. Good-bye. . . .'

5

They walked together to Notting Hill Gate.

'You shouldn't have come without telling me first, mother. I asked you not to,' Daisy said, dully, and without even the animation of anger, as they descended Campden Hill Square, passing the garden, where the trees, burgeoning and budding into April green, were, however, already grimed with soot. They never wore, even for a moment, these London trees, that air of translucent, innocent, and vivid youth with which annually in the country verdure appears; like gutter children, they are tarnished and darkened even in the bud. The birds, too, were grimy; only their fluting voices and animated chirpings suggested youth.

Mrs. Arthur now perceived, though dimly, that she shouldn't have come. She should have asked Daisy first; she saw that now. It had been Milly's fault; Milly had worked her up to it.

'I'm sorry, girl. . . . Aunt Milly's idea, it was. But come, it's done no harm, has it now? I'm sure it all went very nicely.'

'That's no way to speak to your mother, Daisy. She did right to come, and you were wrong all along to try and stop her. Being ashamed of your own mother like that! I'm surprised at you, Daisy, that I am. You own mother, who's been so good to you always, spoiling and pampering you. There'd be more sense in it if you were ashamed of your father, and *his* relatives.'

At that Mrs. Arthur turned on Mrs. Barker with anger, and there ensued one of those sharp, recriminating duels that had always punctuated the relations of these sisters, arising like sudden tempests and subsiding without bitterness owing to the sweetness of Mrs. Arthur's temper. While it raged, Daisy slipped away from them and boarded a bus for Bloomsbury.

Perceiving, near Notting Hill Gate station, that her child had gone, Mrs. Arthur broke down and wept, but was comforted in the train by the gratifying thought of that nice and reliable young fellow who was to make Daisy happy.

6

Daisy let herself into a flat empty of consolations, full of remembered moments of such poignancy that, encountering them when thus wilted with misery, she seemed to crack, like cold glass when it encounters sudden heat. Here Raymond had sat, and here, and there; here lay the ashes of his pipe, knocked out into the grate; there, left on the chimney-piece, was his tobacco-pouch. Mingled mournfully with the aroma of dead cigarettes, the smoke of his dead pipes lingered still on the air. There, on the divan, he had sat, only yesterday, and talked to Daphne of flying dragons who lived in China, and of little climbing dragons who lived in the zoo; to Daphne, whom now he knew never to have lived, to have been a phantom, a dream fled on the wind like a drift of smoke, leaving behind her what? A little heap of ashes, a dusty sediment, that, stirring, built itself into a new, strange figure, a sordid figure, a figure of shams, of cowardly snobberies, of mean, vain lies, the figure of Daisy of East Sheen.

To stay in that room with Raymond and his dead Daphne, she did not dare. She would have begun to weep, and, should she once begin to weep, there seemed no reason why she should ever cease; her tears would submerge and drown her. She could not, dared not stay. Yet she could not go to Raymond, face again that house whose inhabitants (all but the Baltic deputation) now knew so much of her, and in such a way. She did not see how she could go to that house again, even after half a century of oblivion.

She dared not go, she dared not stay; poised between these two bitternesses, she thought of the flat overhead. Geranium was never in the flat for week-ends; had Geranium been in it, she could not have gone there, since Geranium was Raymond's friend. To encounter Geranium would be bitter, like death; to encounter Theo would be to forget, perhaps, bitterness in laughter, friendship, talk, and drink.

Daisy went up to the flat overhead and knocked. Surprisingly, Theo was in, and alone.

'Hullo, my dear.'

'Hullo. What are you going to do this evening? I want to come out with you and get terribly drunk.'

'All right, my love, you shall. It's no trouble or expense to you to do that, is it, and you look as if you needed it. I'm going to the Roast Chestnuts with a crowd; come along and drown yourself.'

Theo was a comfortable friend. She asked no questions, and did not take love seriously. With an expression and manner which assumed that all the world was a cabaret and all the men and women merely players, she went about the business of living as others set out for a fête. One pictured her soul in a jester's cap and the skirts suitable for ballet. Truthful to excess, because without embarrassment, fear, or shame, she yet readily forgave lying. Light tippler and light lover, she was yet dear to many of the sober and the chaste. Mocker of the passions, she yet was episodically subject to them; intelligent, she seldom exercised her brain;

gently born and bred, she used often speech suitable to
courtesans and oaths commonly believed to occur mainly in
stables (one presumes because horses are irritating animals);
with the manners of a rake she combined the face of a
madonna. In short, she was of a type independent of all
fashions and incidental to all periods.

Whatever she was, she restored to Daisy by the evening's
end the universe, relit with faint constellations of hope
which twinkled through the fumes of oblivion like circus-
flares through fog. Daisy, becoming tipsy, believed that
nothing had occurred for tears; that Raymond, if he loved
her as she loved him, would love her still as ever. What if
Raymond should suddenly have appeared before her as a
liar, a snob, of low extraction, advanced years, vulgar
literary output, and common relations who accused her of
seducing him? She would scarcely have noticed it; all these
trifling flaws would have been submerged in the flood of her
love and washed from sight. If Raymond's love was, had
ever been, like hers, he would love Daisy as he loved
Daphne. After all, how could his desire to unite himself
with Daphne fade away because Daphne was, in some
respects, other than he had supposed? Was love like that?

Thus the lost universe was restored to Daisy, swaying a
little and faintly, unsteadily lit.

7

But, waking next morning, with the headache customary
after such a night, she encountered, in place of this universe,
one dubious and dark and lit only by the jagged lightenings
of despair. For Raymond (she knew when she was sober)
did not now love her, if he had ever loved her, with the
abandon with which she loved him, the abandon that
would suffice to obliterate those little flaws which he could
not have failed to observe in her and in her relatives.
Groaning, she pressed her head into the pillow, and
believed that she could not get up.

The Undoing of Daisy

The telephone-bell rang, suddenly and sharply (for this is the way in which telephones always ring). Sitting up in bed Daisy gave it nervous attention.

It was Raymond.

'Hullo. That you? What time am I coming for you to-night?'

She remembered that they were dining together and going on to dance somewhere. His voice was as usual, soft, light, and unhurried. Hers sounded to herself queer and strained, as if all night, instead of revelling, she had wept.

'Oh . . . any time. Do you mind if we don't dance, though? I'm feeling rocky. I don't expect I shall even feel like dinner. But could you get here early – as early as you can? I want to talk to you.'

'Right. I'll be there at seven.' He rang off.

Dizzily Daisy lay back on her pillow.

The bell rang again. It was like a chorus of noisy cicadas chirping – the same cadence and rhythm and impertinent contempt of the repose of others.

'Hullo, Miss Simpson? *Sunday Wire* speaking. An idea for your article this week. Does the modern girl believe in romance? How's that?'

'No,' said Daisy.

'How d'you mean, no? It's not a query, it's a heading for your article. What about it?'

'No.'

'Well, have you got a better idea? What have you thought of?'

'Nothing. I'm not writing any more articles.'

'*What?* How d'you mean, not writing any more articles? For how long?'

'For always. I've stoppped writing articles.'

'I'm afraid I don't quite get that, Miss Simpson. Perhaps you'll write us about it. As you know, of course, there's your contract still not run out. . . .'

'Yes. I'm breaking it. Good-bye.'

What further communications, if any, came from the *Sunday Wire* were lost, for Daisy laid the receiver on the table and herself back in bed. Henceforth the world might assault in vain the tomb where Marjorie Wynne and Daphne, dissimilar twin corpses, lay, and where only Daisy Simpson waked and suffered.

2

Raymond came at seven. He was embarrassed, shy, restrained. Seeing him thus, Daisy's one faint lamp flickered out. He did not love her, then. Had he loved her, he would have been eager to console her in her confusion, instead of being embarrassed by his own.

She mixed cocktails for them both, bracing herself up to talk. For she intended, in spite of his reluctance and her own headache, to explain, once and for all, Daisy and Daphne to Daphne's lover, that he might take Daisy or leave her.

Lying on the divan, built up with cocktails and cigarettes, she began.

'I'm sorry about yesterday, and that idiotic visit.'

He said, 'Why? I don't see why your people shouldn't come and see us. I don't know why you didn't bring them months ago.'

'Don't you?' she asked him, bent on explanatory candour for them both.

To this he agreed, since she wished it.

'Well, yes, I suppose I do know. But why, Daphne? I mean, how can it matter twopence, all that kind of thing? Who's going to care one way or another? As a matter of fact, I rather liked your mother. Though I didn't much care about your aunt; she seemed rather genteel.'

'She is. Mother's not that; all the same, you wouldn't want to see much of her, really. She's jolly and gay and has a sense of humour, but she'd get on your nerves and bore you quite soon; you're too different. However, I admit that's not the point. I lied to you about my people, and it's that you don't like. Well, I lied from the beginning to Mrs. Folyot and all of you, because I wanted you all to think I came of Aunt Monica's and my father's kind of people. I'm illegitimate, you know; my father never married my mother; she was a farmer's daughter, and he met her when he was quite young, and died a little later. I was brought up partly by mother and partly by Aunt Monica. I got to dislike the class mother comes of – not mother, she's just herself, but her class. I disliked it morbidly, in a way you don't unless you *are* partly it. *You* don't mind them, because you don't bother about them. If you saw much of them they'd bore you terribly – they're mostly so muddle-headed and illogical and conventional, and so without ideas. Anyhow the women. They wouldn't understand half you say; they'd go on with their own jobs, and their own thoughts, and just let you talk, as if you were a brook babbling. Women of that kind of bringing up are amazing, Raymond; they sometimes hardly seem to me to be civilised human beings, but more a kind of special creature by themselves. I don't even understand the way their minds work; you'd understand them still less. Oh, they're very nice and kind, lots of them, but *stupid*. . . . Well, I couldn't bear, after living with Aunt Monica, and going to school, and meeting the other kind of person, to be mixed up with that kind. I loved mother – she's such fun, and quite different from the ones I mean, though she's no better educated – but I couldn't bear to be thought one of them or to think myself one of them. It was sheer snobbery, and you'll probably never understand it. So I pretended to every one that my mother was educated, like Aunt Monica, and all that. And once I'd begun that, I couldn't tell you – I hadn't the nerve. Do you understand that?'

Raymond had been listening with the receptive attention of the scientist.

'Quite well. Of course it seems to me nonsense, because I can't see that one can lump people together in classes, like that. I mean, surely they're just individuals, whatever kind

of bringing up they've had. And, anyhow, it doesn't seem
to me to be of the slightest importance what anyone's
family is like. I mean, if you don't like your relations, you
can be different from them, and be accepted for what you
are yourself. But, still, I see your point.'

'Well, then, that's that. For the same kind of reason I hid
my writings from you as long as I could, because I knew
you'd hate that kind of writing. I couldn't, with you, just
treat it as a joke, as I did with lots of people, because I knew
you'd all think them such a bad joke. And I hid all kinds of
other things from you – being frightened and running
away, because the Daphne I'd made for you – (and for
myself; you must try to understand that part of it too,
because it's just as important) – was plucky and behaved
beautifully in danger. That's partly a class thing, too, you
know; women of my mother's class are so often cowards;
they scream.'

'Yes, I've noticed that. Still, anyone may be nervous.'

'It's not being nervous that matters; it's how you behave
when you're nervous. Women like Mrs. Folyot and Aunt
Monica and the girls I was at school with know they
mustn't disgrace themselves in danger, so they usually
don't. Women of my mother's class don't *mind* screaming;
they don't think it *is* a disgrace. It's a different code. . . .
Then, my age. That had nothing to do with class. But I
thought people would like me more if I was twenty-five
than thirty, so I said I was. I even half believed I was.'

'That seems to be quite a common idea people have. I
wonder why it's thought to be finer to have lived a less long
time on the earth. I suppose because, according to average
reckoning, the more you've had the less you've got ahead.
But then, after all, if you look at time fairly, it's as good
to have had it as to be going (possibly) to have it. An odd
idea.'

'I think it's more,' Daisy explained, 'that the younger you
are (within certain limits) the more attractive you are
supposed to be.'

'Still, if you know a person, and see for yourself what he
or she is like, you haven't got to infer their attractiveness

from premises, such as their age. Such as it is, it's before you.'

'You might think it would last longer if they were young.'

'Yes, there's that, of course; I hadn't thought of that. On the other hand, their *minds* are probably better if they are older – again, within limits.'

'Oh, their minds. People don't like girls for their minds . . . anyhow, men don't.'

'I don't agree with you. I should say one largely does. Of course there's the bodily appeal, too, very strongly, but minds count.'

'With you, perhaps. Not with all men. . . . Anyhow, there it is. You and I both waste time analysing and investigating obvious human facts till they look like non-sense. My maternal relations have more sense. *They'd* never discuss why age matters. They'd take it for granted; they just say "*Of course* a woman likes to be thought young. Who wouldn't?" If you asked them why, they wouldn't be able to answer you a single word. They know all about human nature without knowing the reasons for any of it. My stepfather and half-sisters think I'm mad when I talk to them. They'd think you madder – only that in their class men are allowed to be a little mad and women aren't. If a woman disagrees with something that's been said, they think it's rude. They say, "Well, you needn't take me up so sharp." The proper thing is to agree, to say "That's right" to every general statement. An argument means a quarrel to them. It's because they're not interested in abstractions or ideas, so don't think them worth arguing about, like personal things.'

'Perhaps,' Raymond doubtfully assented. 'But,' he added, 'as I said, I'm not at all sure you're being scientifi-cally sound, about all these generalisations. You keep talking of "class," and saying "they," as if every one below a certain economic and educational line was a member of a species, all with certain characteristics. That can't be sound, you know. It's as loose as generalising about the mental characteristics of sexes. Surely it's individuals who matter,

in both cases. I can't help feeling that your personal tastes
and reactions have made you think very loosely and super-
ficially about this.'

'I dare say. I *am* superficial and loose. If you'd read much
of Marjorie Wynne, you'd know that. Anyhow, there it is.
I'm not defending myself; I'm explaining how it was, all
along. And that's how it was. Of course, you'd think it
idiotic from every possible point of view.'

'Well, I don't personally see very much sense in it. But
never mind it now; what does it matter? How are you
feeling? Pretty rotten, I'm afraid?'

Daisy had closed her eyes and stopped talking, for the
room was spinning round her.

'God, I've got a head.'

'You look rotten, poor old thing. Look here, shall I go?
You'd much better go straight to bed.'

'No. Not yet. I've not quite finished yet. Listen,
Raymond. It now remains to break off our engagement.'

'What on earth are you talking about?'

'Our engagement. Breaking it off. Do be intelligent.'

'You might try that, too. What do you want to break it
off for?'

The last little flicker guttered and died. For his tone was
dead; the more dead for the little strain of life he tried to
force into it. They were back again in the garden at Solio,
and Daphne was telling Raymond how she must leave the
island and the Folyots and return to England. He, watching
a lizard on a tree, was saying, politely, indifferently, 'That's
too bad. Must you really go?' He was saying it again now.
For how brief a time had he felt anything else beneath the
incalculable flicker of desire and affection that had been
kindled by proximity and had now died down again,
leaving only a trail of grey ashes in its wake? By what
means, by what episodic progress of disillusion, had Daisy
through this winter succeeded in extinguishing that flicker-
ing, spurious flame that Daphne had somehow lit? What did
it matter, since extinguished and dead it truly now was, and
all that remained was to hold fast to pride and to make a
good end? She could keep him even now if she chose; if,

trampling decent pride and sense to fragments, she should reply, 'I don't want to, unless you do.' She all but said it; her head ached so much as to blind her to all the considerations of the universe but love. But, blind and dizzy, she clung to pride, as to a spar in a submerging sea.

'Because it's over. We're through. You haven't particularly wanted me for some time, and your mother won't want me at all after this – after finding out what I'm really like. So I don't care to go on with it. It's been worth trying, but we're through now.'

He looked at her, unhappy, uncertain, unprotesting, as if he did not know where either of them stood, or what to say.

'I suppose . . . if you feel that. . . . But you know, Daphne, that's nonsense about your mother. And, anyhow, it's not her you're engaged to, it's me.'

'Well, you feel much the same. You don't like liars either. . . . Oh, don't argue, Raymond; don't you see we can't go on? It's all gone, over, phut. It has been for weeks really; this business has only shown it up. Let's chuck it quickly and have done.'

'As you like.' Slowly he got up. 'I suppose I agree that we're neither of us so keen as we were at first.'

'Lucky we found it out in time, wasn't it,' she bitterly commented. 'Lots of people don't till they're married, and then it's not so easy.'

He was standing beside her, looking doubtfully down at her.

'Look here, think it over. You're feeling rotten to-night. Go to bed, and think of it again in the morning.'

'It'll make no difference. I tell you, it's done. And don't put it all on me. We both know it's over.'

He seemed to consider that, fairly.

'Well. . . . I'm frightfully sorry if we've messed it. . . . It was my fault.'

'For beginning it, you mean? I'm not sure you did begin it. Anyhow, what does it matter? We both made a mistake. Hundreds of people do. . . . Look here, you go and get some dinner. I shall go to bed.'

'Yes, do. Good-bye for now, then.'

For now? For always. What situation-shirkers men, even scientists, were!

She stood up, unsteadily.

'Good-bye.'

He hesitated a moment, standing by her side, looking at her in trouble and confusion. Did he want to kiss her, or was she not to have that last bitter sweetness, which might even now drown her unresisting in the flood, carrying her out to sea?

She was not. Probably he did not want to; perhaps he thought she did not, since she had said, It's over.

'I hope your head will be better soon,' he said, and left her without further words.

3

She lay still, and let the floods carry her out to sea, drowning her in grief.

Raymond, she whispered, come back and stay with me. I don't care what you think of me; come back, so that I can see you and hear you and touch you and make you care again. Oh, I can't go on without you; indeed, indeed, I can't.

She could not yet make even the weakest endeavour to do so; instead, she lay and wept.

Looking at the chimney-piece, she saw that he had not taken his tobacco-pouch.

The Immortals

When Marjorie Wynne learnt that her novel, *Summer's Over,* had sold twenty thousand copies in Great Britain and fifty thousand in the United States of America, she perceived that, if she invested the money thereby accruing to her wisely, she need do no more work for quite a long time. Accordingly, after making over a certain sum to her mother, and retaining a larger sum for immediate use, she handed the remainder to a stockbroker and requested him to place it for her to advantage, which, according to the lights vouchsafed to him, he did.

Then she was asked if she would make one of those little lecturing tours in America which are such necessary episodes in the careers of English writers. She had never lectured, and had no reason to believe that she could lecture; however, she felt that such an enterprise would, as the saying goes, make a change, so, since it seemed that America had need of her, she consented to visit and address it.

America is, after all, a New World (in the subjective and egotistic parlance of Europeans, who, ignoring Red Indians, Patagonians, Greenlanders, and all the other ancient inhabitants of this continent, can remember only that they themselves made its acquaintance under five centuries ago), and, as such, it presents to those who have, for whatever reason, conceived a distaste for the Old World, a fallacious promise of being very different.

As to the Atlantic Ocean, that shocking mass of water would, surely, roll very effectively between one who had crossed it and that which she had left behind, whether in East Sheen or Campden Hill Square. Daisy of East Sheen, Daphne of Maynard Buildings, these two should depart, incongruous and ill-fated young ladies, from the spheres

where they had so far functioned. In East Sheen Daisy could
not now endure to be; to Campden Hill Square Daphne
could not, Daisy would not go. Blindly turning from the
curtained years ahead, they decided that Marjorie Wynne
(who had, at least, excelled her sisters in that she had made
good, that is to say, money) should visit the American
continent.

So, under the name of Miss Marjorie Wynne (for her
agents thought this best), she boarded a Cunard liner one
fine May morning and struck west.

2

It is curious, she thought, as they lost touch, one by one,
with all the odd juts and fragments of land that are the last
outposts of the unsubmerged mass we call Europe, and,
giving themselves without reserve to temporary marine
conditions, the voyagers plunged into the fantastic, amusing life lived on liners, it is curious to be on the ocean, with a
ticket, a passport, several trunks, and a name, but without,
however, a personality. For, in point of fact, who was this
Miss Wynne? An inferior but popular novelist, who
intended to emit remarks from platforms in various cities in
the United States, to whomsoever might be induced to
listen. But did she feel herself to be this Wynne? She did
not. With Miss Wynne she had never had more than a pen
acquaintance. Neither did she feel herself to be Daphne, for
poor Daphne had been too much shattered and demolished
by her recent experiences to be as yet fit for ocean travel.
Neither, surely, was she Daisy Simpson, that tortuous,
evasive, and frightened snob digged out of the East Sheen
pit. Disembodied, disensouled, she seemed to herself to be a
cypher, drifting phantom-like across the ocean towards
that startling mass of land on its farther side. On that mass
of land they would take her for Marjorie Wynne; they
would cage her firmly and immediately within the form of
that foolish puppet who would stand on platforms and
babble to them, probably despised for coming at all,
certainly despised for coming in May. (Why did you come

in May? they would all say. Because it was May when I
came, was her only answer.) Anyhow, such as she was, she
would be Marjorie Wynne to them, and would become,
surely, Marjorie Wynne to herself. Then she would have
attained, at least, a personality. . . .

Dreamily, abstractedly, she reflected thus, standing by
the rail and watching the surging mass of that strange fluid
whence all came, to which all will, no doubt, at last return.

3

Someone spoke at her side.

'It *is* Miss Marjorie Wynne, isn't it?'

Turning, she saw two young ladies; one was plump and
white, and short, the other tall and thin and pink.

However inaccurate the statement, she could not, or did
not, deny it. One must, after all, be someone.

'Oh,' said the pink young lady, 'I do hope you don't
think it cheek of us, but we felt we simply *must* come and
speak to you. You see, we simply adore your books. We
read *Summer's Over* as it came out in the *Sunday Wire,* and
then again when it was published, and we do love it so.'

Miss Wynne made those little sounds which indicate
gratitude and pleasure, and the conversation proceeded on
normal lines. After having eagerly inquired how Miss
Wynne thought of her plots, how ideas visited her, and if
she was going across to America, the young ladies departed
to play quoits.

Oh, God, Miss Wynne muttered, and turned again to the
ocean.

Revolt took her by the throat, like sea-sickness. *Was* Miss
Wynne, after all, going across to America? The fatuous
inquiry suddenly acquired meaning, and was capable of
being answered by a yes or a no. Must she visit the United
States of America under the aegis of this tawdry novelist,
whom such young ladies read first in serial, then in volume
form? Must she indeed be this Wynne? Must Wynne cross
the ocean, there to face the crowds who, by the fact of
admiring her books, showed themselves no better than

herself? Could Wynne not, instead, be cast from the ship
and drowned, so that her creator should be delivered for
ever from that burden? What had Frankenstein done to rid
himself of the monster which he had brought to life? Ill-read
young woman, she could not recollect. But, with regard to
her own monstrous creation, intention took definite and
gynicidal shape. She knew in that hour how murderers
conceive their crimes; how little angers, little distastes,
ferment into vast disgusts, breed fevered dreams of assault,
how the vision passes into the plan and the intention, till
intention at last takes shape in deadly deed, and lo, the
murderer stands free of his foe, who, however, seeks
vengeance even from the grave.

But Marjorie Wynne, fatuous and condemned girl,
would seek no vengeance; cast into the Atlantic, in the
Atlantic she would remain, and her creator and slayer
would speed westward without her, anonymous and free.

She was, after all, passported as Daphne Daisy Simpson;
Daphne Daisy Simpson, then, she would henceforth be. As
such she would land; as such she would face Miss Wynne's
lecture-agents, who would meet her at New York, and
inform them, doubtless to their relief and to that of
America, that Miss Wynne had ceased to exist, and could
not, therefore, deliver lectures. She would hasten then from
New York by the next train, dashing across a great continent with the haste of an Orestes pursued by all the furies
of a misspent past, making for the plains of Texas and
Arizona, and for Mexico, on whose inhabitants, frail and
erring as they may in some respects be, God has yet
bestowed as much intelligence as enables them, wise
descendants of Aztecs and Spaniards, to refrain from listening to lectures. And so southwards, each mile traversed
satisfying old dreams with fulfilments richer than imagination could devise; running between the Gulf of Mexico and
the Pacific Ocean, between the Sierra Madre ranges,
between Vera Cruz and the Gulf of Tehuantepec, among
volcanoes and greasers and cattle and revolutions and Aztec
remains, and so, with the Caribbean Sea lapping warmly on
one's left, down the slender stalk that holds a continent

pendant like a great pear, the miraculous isthmus that
conducts one into South America as the narrow corridor of
death ushers one into paradise.

Whatever those eleven – or were they twelve? – republics
of Southern America were in truth like, it would not be
Daphne, nor Daisy, nor yet Marjorie Wynne, who would
behold them, but some new, as yet scarcely born creature,
who might be called by any of their names, but who would
not be any of these persons. A creature unhampered by East
Sheen or by Campden Hill or by Fleet Street, by Daisy's
home or Daphne's friends or Marjorie's public; a creature
cut loose from chains forged in the past, from obligations
overhanging the future; a creature who would be herself,
impacted on by what she would see and hear of the world
about her, making her own commentary, her own
individual gesture to the universe. She would see Brazilian
rivers, forests, armadilloes, and nuts, Bolivian humming-
birds, condors, and coffee, Venezuelan sugar-canes,
vanilla, divi-divi, and flying squirrels, mysterious Patagonians and beautiful Spaniards of Argentina, the huge
Andes and huger Pacific that shut Chile, the revolutions,
jungles, and equator of Ecuador, and all the odd, amazing
variety show of this unparalleled continent (so nicely cal-
culated to heal a broken heart), with her own eyes, those
two little windows passed down to her through aeons of
time, through billions of ancestors, that she, this tiny speck
in time and space which the forces of the universe had
conspired together so long and with such enthusiasm to
produce, might receive her own impressions.

One was, after all, oneself: one had a right to be oneself.
One moulded oneself to suit others, and all failed, collaps-
ing like a house of cards about one's head. The thing was
not to give a damn what other people thought, but to take
one's own path, pursue one's own private adventure
through the maze. Not to love over much; to love was too
painful. In any case, she believed that she could not love
again; Daisy had spent all that for the firm and had gone
bankrupt. But to see and hear and touch and taste, to react in
one's own private way to the universe, to enjoy it, and yet

to hold it lightly at its proper value, never permitting oneself to be entangled or involved, but to keep an eye, as it were, through gaps in the walls, on the luminous, half-discerned view that stretched always beyond it – here was the adventure which this newly-born, anonymous, still shivering and crying creature should make, the game which she should play with the world, when she should have ceased to shiver and to cry for lost love and should be able to make any adventure or to play any game at all.

But at present she did not desire to play even deck-cricket, or quoits, or join in those little competitions in speedily running along the deck to thread needles, or accurately marking the eyes of pigs drawn in chalk, which make voyages on large liners the vivacious entertainments that they are. No; at present she was not at all armoured, this shivering and bewildered creature, to meet the world in which she must live.

4

One day – they were within twenty-four hours of New York – a woman of letters accosted her, having, experienced traveller, discreetly waited until the last day to do so.

'It's Miss Daphne Simpson, isn't it? We met once at the P.E.N. Club, do you remember? And I've heard of you from my niece, Geranium Brown. I used to know your aunt a little, too. So, you see, I have at least three bad pretexts for making your acquaintance, besides our both being in this curious state of transit. Do you enjoy it?'

'I do rather. It's amusing. . . .'

Daphne, fresh, vivacious girl, charming young traveller, who found everything amusing, rushed back to her post, summoned from exile by the agreeable, intelligent voice.

'Are you going to lecture? An absurd business, but we all do it.'

'I'm engaged to,' said Daphne. 'But I don't want to. I want to leave New York at once and go south instead. I want to spend the time in South America.'

'You're very wise. But I expect you'll find your New York friends hale you off to Long Island or some country holiday spot for a time first. They're so nice and hospitable and friendly.'

'Aren't they,' said Daphne, who was friends with half literary New York, though Daisy knew no one in that city.

'Well, I hope we shall come across one another in New York or elsewhere,' the other pleasantly averred. 'You're not going south by yourself, I suppose, are you?'

'No, I expect with friends.' Daphne, sociable and loved young person, had so many friends who would be eager to travel south with her.

The gong sounded for lunch, and they parted.

5

It was Daphne who walked in to lunch and sat down in her place. Daphne, recalled by so light a touch, was not, then, dead after all, nor had she fled far, for all the assaults on her integrity. A casual beckon from a stranger, and here again was Daphne, debonair, youthful, and beloved. And with her came Daisy, her shadow, weaving with lies the garments in which she appeared, building with deceits the floor on which she stood. Daisy and Daphne were not dead: they were immortal.

And what of Miss Wynne? Perhaps she, too, would live; perhaps, after all, she was even to lecture. . . .

Oh, what am I to do? whispered the little bewildered voice that belonged to none of these three, and with the frightened whisper a frail little spirit, overshadowed by the three who formed its cage, fled shivering for cover.

Life is so complicated. What, if it comes to that, are any human beings to do, since all are, in a manner of speaking, in the same quandary?

*Also available by Rose Macaulay
from Carroll & Graf Publishers*

CREWE TRAIN

The heroine of *Crewe Train,* Denham Dobie, has been brought up in Andora by her reclusive father, a retired English clergyman. The father's sudden death coincides with a visit from Denham's sophisticated London relatives, the Greshams, and Denham finds herself whisked back to England and dropped into the busy pond of the Gresham's social life. She is surrounded by publishers, conversationalists, concert-goers; she is introduced to inexplicable social customs—dinners, parties, weekends away; she is expected to become a socialite and she cannot see the point of any of it.

Denham's childlike directness is the vehicle for Rose Macaulay's sparkling and devasting portrait of the social ant-heap. Originally published in 1926, it endures as irresistible proof of her wit and literary vitality.

DANGEROUS AGES

Four generations of women are the focus for Rose Macaulay's absorbing study of discontented and frightened people. There is Mrs Hilary, selfish and petulant, facing the emptiness of old age; her lithe, beautiful daughter Neville, who at 43 carries a wistful sense of unrealized ambitions; her youngest daughter Nan, independent and cynical, in search of stability and purpose; and Neville's delicate daughter Gerda, who belongs to the new generation and holds advanced views that threaten trouble. Each woman is assailed by the problems of age, temperament, and the impingement made upon her by each of the other women. Only grandmamma, at 84, is able serenely to survey her family in a dignified state of peace.

Dangerous Ages was awarded the Femina-Vie Heureuse prize in 1922 and now stands among the most enduring and memorable of this remarkable author's works.

FINE WORKS OF FICTION AND NON-FICTION AVAILABLE IN QUALITY PAPERBACK EDITIONS FROM CARROLL & GRAF

☐ Anderson, Nancy/WORK WITH PASSION
$8.95, Cloth $15.95
☐ Appel, Allen/TIME AFTER TIME   Cloth $17.95
☐ Asch, Sholem/THE APOSTLE $10.95
☐ Asch, Sholem/EAST RIVER $8.95
☐ Asch, Sholem/MARY $10.95
☐ Asch, Sholem/THE NAZARENE
$10.95 Cloth $21.95
☐ Asch, Sholem/THREE CITIES $10.50
☐ Athill, Diana/INSTEAD OF A LETTER
$7.95 Cloth $15.95
☐ Babel, Issac/YOU MUST KNOW EVERYTHING
$8.95
☐ Bedford, Sybille/ALDOUS HUXLEY $14.95
☐ Bellaman, Henry/KINGS ROW $8.95
☐ Bernanos, Georges/DIARY OF A
COUNTRY PRIEST $7.95
☐ Berton, Pierre/KLONDIKE FEVER $10.95
☐ Blanch, Lesley/PIERRE LOTI $10.95
☐ Blanch, Lesley/THE SABRES OF PARADISE $9.95
☐ Blanch, Lesley/THE WILDER SHORES OF LOVE
$8.95
☐ Bowers, John/IN THE LAND OF NYX $7.95
☐ Buchan, John/PILGRIM'S WAY $10.95
☐ Carr, Virginia Spencer/THE LONELY HUNTER: A
BIOGRAPHY OF CARSON McCULLERS $12.95
☐ Chekov, Anton/LATE BLOOMING FLOWERS
$8.95
☐ Conot, Robert/JUSTICE AT NUREMBURG$10.95
☐ Conrad, Joseph/SEA STORIES $8.95
☐ Conrad, Joseph & Ford Madox Ford/
THE INHERITORS $7.95
☐ Conrad, Joseph & Ford Madox Ford/ROMANCE
$8.95

- Poncins, Gontran de/KABLOONA $9.95
- Prince, Peter/THE GOOD FATHER Cloth $13.95
- Proffitt, Nicholas/GARDENS OF STONE
  Cloth $14.95
- Proust, Marcel/ON ART AND LITERATURE $8.95
- Rechy, John/BODIES AND SOULS
  $8.95 Cloth $17.95
- Richelson, Hildy & Stan/INCOME WITHOUT TAXES Cloth $16.95
- Rowse, A.L./HOMOSEXUALS IN HISTORY$9.95
- Roy, Jules/THE BATTLE OF DIENBIENPHU$8.95
- Russel, Robert A./WINNING THE FUTURE
  Cloth $16.95
- Russell, Franklin/THE HUNTING ANIMAL $7.95
- Salisbury, Harrison/A JOURNEY FOR OUR TIMES
  $10.95
- Scott, Evelyn/THE WAVE $9.95
- Service, William/OWL $8.95
- Sigal, Clancy/GOING AWAY $9.95
- Silverstein, Fanny/MY MOTHER'S COOKBOOK
  Cloth $16.95
- Singer, I.J./THE BROTHERS ASHKENAZI $9.95
- Sloan, Allan/THREE PLUS ONE EQUALS BILLIONS $8.95
- Stein, Leon/THE TRIANGLE FIRE $7.95
- Taylor, Peter/IN THE MIRO DISTRICT $7.95
- Tolstoy, Leo/TALES OF COURAGE AND CONFLICT $11.95
- Wassermann, Jacob/CASPAR HAUSER $9.95
- Wassermann, Jacob/THE MAURIZIUS CASE $9.95
- Werfel, Franz/THE FORTY DAYS OF MUSA DAGH $9.95
- Werth, Alexander/RUSSIA AT WAR: 1941–1945
  $15.95
- Zuckmayer, Carl/A PART OF MYSELF $9.95

Available at fine bookstores everywhere

To order direct from the publishers please send check or money order including the price of the book plus $1.75 per title for postage and handling. N.Y. State Residents please add 8¼% sales tax.

Carroll & Graf Publishers, Inc.
260 Fifth Avenue, New York, N.Y. 10001